THE
WREN HUNT

MARY WATSON

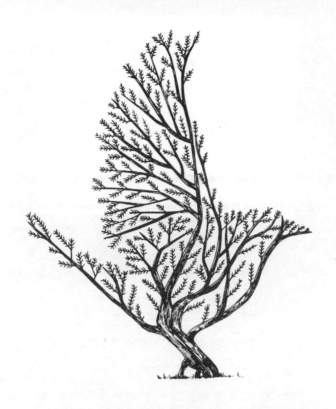

THE
WREN HUNT

MARY WATSON

BLOOMSBURY
LONDON OXFORD NEW YORK NEW DELHI SYDNEY

Bloomsbury [...] Sydney

First publis[...] [...]hing Plc

50 Bedford Square, London WC1B 3DP

www.bloomsbury.com

BLOOMSBURY is a registered trademark of Bloomsbury Publishing Plc

ISBN 978 1 4088 8493 5

MIX
Paper from
responsible sources
FSC   FSC® C020471
www.fsc.org

Typeset by RefineCatch Limited, Bungay, Suffolk
Printed and bound in Great Britain by CPI Group (UK) Ltd, Croydon CR0 4YY

1 3 5 7 9 10 8 6 4 2

For Cathal

The wran, the wran, the king of all birds,
On St Stephen's Day was caught in the furze.
Her clothes were all torn, her shoes all worn,
We chased her all night, right through until dawn.

Dreoilín, Dreoilín, where is your nest?
It's in the bush you all know best.
Between the holly and the ivy tree,
Where all the boys do follow me.

We followed the wran three miles from home,
Through hedges and ditches and piles of stone.
We caught her at last and we broke her knee,
And hung her up in a hawthorn tree.

For we are the boys that came your way,
To bury the wran on Stephen's Day.
So up with the kettle and down with the pan,
Give us a penny to bury the wran.

Traditional, as sung in Kilshamble

ONE
With honey

You catch more flies with honey.

Maeve's words chased through my head as I walked towards the village, her flowery bag slung over my shoulder. Good girl gone looking for trouble.

It was quiet in the main street. It always was the day after Christmas. In other towns the wren hunt was a happy occasion with dancing and music. Wrenboys in costumes with loud banging drums. Delighted crowds looking on. But things were a little more bloody in Kilshamble. That's how it goes in a village built around an open-air slaughterhouse.

The Spar was shut, the handwritten sign at the Gargoyle turned to '*closed*'. The twinkling lights outside the pub only emphasised the quiet: no laughter, no music spilled from inside. I paused, scanning the village green. They liked to hide around there. They'd fold out of the shadows, from the church's stone façade, from the thick hedge.

I passed the butcher's, the hotel, until I came to the ghost estate on the outskirts: semi-detached houses that had been hastily assembled in the boom years and now stood empty, running to ruin. No one wanted to move out here. Not if they didn't have to.

This wasn't how it was supposed to work. The boys usually came looking for me, not the other way round. But earlier that afternoon, Maeve had found me in the kitchen, where I'd been staring at burned toast.

'You catch more flies with honey,' she'd said, handing me the flowery bag, the one she used at the Spar for bread, cheese and a naggin of Powers. She stepped closer, conspiratorially.

In the bag was a bottle of whiskey and a loaf of Maeve's apple bread.

'I think you should talk to them,' Maeve had said. Backlit by the window, her fuzzy hair was framed by the dark clouds and their silver linings. 'Reason with them. They're older now. The game has run its course.'

'Smith said to stay home.'

'Smith also says that facing up to problems,' Maeve looked at the burned toast in my hand, 'is better than hiding from them.'

Hiding seemed pretty appealing to me. But if I didn't go out today, they'd wait. They'd come to the cottage tonight, throw stones at my window, signalling the beginning of the hunt. And the anticipation of when they would finish, maybe on my way home from the shop tomorrow or out at the weekend, was worse.

She frowned, and standing there in her dress with its crazy flowers Maeve looked strangely dangerous.

'I'll go.' Before Smith woke from his nap.

'This ends today,' Maeve had said. She spoke so fiercely it seemed like it was possible. That I would give them gifts and it would stop.

Taking my face in both hands, Maeve kissed my forehead. I had to dip to let her. Her roots were showing grey again.

'This ends today,' she repeated. But it lacked the fervour of the first time.

Dropping the toast in the slop bucket, I searched the junk drawer for the letter opener I'd stashed there. Then Maeve hustled me out, jacket in hand.

She sent me into the dark day to catch some flies.

And there I was, alone in the ghost estate, feeling the creeping cold. I ran my eyes over the houses, wishing I wasn't the stand-in bird in this warped version of the hunt. It struck me as odd that I'd never seen a real wren hunt, except on TV, and there the masked wrenboys parading the streets with the plastic bird made it look like such a merry, rousing thing. Not like this, this secret hunt that none of the villagers seemed to notice, this chase that was so dark and unhappy. On TV, the masks and music were mysterious and thrilling, but here they felt sinister.

'David.' I cupped my hands around my mouth. My voice echoed through the untended square. The houses stared back with empty eyes.

No trace of the boys. Just an old Coke can in the middle of the road.

It was always the thrill of the chase for them. Those final exhilarating minutes when they closed the distance between us. It didn't happen often, but there'd been years when I won. When I got away, gasping for breath as I ran through the cottage gate while David watched from the trees.

But most of the time, they caught me. Tracked me through the village, the forest, even down by the lake. And they'd make me sit with them while they drank beer and decided on their trophy.

A dull, echoing scrabble that might have been boots against loose stone came from the other side of the rubble heap. My immediate reaction, deeply ingrained, was to run. I held my body rigid and refused to turn away.

'David.' My voice was loud and angry.

The sound of high-pitched male laughter echoed through the empty space. I moved towards the running footsteps. By the time I climbed the rubble heap, they were gone.

Not for the first time, I cursed my name.

Wren.

Might as well stick a sign on my back saying, '*Please hassle me on Stephen's Day.*' It was the only thing my mother had given me before she ran off with a man from God knows where when I was a few days old. Fallen in with a bad crowd, her judgement had been clouded by an addiction to heroin. She'd taken money and jewellery and left me behind.

I jumped down from the rubble and kicked the Coke can, watching it rattle away. Walking on, I heard deliberate noises from just beyond: scuffling, some rustling. But when I turned and called out, no one was there. Purple clouds hung low, making the near darkness tighter.

Talk to them, Maeve had said. When I left the cottage, flowery bag in hand, I was sure I would find the boys, hand over whiskey and cake, and reason with them. But that was before the darkness started settling in. That was before they started playing hide-and-seek.

A distant noise broke the silence. It could have been an echo of laughter or a cry from somewhere in the woods. A fox, I hoped.

The faint smell of cigarette smoke wafted over, and then it was gone.

In the village, they said that the woods weren't friendly after sundown. They said that bad things lurked in the forest, hidden behind the dank, fallen boughs. The good people of Kilshamble liked nothing more than blood and gore. We were fed gruesome stories with mother's milk.

We loved best the stories of the bloodthirsty tuanacul, the people of the forest, who would crush you in their embrace. Beautiful, strong tree men with roped muscles, who kissed you until you withered. Women with lips of petal, who lured you close and wrapped vine-like arms around you, choking the life out of you.

I believed these stories as much as I believed in aliens and ghosts, so barely at all. Except on those days when the light was violet and the wind blew wild and the forest and fields felt restless.

'Wran.'

He said my name the way they did in the old song.

My tormentor.

While I was fixed on imaginary dangers, the real trouble had nestled in close. He spoke my name as gentle as a caress.

Wran.

He almost sighed it.

I felt a hand on my shoulder.

'David.' Maybe I could pretend that this was a normal chat between neighbours. 'You have a good Christmas?'

He reached out his other hand and steered me to face him.

'Sure.' He leaned in, smiling. 'But I prefer Stephen's Day.'

He was good-looking, tall, with the back and shoulders of a rower. For the last three years, he'd attended a posh boarding school overseas. He had that easy confidence that came from wealth. From being told that he deserved the best and no one else mattered. But it was more than his rich-boy arrogance that made me despise him.

He was one of *them*.

If it wasn't so awful, it might almost be funny, David's instinct to target me. That somehow, blindly, in playing this game, he'd stumbled upon his true enemy. I was the Capulet to his Montague, the hot to his cold, the white queen to his black knight. I was the oil to his water, the bleach to his ammonia, the salt to his wound. We were everything that was anathema to the other.

I was augur to his judge.

We would never be friends.

David didn't know what I was, yet he sensed something was amiss. Something about me vexed him. Something he couldn't quite put his finger on. He didn't know that from that very first chase years ago he'd unwittingly recognised me. This game was blueprinted in hundreds of years of hostility between judges and augurs.

'About that,' I said. 'About the *game*.' I said the word carefully, hoping he couldn't read my fear. 'It's been enough.'

'Enough?'

'Yes. No more. This ends today.' Maeve's words sounded weak and watery when I said them.

'Yeah?' David seemed to have come closer without having moved at all. 'What are you going to do about it?' He took a drag of his cigarette before crushing it under his shoe. 'Run?'

'Nothing to chase if I'm not running.' If only it were that simple. Better to be a hunted wren than a sitting duck.

I pulled the whiskey from the flowery bag. But looking at David, something seemed different. He was cooler than usual. Smirkier. Behind stood his toadies, Brian and Ryan. All muscle and no brain.

'I'm calling a truce, David.' I handed over the whiskey.

David smiled, then examined the bottle.

'I'm after passing my exams,' he said. 'In the mood for a little celebration.'

He twisted the cap open.

'I'm getting a new tattoo to mark the occasion. Maybe a wren?' He paused as he held the bottle to his lips. 'In a cage. What do you think?'

He took a slug, and slowly screwed the cap back on. He held out his hand to shake mine. Reluctant, I placed a tentative hand in his large, rough one. He closed on my fingers and pulled me towards him, whispering in my ear with whiskey-flavoured breath, 'You better fly, little bird.'

Pulling away, I stood my ground, holding myself stiff so that my legs wouldn't just run, run, run, as everything inside was braced to do.

'Game over,' I said.

'Little Wren, the game is just beginning.' And there it was again, that cool assurance, which made me think that the stakes were somehow raised this year.

I searched his face to see if he'd finally figured out why he hated me so much. As I stared, I saw a flicker of distaste, his sense that something about me was just plain wrong.

But he didn't know.

He came closer. I didn't move. This close, I could feel the heat from his chest. He reached out a hand to clamp my wrist.

'Maybe we should see if your friend wants to play. What's her name again? The pretty blonde one?'

Nearly dropping the flowery bag, I pulled away. But damn it if I was going to let him bring Aisling into his crazy game. Even as a child playing in the woods or quarry, Aisling had never liked to run. No way would anyone do this to her.

I turned on my heel and fled.

'I'll give you to fifty,' David called after me.

I was out of reach by three. I could hear him counting slowly, as if we really were playing hide-and-seek and he was being especially patient.

It would be quicker to cut through the woods. But I wasn't the idiot girl in the movies who hurled herself into the arms of the axe-wielding maniac by going into dark places.

David and the others were right behind. They were gaining on me fast. Night would fall within the hour. I picked up my pace.

Turning the bend, I saw the boy standing in the road. Waiting. His clothes were dark and the way he stood, still and slightly hunched, made me think of the tuanacul. He was like a tree come to life, sorrowful and ancient. He turned his head, and it was Cillian, wearing a mummer's mask. The surprised, painted eyes stared at me. Of the four bullies, he was the one most likely to become a finger-severing psychopath once he graduated from terrorising girls. That boy put the kill into Cillian.

He began the slow whistling of the song I had come to hate: *The wran, the wran, the king of all birds.*

Of course they had split up. That's why David had given me such a generous start. Cillian was ahead, waiting. To the right was the McNally farm, Cillian's family. I couldn't go there. Behind me, the other boys were getting closer. I could hear their answering call, fast and raucous: '*Up with the kettle and down with the pan. Give us a penny to bury the wran.*'

So, like the idiot girl in the movies, the one who ends up hacked to bits, I ran into the woods.

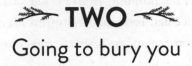

TWO
Going to bury you

The peonies are a study in colour: blood red on green.
AdC

It was darker among the trees. Moss-covered stones and exposed tree roots slowed me down, but I pushed on. Every now and then I would hear calling or whistling as they drew closer. Or maybe I imagined it. It was easy to imagine things there in the forest, there beneath the thick canopy of leaves.

I had to get to the river, it was the easiest route home. I knew the terrain well. I'd run there in frost, rain and fog. But it was different today. It always felt different with the boys at my back. My feet were less sure. The trees had rearranged themselves, closing over the paths I knew. Ahead, I could see the crumbled outline of the ruined cottage. Behind me, whistling through the woods, was that jolly, awful tune.

For we are the boys that come your way,
To bury the wran on Stephen's Day.

I pushed harder, stumbling over the uneven ground until a partially concealed root sent me sprawling, face to dirt. I pulled myself up. Steadying against a tree, I breathed deeply. There it was, that faint whistle. I pressed on, running through the trees, the thin branches scraping at my face and the wet leaves slippery beneath my feet.

I reached a fallen bough that blocked the path, and was about to climb over when I saw something near the ruin. It could be just another dark forest shadow shape. Or it could be one of them. I crouched down, watching from behind the bough, taking air deep into my lungs. Nothing moved ahead and I couldn't hear anyone behind me. But that was how David liked to play it. That was the fun of the chase: to let me get away first.

From behind the bough, I paused to think. The river was too obvious. There were more of them and they were faster. I would almost certainly run into an ambush. But if I headed back towards the road, they might not expect that.

My eye traced the outline of the ruin. No one ever went there. Most people in the village were wary of it, but the cottage had never bothered me. And just behind it was an overgrown path back to the road.

Having a plan instead of running helter-skelter gave me confidence. I would do this. I would evade them. They'd had their chase. The thought of getting away brought new energy. They wouldn't catch me this year.

I left the path, ducking in between the trees on the slope. It slowed me down, but stealth above speed. Watching carefully, I reached the ruined cottage. Hardly a cottage, there were only the remains of four walls overgrown with moss and ivy.

In the 1800s, the mad girl artist had lived there. Arabella de Courcy. She'd fallen in love with a tree man, the prince of the tuanacul, who lured her to the cottage. He didn't mean to kill her, but every time he loved her he drew vitality from her. Some would swear to seeing a blonde girl in old-fashioned white petticoats between the trees, her hair like tangled branches. With lips of petals and skin as rough as bark.

But these were just stories. Of that I was certain. Because I knew magic, and it wasn't ghost stories about a tree girl in a ruined cottage.

A yew had split the back wall and I pulled myself up on the trunk and climbed. From the high branches, I scanned the ground, not seeing anyone. The cold settling through my jacket, I waited.

They came up from the river, flitting through the trees. His face now hidden by a mummer's mask, David prowled closer. There were two figures behind him and one coming along the slope. Using hand signals, they conferred. One continued on the slope, the two behind split up, one retracing his steps and the other pressing forward with David. They moved quietly, surefooted on the uneven ground. One last look back from David, the fixed smile on his masked face turned in my direction. Then they were gone.

Out of my hiding place, I sprinted uphill, away from the boys. Steep, the ground loose, I slipped a few times as I scrabbled forward. The woods were thinner and brighter here. There were fewer places to hide.

The beginnings of a cramp started in my side and I breathed through the pain. In the distance, the grey road appeared. The sound of a car nearby. The trees at the edge lit up, and the car passed. I ran, nearly falling over a broken tricycle that had been dumped behind a tree, its glittery pink streamers lifting in the wind. Pushing on, I went towards the road, hating the chase, hating that this still happened. Every year, and I didn't know how to make it stop.

I heard nothing, saw nothing until I was down. I knew only the slam of bone against bone, hard, gritty ground on my face. David's head cracked against mine and we fell together. My cheek scraped stones and twigs and dirt; something sharp cut the skin on my temple. Pain strobed through my skull. Dazed, nonsense words echoed inside: *Wren has left the building!* And in my mind's eye, I saw the mesmerising swing of a stone pendant on a worn gold chain moving sweetly from side to side.

I felt David's weight on me, crushing the air from my lungs. His mask scraped my cheek. Fear throbbed through me. I was caught.

I tried to twist out from under him, my terror lending me strength. I crept forward, first one inch, then another. But he tightened his grip, holding me still. Along with earth and wood, I smelled the whiskey and cigarette smoke that clung to his clothes and hair.

'Gotcha.' He sat up to his knees.

He pushed the mask off his face and smiled. 'Just a bit of fun, eh, Wren? No real harm done.' The bruises faded, the cuts healed. I couldn't pinpoint the moment when it had shifted from a game that I didn't enjoy but could tolerate, into this. My heartbeat was loud and fast and I struggled to catch my breath. I repeated Maeve's words like they were a charm or a prayer: this ends today. But how?

David pulled me up, gripping my arms. In passing him on the streets, I might have noticed the bit of stubble, the gradual change from solid boy to thickset teen. I saw it properly now, facing all four of them, unnervingly no longer boys but not yet adults. They were bulked out, big arms and thick thighs. With shorn hair and underage tattoos, they were terrifying.

They won't hurt me, I told myself. But it didn't stop the fear.

'We're not really going to bury you,' David said.

He was every inch the village princeling. Most of our neighbours wouldn't understand the significance of his position in the hierarchy of judges, that as nephew of Calista Harkness he was as good as royal. But they understood that David was rich. That his family owned much of the land in and around Kilshamble.

The other three boys looked on, smiling.

'What do you want?' I tried to sound bored.

Whenever they caught me, they took a trophy. Maybe a button from my dress, a thread of unravelled wool. Last year, it was a lace from my shoe. This time, I wore a cheap string of charms around my wrist, feather earrings from the Saturday market. I worried that these useless objects could whisper my secrets. That if David listened hard enough, he'd know the truth that eluded him so.

'Do you know, in the old tradition, why they chased the wren?' David said. He pushed his hand into my hair and then twisted it around his fingers. My ear scraped the tree as he pulled me towards him.

'Because it's so strong and manly to hunt a small defence-less bird?' I said.

But it didn't sound as glib as I intended. My eyes were stinging from my pulled hair. I could feel every bang and scrape from when they first started chasing me. My temple hurt like buggery. I was not in the mood to play Q&A.

'The knife,' David said to Cillian. His hand tightened around my hair. The flowery bag fell to the ground.

'They chased her because the wren is a treacherous creature who betrays those that trust her.' He took the knife from Cillian.

'How can I betray you if I'm not on your side?' I said, feeling his fist against my scalp. Pulling hair was such a dirty trick.

'The wrenboys would punish her by taking her feathers.'

They did so love to go on about punishment, the judges.

Then David lined the knife on my hair and I realised what he meant to do. I reached for the flowery bag but he had me at an awkward angle. Should have put the letter opener in my pocket.

'Just one dark chunk,' David said, working the blade through my hair. 'You won't even miss it.'

I didn't want him taking my hair. This year's trophy was different. David had intent, which I'd never seen before.

This wasn't a useless object to be tossed into a drawer and forgotten. By taking my hair, David would take a part of me. An augur could never allow a judge to own a piece of her. Who knew what dark magic he might do with my hair?

I brushed the fabric of the bag. The tip of the letter opener was between my left fore and middle fingers. I pulled it up a little more until I had a better grip. David's knife pressed against the hair twisted in his hand. The blade sawed through a few more strands.

I jabbed the sharpened edge of the letter opener deep into his hand. It was an awkward, messy stab. David snarled as he dropped the knife and let go his hold. Long, blunt ribs of hair were wrapped around his fingers.

'What the hell, Wren?' he spat. As if in slow motion, I saw his blood fall. In the dim light, I thought I saw three drops hit the dirty leaves, then a more steady stream. David slipped my hair into his pocket.

As the first drop touched the ground, I felt it coming in a powerful wave. Then a second drop seeped into the dirt and mulch. The skin on my palms began to prick ever so slightly. I was transfixed by the pretty pattern. It was like a lens coming into focus. Just a little more, then I would see.

'What's wrong with her?' I heard one of them say.

'She's having convulsions, man.'

'I'm out of here.' Brian's words were muffled, as though he had already turned away. I barely registered the sound of the other boys following.

When the third drop hit, the pattern was complete. The dirt, the mulch, the exposed root of the tree and the blood. The soft edges of a sweet kind of bliss. I knew I should stop, but I couldn't. I focused on the pattern of blood against the leaves. The lines blurred, and suddenly I could see the secret picture inside. And with it came the head rush. This was stronger than anything I'd ever felt before. My eyes rolled back in my head as I heard the last set of footsteps running off.

As I fell, I saw a large table made of solid wood, laden with ripe fruit. Pitchers of wine and bowls of rich gravy and sauce. A crowd gathered around a large, roasted animal, tearing chunks of meat. I couldn't tell who it was that stuffed food into their mouths with both hands, barely chewing. Someone shifted and then I saw her.

Sorcha.

My long-lost mother.

Laid out on the table, adorned with slices of orange. Cocktail umbrellas in her hair. And, at her heart, a stone pendant on a worn gold chain, like an unseeing third eye. She was missing chunks from her legs and arms. A large bite mark on her shoulder. I heard cartilage tear as her arm came off the socket. A large hand reached towards the stone. The image of Sorcha fuzzed over, and for a brief moment I thought I saw her hair change from red to dark waves. For a second, it wasn't Sorcha on the table. It was me.

The hand closed over the stone and pulled. But as it pulled, the stone splintered into a thousand shards. And then I lost consciousness.

❧ THREE ❧
And then they ate her

The Gallagher boys have left to defend the Rose.
My beloved Elizabeth longs to follow her brothers as
they subdue the brutish Grovers who wreak havoc
across the country.
AdC

I sat in the growing dark. The chase had left me utterly
drained. There was blood on my shirt, and my scalp still
ached from where David had pulled my hair. I touched my
temple, feeling the graze where I'd hit the ground. Troubled
by the vision of Sorcha, I began the slow walk home. I
didn't know how to begin explaining it to Smith. I didn't
want to tell him at all. Seventeen years, and Sorcha still
caused him pain.

When Sorcha ran away, she'd stolen jewellery from the
house. All I had of my mother was a list of things we no
longer owned: a man's watch with a leather strap, two rose-
gold ladybird earrings (wings aflutter) and an old necklace

with an unpolished stone. The necklace I'd seen in the vision. Smith had tried to find her, but I was a sickly baby and demanded all his attention. He never said, but I guessed my failure to thrive came from Sorcha's addiction.

During those months, in and out of hospital, we'd met Maeve, then a nurse. By the time I was on the mend, any trail Sorcha had left was cold. So Smith and I had settled in the cottage at the edge of the village, surrounded by the sprawling wood and farmland. Further up, the old abandoned quarry.

Moving here was an act of defiance; the judges didn't want augurs in Kilshamble. A few, like the Laceys, who were more than a little fearless, might settle in the townlands right outside. But the village, from the quarry to the lake, was judge territory. It hadn't always been like that, not in the days when augurs divined through blood and guts on the old green.

Most people in the village didn't realise we were different. There was a lazy, half-awareness of something a little other. Like it was in the wind or the soil or the water, that sense of a different kind of normal, living alongside them. It leached through, like the taint of copper coins on a wet sink. We were an infection that the rest of the body didn't quite know what to make of, so they closed around as if nothing were otherwise.

For years, Smith presented himself as the amiable geography teacher, now retired. Keeping our identity secret, we were able to watch them. To keep an eye on our enemy in this sleeping war. Smith, who knew such things, had found the best place where we could observe without being seen. When the house next door became free, Maeve and her two girls moved in.

Sometimes I envied the judge children, especially when I saw how close they were; how they distanced themselves from the other village children, that air of secrecy around them. I wanted to tell them that I wasn't just an ordinary village child who knew nothing of draoithe and their nemeta and rituals. I wanted to remind them that judges and augurs, for all our differences, were once united. That despite our conflict, we all needed nemeta to preserve the old ways and feed the rituals that had been passed through the generations. I longed to tell the judge kids that I was like them. Kind of. Apart from the enemy thing.

But Smith had forbidden it. And even though I felt lonely, we weren't alone. Far beyond the dark fields and distant lights, other augurs were spread out over the neighbouring townlands and into the surrounding villages. Our grove. Fifteen families, and we were tight.

'You OK, honey?' Maeve's voice came from the bench in

her garden. She always went overboard with the fairy lights at the winter solstice. 'Did you talk to them?'

Through the window, I saw Smith in his armchair. I buttoned my jacket, hiding streaks of muck and blood, and turned to Maeve.

'Yeah, we talked.' No lies there. 'What you doing out in the cold?'

'Looking at stars.' She gestured above. Maeve always had an eye on the sky. 'Watching for you.'

I should have known she would be waiting. From my earliest memories, Maeve was there. Her relationship with Smith was for a long time platonic, until one day it wasn't. It was Maeve who'd stood in Sorcha's place at my coming-of-age ceremony when I turned sixteen, who'd guided me through the ritual while I stared at my inner forearm in dismay.

Maeve had shown me the old ways, the secret traditions passed down through generations. Some of them so old they came from the time when draoithe were one, with no division, no hostility. A time when we worked together as the prophets, poets, arbiters and advisers to kings.

But that was before we began dividing among ourselves, distinguishing between draoithe who worked patterns, the astrologers, healers, architects, metal-workers and alchemists, and the draoithe who upheld the law. The augurs and the judges. That was before we started fighting each other.

'I'm grand, Maeve. Go on in. You'll catch a cold,' I scolded, grateful for the dimly lit path.

My hand on the doorknob, I glanced up but could see no stars.

Just inside, I could hear the singsong voice of the newsreader: 'And in other news, Basil Lucas, prize-winning geologist and media personality, died unexpectedly at his home in Galway.' Smith was watching intently and I used his distraction to cross the living room.

'Wren,' he said, holding out a hand like a traffic officer on a wet Monday morning. 'You should listen to this.'

I paused, not turning round. If I hugged the shadows, maybe he wouldn't see the dirt, the blood and grazes. But I got as far as the passage before my curiosity about Lucas won out.

'Earlier this year, Basil Lucas bequeathed his archive, valued in excess of five million euros, to the Harkness Foundation, effective upon his death. Calista Harkness, director of the Harkness Foundation, expressed her sympathy to the Lucas family.'

The report switched to a clip where Calista Harkness tried to contain her glee at acquiring the archive. She had the same pinched nose as her nephew David, whose blood currently stained my shirt.

'It's happening,' Smith said. 'Just as you said.'

Foretelling Basil Lucas's death at Christmastime had been one of my better moments as an augur. I'd seen him lying in a coffin. Not an ordinary coffin, one wrapped in Christmas paper and tied up with a bow. Like a dead-man-shaped Christmas present. I'd seen it while staring at the peeling paint on the walls of Dr Kelly's waiting room, and it took all my control to not shriek like a loon. In the village, they already found me more than a little odd.

'Wren?'

I turned round. Smith broke off, breathing hard, as he looked at my face.

'It's Boxing Day,' he said. He rubbed his jaw with his hand. 'Why didn't you stay in?'

I shook my head, no use rehashing the afternoon. Behind him, the newsreader was smiling: 'And to end this evening's broadcast ...'

'I'll get the tin.' He raised himself from the large armchair and went into the kitchen.

'... a round-up of wren hunts from around the country.' The newscaster beamed and my nausea rose as the song began, '*The wran, the wran the king of all birds.*'

I didn't want to look, but couldn't help myself. The

swirling colour of the parades, the straw-clad dancers and musicians. Bright ribbons streaming from the fake bird carried on a holly bush by masked boys. The deep, regular drumbeats and laughing flute. A boy explained that they were collecting money for the wren's funeral. After they'd symbolically killed her and decorated her with ribbons.

I turned off the TV, hitting the button harder than was necessary.

Smith came back, balancing an old cake tin that said *First Aid Kit* in a faded script with a glass of whiskey and a bowl of steaming water.

He took a piece of cotton wool and dipped it in water. Reaching inside the cake tin, he pulled out a tube of ointment that looked like it had been bought when Sorcha was a girl.

'How bad?' Smith dabbed the cuts on my face with the beige stuff.

'The usual.' I didn't want to talk about it.

'Did they hurt you?' His blue eyes held mine.

'I'm fine, Smith.'

His eyes flicked to my temple.

'I fell.' I touched my hand to the graze, glad he couldn't see my shirt. 'It's nothing.'

'You should have stayed home.' Never had a graze been so thoroughly cleaned.

'I saw something,' I said. 'There was blood.' And hair. I couldn't tell Smith that David had taken my hair. What if it meant something? Maeve would fret and Smith would glower. I couldn't handle their worrying. Or maybe it was that I didn't want to bring scrutiny to the unwelcome intimacy of it, that David had stolen a part of me.

'Blood?' His hand faltered slightly and then dabbed briskly again.

'Not mine.' Not most of it, anyway.

'What happened?' He took a huge gulp from his tumbler.

This close, I could smell whiskey and a faint scent of mould. He never aired his clothes properly when he washed them. He was always folding them away before they completely dried. Smith stopped his dabbing but kept his eyes on the graze on my forehead.

'I took the letter opener. Just in case.' Sharpened down to a stiletto. Because really, no one ever used the wretched thing. Not for opening letters anyway. It was an entirely unnecessary instrument, I thought, shrugging out of my jacket.

'And what did you do with the letter opener?'

'Skewered his hand like a kebab.' Was it bad that I smiled?

Smith sighed. 'If David tells his dad …'

He turned to pick up another ball of cotton wool soaked with stinky beige ointment, but I saw the small smile. Not every girl had a grandfather who'd be proud of her for stabbing someone in the hand.

'He's all right. Ouch.' I pulled away as Smith started on my shoulder. 'He'll live.'

The silence stretched. Smith was trying not to ask but eventually he couldn't help it. 'You saw something?'

'Sorcha.' I dreaded saying it. 'With a stone.'

Smith busied himself, throwing the used cotton wool balls in the wastepaper basket. He took his time screwing the cap on the tube of ointment. A useless endeavour, it leaked out of the sides in three different places.

'A Daragishka stone?'

I nodded. The one she'd stolen. Smith turned away. He bent over the old cake tin as if he were looking for something inside it. Something that could cure heartbreak.

'It happened quickly. She was,' I paused while trying to find a delicate way to put it, 'laid out on a table wearing the stone. A bunch of people around her. But it was like they were using her to get to the stone. They cut into her body and served it up. And then they ate her.' So much for delicacy.

Smith snapped the lid of the cake tin down, his long fingers on the rim, carefully sealing it. I could see his mind working. He was figuring how this affected the plan. Just how ominous it really was. I didn't tell him that for the briefest flash I'd seen myself on the table. Now that I was home, I wasn't sure I'd seen it at all.

'What do you think it means?'

He picked up his whiskey, swirling the melting ice.

'It means we have to find those stones. Soon.'

From when I was little, Smith had taught me that it wasn't answers that mattered but knowing the right questions to ask. Which made questions seem very important. So the words rasped against my throat: 'What happens if we don't?'

Smith gestured to the TV. 'You saw the news. Calista Harkness owns the Lucas Archive now. If we don't get into it and find Lucas's map of the Daragishka stones, they will.'

'Would that be so bad?' I hated how timid I sounded.

'The stones are our only hope. If we don't get them, it's the beginning of the end for us. It happened to the bards, don't think it won't happen to us.'

Smith drained the glass and set it on top of the tin. No one liked thinking about the bards, the third group of draoithe, who'd wanted no part in the fight between the judges and augurs. No one liked to talk about how, after losing their nemeta, the bards' songs and poems lost their magic. Their numbers dwindled and then they were no more. Not with a bang but a whimper.

'And the internship is the only way.'

Smith had ensured the internship would go to one of his girls. Someone either owed him a favour or wanted to keep a secret. That was how things were done in Kilshamble. I dreaded the thought of me or Aisling going undercover at Harkness House. The place where David and the wrenboys worked. All of them, whether it was David or Calista Harkness or any other judge, had a burning hostility towards us.

'I can't tell the future,' Smith said, his face soft with concern and perhaps remorse. He didn't need to touch or hug me, his face was unguarded in that moment and I felt loved, cared for. 'But from mapping the situation, the possible options and outcomes, this is really our best chance.'

'Then we do it.'

He turned to the kitchen, clearly in search of more whiskey.

'Who do you think they were?' I stopped him. 'The people. Who fed on her.' Those hands, grabbing at Sorcha. At me.

Smith paused in the wide squared frame leading to the kitchen. He turned slightly. 'Why, the judges. Of course.'

Before I reached the stairs, he spoke again, still framed by the square. 'That was a blood vision, Wren.'

I gave a short nod. There would be consequences, I knew that. There were always consequences, usually teeny tiny consequences that you hardly noticed. But the small things added up over time, until eventually they formed one big thing that could crush you beneath its weight.

FOUR
Ritual at dawn

When I observe the flowers I draw, it is as though I can see beyond them. The details reveal themselves to me as a perfect design.

AdC

We left at sunrise. The morning was clear and dry after a night drawn so deep inside my dreams that waking felt like surviving.

Maeve was waiting in the kitchen. I smiled at Aisling's golden head resting on the kitchen table. She was not a morning person, and especially not before breakfast. Mrs Lacey and her daughter had gone ahead, they told me. Mrs Lacey's hip was sticky again, so we'd catch up easily.

'Where's Sibéal?' I said. I reached for the juice carton in the fridge, trying to shake off the sleep fug that lingered.

'Finding her best ritual–at–dawn outfit.' Maeve took the carton from my hand and shut it back inside the fridge. 'Later. You can have some later.'

I should have remembered: first the trees, then food and drink.

We went out in the cold morning, our feet crunching the stones beneath. The front gate was hanging off its hinge and I stopped to hook it up to the rotting wood post. A useless gesture to protect Smith, who was sleeping inside. Like a closed gate would keep the monsters in my head at bay. My dreams had left me wary.

Sibéal tumbled out of Maeve's house. Her coat was undone and her hair flew wild. A dress that resembled a curtain peeked out beneath her coat.

'Party time,' she shouted. Sibéal loved rituals. We didn't do them nearly enough to keep her satisfied. But we couldn't. Rituals drew from the nemeta and we were on rations. This morning's ritual was small, with only a handful of us taking part. I guessed that's how Maeve justified doing one when we could so ill afford it.

'Shhh,' Aisling said. A knee-jerk, sisterly impulse to argue. 'You don't have to scream it to the whole village.'

'Do you see anyone around here?' Sibéal was incredulous as she gestured to the empty fields. 'I could shout a load of filth and no one would hear.' She looked like she was about to prove it.

'Don't.' Maeve put a lot of weight into the single word and went a few steps ahead, her long puffy coat flaring out like a cape. She pulled herself up to her full height, all five feet one inch of it, and in her bearing I could see the ard-draoi of the Whitethorn Grove about to lead a ritual.

Following Maeve, we set off down the road, heading away from the village. We cut across Brannigan's field and up the hill. In the soft dawn light, Ruth Lacey laboured up the steep slope. Annie walked slowly beside her like a restrained terrier. I felt sorry for Mrs Lacey with her gammy hip, out so early when it was so cold. Really, they were only there to make up the numbers. For an Ask, there had to be six of us on the sixth day of the new moon.

We walked up the hill. We were headed towards the copse above the old abandoned quarry to perform the Ask. They didn't happen often, Asks, only when we found ourselves stuck.

And we were stuck. Aisling and I were locked in a battle of wills about who would risk the internship with Calista Harkness, and neither would back down. Maeve had decided to resolve it the traditional way. We were going to ask nature.

There wasn't much to set us aside from people who weren't draoithe. We augurs lived normal lives with mainly our talents, our way with patterns, to distinguish us. We had our secret history, the stories of ourselves that had been passed down the generations. And our groves, the communities where we observed the old ways, where we performed the old rituals.

At the top of the hill, I went beyond the copse, where Maeve was unpacking stones from her flowery bag, and stood at the edge, looking down into the quarry. As always, I felt that familiar rush. Maeve would say it was because the hill was a nemeton, one of those places where the threshold between this world and the unknown was worn thin. Where magic leaked through. Or at least it had been, before half the hill had been eaten away by greedy machines. That crackle or spark or buzz that always zinged through nemeta was faint, the hill wasn't as strong as it had once been. It wasn't as strong as we needed it to be. Later in the morning, once the ritual was complete, that buzz and zing would be even further diminished. But still, those bare stone walls below. They'd always stirred something in me.

'It should be me, Wren,' Aisling said. 'Let me go to Harkness House.'

I wasn't sure if it was the morning shadows, or if her face really was that pinched. Almost cross.

'You're too nice.' I shrugged, keeping it light. 'The nastier girl has to do it. And that's me. The Ask will confirm. Just you see.'

'I'm infinitely more terrible than you.' And she was. But her terribleness was grand and beautiful. I was meaner, baser and more selfish. Which meant I was better suited to blending in with judges and maintaining deception. Because if they found out, the wrath of the judges would be unleashed. Not only would they target the one who deceived them, but they would act against our grove.

'It's out of our hands now.' I gestured to the stones that Maeve was placing in the centre of the ring of trees. But I worried. It had to be me. Three months among judges, among Calista Harkness and David and his wrenboys, would damage Aisling far more than it would me.

Aisling looked down into the quarry, at the deep pools of water and the brown ragged walls. Her anxiety was marked in her shoulders, her eyes, the set of her mouth.

'Wren, draw the circle, there's a good girl,' Maeve called from the trees.

'You'll have to face David every day.' Aisling seemed defeated, like she knew how the Ask would play out.

At the trees, Maeve stood, shoulders bent as she counted the stones. I knew she was worried; performing rituals was like feeding a hungry family from a diminished pot. Nemeta could replenish, usually through natural events like storms or an eclipse or a solstice. But never enough to get us out of the red.

'I can handle David.' It almost sounded convincing.

Aisling said nothing, just looked down at a dumped mattress in the quarry below. There was a large russet stain on it, like someone had bled out there.

'Maybe we should just do a bloody virgin sacrifice,' I muttered, but it sounded gloomy rather than funny. 'See if that gets the nemeta going again.'

'A wicker man,' Aisling said, referring to the old, forbidden practice of stuffing someone inside a giant straw effigy and then burning them alive. 'I've heard they've started doing it again, the judges. That's why they're getting so strong.'

'Human sacrifice?' My head jerked towards her.

Aisling shrugged. 'That's what I've heard.'

'No way.'

'Wren,' Maeve called me again.

'You know what they're like,' Aisling continued. 'They take punishment seriously.'

Neither of us needed to be reminded how seriously the judges took punishment. Not while we decided who was going to deceive them for three months and then steal something valuable.

'Wren Silke, the circle.'

Hearing the shrill end of Maeve's voice, I hurried to her, thinking about Calista Harkness and imagining the smell of charred flesh.

Sibéal had wrapped her long cotton shawl around her shoulders, dramatically covering her mouth. Shrugging out of my coat, I picked up mine and let it fall loosely over my head. It wasn't my best look.

Maeve pushed a carved staff into my hand and I walked around the wide ring of trees, whispering the words I knew so well. I went around a second time, sealing us within the circle of the trees.

The circle complete, I joined the women beneath the trees. Maeve chanted the words I knew from my earliest childhood. Always, something like peace infused me when I stood inside the circle, listening to the Old Irish. I felt embraced by family, by history.

When it was time, Maeve spoke: 'We will use four rounds. If there is a tie, we'll break it with a fifth. If there is an unbroken run, the matter will be decided after three. The first round is stones in a circle.'

Maeve gestured to the twelve stones and Aisling chose one. I held my hand over the stones. They were all marked with Ogham symbols on their undersides, each the name of a tree. But only one had the diamond shape with the line running down. Gold.

I moved my hand to the right and picked up a stone that was neither too big nor too small.

'Iompaigh thart iad,' Maeve spoke in Irish. *Turn them over.*

Aisling turned hers and saw two perpendicular lines: 'Oak.' We would keep drawing stones until one of us found gold.

I held mine, hoping for Ash. Ash was my lucky tree. I turned it over.

'Gold.' The diamond with the line running down.

'First marker to Wren,' Maeve said, packing the remaining stones into her flowery bag. 'Second round is bird in a tree.'

I didn't believe that picking stones or placing them at the bottom of the tree meant that we were being whispered secret answers by powers we couldn't understand. Even as I took my stone and considered the trees, I didn't think that some nature spirit was choosing between me and Aisling. But it was hard to believe that there wasn't *something*. An unnameable, unknowable magic that pulsed, touching lightly and leaving things subtly altered.

And I could feel it, the changed air, the sense of something other that curled between us like smoke. I looked over at the others: the near rapture on Sibéal's face and the intense concentration on Aisling's.

Whatever it was, this magic pooled in the nemeta. And its expression was our talents.

The autumn Aisling had turned sixteen, she narrowed her eyes at me and said, 'Wow, Wren, you're buzzing.'

I laughed at her.

'No, seriously, Wren. Your whole body is singing a tune. Except here.' And she touched my throat. 'It's odd here. Wrong.'

'You must be coming down with something. You're delirious.'

But it wasn't Aisling who was sick. The next day, I was in bed with strep throat.

From early times, divination occurred through the reading of patterns, either in the stars, or in the flight patterns of birds. Or the dance between fire and smoke, the flow of water in a stream. And here was the heart of augur magic: this affinity for patterns.

But hardly anyone saw the future any more. Some could scry for the past and present through the interpretation of patterns. Maeve, a nephomancer, read through the movement of clouds and their position in the sky; I'd met augurs who interpreted fire and smoke, plant foliage across seasons, eggs, the movement of water, weather patterns. But most, like Smith, whose talent was mapping, didn't scry. Instead, through their uncanny instinct for a pattern, they became unnaturally good at something. Like a doctor who knew her patient was sick because she could sense an anomaly in the body. Or the explorer who knew a landscape because the sense of it thrummed inside him. Most things, if you looked hard enough, had an underlying pattern, and we had an instinct for it. Rather, most augurs did. Just not me.

'It's happening to you,' I'd told Aisling, my voice scratchy. It wasn't the first time I'd been jealous of her. Everyone always said that Aisling looked like an angel, with her delicate features, her dirty-blonde hair, large brown eyes and flawless skin. And I was her dark reflection, the necessary demon to balance out such light. With eyes as green as envy.

'And it will happen to you,' Aisling said. But she couldn't be sure. With our nemeta depleted and unable to do the rituals that fuelled us, more and more augur children remained blank.

'It's the best, healing,' I told her. It was my biggest wish: I wanted nothing more than to be a doctor in a hospital, where I could take on the human body like a Rubik's cube, figure it out, solve it. I wanted to be able to intuit the tumours, the fractures and fissures just by looking at the patient.

'It's all right,' she said. But I knew she'd been hoping for music.

'At least you won't be a butcher, reading secret messages in sheep guts.'

We had declared this the worst possible fate. Maeve had

tried to tell us that haruspicy, divination through animal entrails, was one of the most respected talents. But we wouldn't hear it.

'Blood is gross.' Aisling was squeamish. 'I won't get the points for medicine. I don't even want to study medicine.' She picked at invisible fluff on her jeans. 'Mam's hoping I'll get into nursing.' Even though she didn't practise any more, was Aisling's unspoken accusation.

'You don't have to,' I told her. 'There are other ways to be a healer.'

'It should have been you.'

'It might be.' I tried to cheer up. It wasn't like Aisling had used up healing. I still had a chance. 'And there are other talents.' Ruth Lacey's was weather, Annie Lacey had numbers and wanted to be a cryptographer or an actuary, while her brother Simon had an uncanny ability to read body language. He picked up on physical cues and knew with some certainty how a person was feeling, even what they were thinking. Whatever my talent, I'd find a way to study medicine.

'Wren?' Aisling's voice drew me out of my thoughts. I placed my stone beneath the whitethorn and walked back to the centre.

'What are you thinking about?' she whispered. Maeve was watching above, searching the sky for birds. When a bird settled in one of the trees above a stone, that was the second marker.

'Our talents,' I said, keeping an eye on my tree. From this angle it resembled a woman, the trunk a long, thin torso with a slight swelling near the top. Branches like arms held out and the thin, bare twigs were a wild tangle of hair. I glanced at Aisling, and there it was, that sympathetic look I always received.

More than a year after Aisling's talent emerged, there had been no sign of mine. March arrived and I was quietly freaking out, trying to ignore those sorry looks from Maeve and Aisling.

When the daffodils started to wilt, I was ready to take on animal guts. Hell, I *wanted* animal guts. I could barely wait to get my hands on eviscerated pigs. My birthday was in April, and if my talent didn't waken before then, it wasn't going to happen.

Then, the day before my sixteenth birthday, I was outdoors with Aisling and Smith, clearing weeds from the chip-and-tar drive. I'd spread the poison liberally. I kept my head bent over the drive, transfixed by the small stones. When I saw them shiver, I dropped the jerrycan of weedkiller. The ripple began to form a shape: slithering towards me was a snake made of gold chip. My hands started to hurt, just on the inside, at the centre of my palm.

'Fuck!' I shouted, recoiling.

'Wren.' Smith's reprimand was token. I had an allowance of three dirty words a month. More than that, he said, and I'd get lazy.

I scrambled back as the snake raised itself up, spattering small stones as its body arched. But then I saw at the base of its throat the snake had split in two. A second snakehead reared.

'Snake!' I pointed.

'There are no snakes in Ireland.' And certainly no two-headed snakes. Smith was always the voice of reason. He came towards me, clearly oblivious to the snake in the stones.

I stumbled against the rail fence. As I fell I saw two open snake mouths hissing at me. They moved closer, poised to strike. And then, instead of forked tongues, two grey marbles pushed forward from inside the mouths. Like the special effects in some B-grade horror, the mouths shifted into eyes. Grey with long thick lashes, they stared at me with surprising gentleness.

The snakes lurched forward and the eyes shot venom. The poison puckered my skin and the eyelashes blinked slowly. The skin on the inside of my forearm, where the venom struck, sizzled and burned. I fainted.

The night of the first vision, Smith and Maeve seated me

at the kitchen table. If I'd come home drunk and drugged with 'whore' tattooed across my chest they couldn't have been more disappointed. The skin on my inner forearm was mottled and ugly and I stared at it while they explained. It turned out that there was something worse than animal entrails.

My talent was apophenia. It was more commonly called, with some derision, spinny eye: the ability to perceive patterns in random things. And with it, I might see the future. But I didn't care to know the future. No point in warning me to hide from an imminent apocalypse; I'd want to go, to dance between the falling rubble.

It wore on you after a while, seeing significance in everyday things. The hidden pictures in soup, muck, gravel, fallen leaves, TV snow, branches on a tree and pee stains on toilet floors. The arrangement of peas and chicken in the vomit on the city streets on Saturday mornings. It was the road to madness, finding patterns in every random arrangement.

Apophenia was rare, but pretty much everyone who'd had this talent ended up losing their minds. The only way to stay sane was to shut it out. The visions were a powerful hit, like a drug high. So, even as I tried to block them, my body craved them. The more I tried to see Hello Kitty in the bathroom mould, the more unhinged I would become.

The hidden pictures beneath, which opened my glimpse into the future, were wild and not always easy to interpret. Sometimes they seemed to deceive me, deliberately twisting details.

I could have lived with all of this. I could have gone with the occasional wood-whorl vision, carefully controlling how I indulged, so that I plotted my path to madness with precision and elegance. But what undid me was that any vision emerging through bodily fluids was forbidden. And most dangerous of all were the blood visions. These were wilder and stronger, but took their toll on the seer's body. In the past, they'd killed augurs through convulsions and strokes, and so were banned by all groves. I was the girl who couldn't look at her own toothpaste spit. There was no way on earth I could become a doctor.

'Second marker to Wren,' Maeve called out. I looked up. I hadn't been watching.

There, on the tree above my stone, sat a single magpie. Fastest response ever. Asks had been known to take all day when watching for birds to settle. Another magpie landed on my tree, as if to reiterate, yes, we meant Wren. I stared at my tree, still seeing the illusion of a woman, now with birds in her hair. Moving closer, I could almost make out details of a face.

'What's the third round, Mam?' Aisling said. There were

twelve possible rounds; the more serious the matter, the more we used. We'd completed two of four: stones in a circle, bird on a tree, and it wasn't looking good for me.

'Stone on skin.'

Aisling looked up sharply. Stone on skin wasn't commonly used. Even though it had been toned down from the days when augurs aimed to hurt, it still felt barbaric.

'It's a strong round, Ash,' Maeve said. Stone on skin carried more risk for augurs and so it drew less from the nemeton.

Aisling and I walked towards the edge of the hill. She didn't look happy. Most people wouldn't be, having stones thrown at them. But simple reasoning, the distance between us, the size of the stone, Maeve's lack of muscle tone, meant it was unlikely to come anywhere near us.

'Have you seen your mother's aim?' I tried to lighten the mood. 'I'm betting she'll hit that tree over there.'

But when we turned to face the women, it wasn't Maeve holding the stones. It was Sibéal. Sibéal who tried so hard not to be athletic. She disdained sport, and yet her body leaned naturally to it, eager for the chance to run, throw, jump.

'First to Aisling,' Maeve called.

Sibéal stared at Aisling and then turned the stone as if she was warming it in her hand. Her face was set in concentration and she raised it, then threw. The stone whipped through the air and landed inches from Aisling's feet. A perfect shot.

A small smile on Aisling's face. It could still be her.

'Now to Wren.' Maeve's voice rang through the air.

Sibéal's shawl had slipped down. She pulled it up over her hair. Inexplicably, I felt unsettled. The intense stare on Sibéal's face was cold and dispassionate. The stone was whipping through the air towards me. My hands flew up in front of my face and I felt a sharp pain just beneath my collarbone, muted by my shawl. I touched my hand to it, shocked. The stones were supposed to avoid the upper body. Sibéal was still staring at me in that strange way, and then she was running, screaming, 'Oh my God, oh my God,' like some kind of chant, her shawl and curtain dress flying out behind her.

'Are you crazy?' Aisling was shouting. 'You hit her. Why did you aim so high?'

'I didn't,' Sibéal was saying. 'I swear I aimed for the ground like I did with you. I don't know what happened. It's like the stone flew by itself.' She touched me with a tentative hand, pulling at my shawl to see the bloody skin beneath.

'It's OK,' I said. 'I have a crap aim too.' I tightened the cotton wrap around my chest.

'Marker three to Wren,' Maeve's voice rang across the hilltop and seemed to echo down into the quarry. 'An unbroken run. It is decided.' Then more anxiously, 'Did the stone hurt you, Wren?' Her maternal instinct temporarily overtaking her role as head of grove.

'Just the tiniest graze,' I lied, my skin throbbing.

We returned to the centre to close the ritual, Sibéal uncharacteristically quiet. We were all somehow more than we were before. All of us a little stronger. The ritual had done that. But, in exchange, that strange faint buzz was reduced, the frequency moving in and out of phase.

Starting back down the hill, we listened to Ruth Lacey complain about the new doctor down at Kelly's practice, that Simon, her younger boy, wanted to get his truck-driving licence, and how Mr Lacey was dreading the lambing that year. It was all so normal, so ordinary and re-assuring. We'd go back to the cottage for tea and Maeve's scones.

There'd been three immediate markers. If there really was anyone out there answering our petty questions, they'd made it abundantly clear: it was me. I was it. I turned for a last look at the copse, and in my tree, the one where I'd placed the stone, I counted five magpies. I felt a slight chill, the faintest shiver. A sixth bird landed, closely followed by a seventh.

We were always told: when something repeats, it gains significance. This is how a pattern is formed. And it felt like something was forming around me. Like I was being woven into something and couldn't work my way out.

FIVE
The worst that could happen

Today we visited Lady Catherine. She is brown with
freckles and there are callouses on her hands. She offered
to show me her garden.

AdC

Smith was outside with Simon, replacing the worn gate
pole.

We didn't need to tell them; it was obvious from the way
the girls flanked me. Aisling and Sibéal walked just beside
me, their arms brushing mine every few steps. Maeve was
behind, as if by forming this triangle they could protect me
in the coming months.

'I'm so, so sorry, Wren,' Sibéal whispered. She was never
contrite and a perverse part of me was enjoying the squirm.
But her apology was muted by the sound of Simon dropping the heavy post pounder on to the pole.

'Forget about it,' I said, feeling the throb where the stone
had hit. I looked down and saw, beneath the collar of my

coat, blood had seeped on to my top. Again with the blood-stained clothes. Simon glanced at the blood as he lifted the pounder.

'I didn't …' Sibéal started. The pounder struck down, the clunk of metal against wood inhibiting conversation.

'… mean to hurt you,' she finished louder as the pounder stilled. The sudden silence highlighted those words: mean to hurt you. I thought of David and his wren-boys. Mean to hurt you. They never did, mean to hurt. Always just happened.

'Yeah, if you'd hit a bit higher,' I tried for a joke, 'maybe I'd be in hospital and the old folks would forget the plan.' But my words sounded brittle.

Simon lifted the heavy pounder and drove it down again, lifted and dropped.

'Only three months,' he said, voice catching as he raised the pounder, his fingers curled tightly around the handle. 'Sure, that's no time at all.'

He brought the pounder down with force and the pole sank deep.

'Here, easy with that, Simon,' Mrs Lacey said. 'Come on in for a cup of tea.'

'Nearly done, Mam.' Simon raised the tool, both hands high as his head, like he was about to strike the killer blow.

I turned from Mrs Lacey's fretting over her son, who

seemed to be confusing pole driving with punishment.

'You OK with this?' Smith said as we walked around the side of Maeve's house. But it didn't matter. If a ritual decided something – suck it up, princess.

'What's the worst that could happen?' I was out of my depth. This creeping sense of inadequacy was confirmed when I caught my reflection in the window. Smith was tall and capable beside me. I was so much smaller, my face warped by the glass. How could a girl like me deceive a woman like Calista Harkness? I'd fumble it, and then we'd be worse off than now.

Smith was pensive as he decided how to answer. He didn't want to dwell on the dangers, because he didn't want to alarm me. But he didn't want me to underestimate the situation either.

'There was trouble last night down in Abbyvale,' Simon's voice came from behind us. His eyes swept over me, reading my posture, my fingers looped in my belt holes, checking to see if I was ready to hear this. His talent for reading body language was pretty strong, but not always convenient.

Smith interjected, 'Simon, I don't think …'

'What happened?' I said to Simon.

'Three of them from Rowan Grove were caught on a judge farm. There's a pillar stone there. A strong nemeton.

They found it by accident last summer. Been going in at night for months, trying to bind to it.'

'How many months?' I interrupted, thinking of the augurs quietly humming the binding songs under the cover of darkness, their fingers working the patterns. Forming a bind was like filling a large pool with a small cup. Slow.

'A little under six. Three men every night.'

It took around six months for a grove to form binds to a nemeton. Rituals were flat and without magic if there was no bind.

'And was it working?'

'There was a change all right. But last night Calista's boys got to them.'

'David and his crowd?' I was surprised. Abbyvale was a near derelict town thirty minutes away. 'Surely Calista Harkness wouldn't worry about a gairdín all the way out in Abbyvale?'

It irked me that the group name for judges was not swarm or murder, but gairdín. A garden of judges. Which made them sound all flowers and sunshine, and that couldn't be further from the truth.

'It's strange all right,' Simon agreed.

'What happened?'

Simon paused. Smith shifted his weight from one foot to the other.

'Calista's boys roughed them up really bad.'

'How bad?' I stepped towards Simon.

'They'll be OK,' Smith said. 'They're strong men themselves.'

But I could tell from the way that Simon was standing so rigid that the three augurs weren't OK, strong men or not. That 'roughed them up really bad' was understating things. Again, I felt a surge of hate towards David.

'That won't happen to me.' My jaw was clenched.

'What they did to those men last night was a message,' Simon said. 'A warning of what happens to augurs who cross them.'

My unease grew. The tension between judges and augurs was rising because we were feeling the pinch of our depleted nemeta. Judges were smug, augurs were angry. Things had become volatile. Wouldn't take much to trigger open conflict.

'If Calista Harkness finds out that you're deceiving her …'

'She won't find out.' I had to believe it.

I turned away from them and their frowns.

'It's a completely different situation,' Smith was arguing to Simon as I walked off.

The news from Abbyvale had cranked up my anxiety. There was nothing to give me away, I reassured myself.

We'd spent the last sixteen years hiding in plain sight. Calista Harkness lorded over the judges from Harkness House. She wouldn't know our faces or names. No one in the village knew we were augurs, while we knew every single judge family here. Smith was smart, the plan was solid. Sure, the struggle was uneven, but stealth was our secret weapon. Still, I couldn't shake my worry.

Maeve was serving scones in her kitchen. Something sweet and cinnamony was in the oven. Cake on the counter. None of them appealed. It felt like there were rocks in my stomach.

On the other side of the large room Smith's research was mapped out on the dinner table. Charts, tables, diagrams, notes documenting exactly how we would lie and steal so that we could save ourselves. To stop an otherwise sure path to ruin. Already, families with weak or no talents were distancing themselves from their groves. With their rituals losing meaning, they no longer sensed the patterns of things. Shame or apathy made them turn away from their history and choose to live as if they weren't draoithe. Groves were shrinking at an alarming rate. We had to act before we disappeared completely.

Ignoring the background clatter of tea being made, cups brought out, the search for clean teaspoons, I went to the dinner table. Neon tags pointed from this thing to that.

Colourful pinheads connected string from one possibility to another and then on to another.

Heaps of notes, but the bottom line was simple: get into the archive at Harkness House, retrieve the map, locate the stones. And, bonus prize, find runaway mother.

In the top left corner was the root of the problem: the nemeta. Our sacred sanctuaries. Sibéal had drawn a dolmen, a mound, an old oak, a circle of trees. Groves all over the country had lost their binds to nemeta. Either because a road ran where an ancient maze once was or because a dolmen had become a tourist attraction, its energy leached. But mainly because the most powerful nemeta were now privately owned by judges, their locations a closely guarded secret. They'd taken the best, and the leftovers were too weak to sustain us.

'... must be another way.' Aisling's voice, both hissed and raised, carried across the room.

I glanced up and saw her in the corner of the kitchen, talking to Simon. Their bodies were jagged angles and their faces tight. Her hand crept to her neck, as it did when she was agitated. Mrs Lacey, seated on the faded green armchair, blinked slowly.

'Your cup is empty there, Ruth.' Maeve smoothed over the awkwardness, carrying the teapot to Mrs Lacey. 'And, Simon, you haven't tried my coffee cake. Another slice, Ash?'

Simon obliged and cut a huge piece of cake. Aisling, looking a little less blotchy, didn't.

Aisling was wrong, there wasn't another way. I looked again at the map.

In the bottom right corner Sibéal had drawn something like a triquetra, but not the usual three-cornered knot. Hers was looser, simpler: the Daragishka Knot. The solution to our problem.

When she'd stolen her mother's jewellery, Sorcha had taken one of the three Daragishka stones on the worn gold necklace. It had been in Smith's family since his ancestor Ruairí Ó Cróinín found all three in the Red River, the Daragishka, on Hy-Breasil, the island that appeared through the mist every seven years. The original home of the druids.

Together the three stones made the Daragishka Knot and were charged with the same energy that hummed through the nemeta, but on steroids. By forming the Knot we'd strengthen our nemeta and help other groves restore theirs. Problem was, the other two stones had been lost centuries ago.

When Basil Lucas, the judge geologist and media whore, hinted that he could form the Daragishka Knot, Smith began to watch him. We discovered that he'd marked the locations of the stones on a map. After my premonition of his death at Christmas, we knew we had to find a way into his archive and get the map. We couldn't let the judges find the stones. Not only would the Knot amplify our nemeta, tracking down Smith's stolen stone would most likely lead us to Sorcha.

'Wren, tea.' Maeve pushed a cup into my hand and stood beside me.

I sorted through the pages, passing over Maeve's research into new ways of binding nemeta, Smith's timeline for meeting targets, profiles on Calista Harkness, Jarlath Creagh and other influential judges. Beneath the carefully collected information, I found it. The plan of a house, Harkness House, the headquarters of the Rose Gairdín, with the Lucas Archive in the basement library.

Where I would be spending the next three months.

Unbidden, I saw my vision of the hands grabbing at the food-laden table. But not at Sorcha, with her long red hair. It was me stretched out on the feast table. Me with cocktail umbrellas in my hair. Me being fed upon. I shuddered, and from across the room Simon looked over with sympathy.

Sibéal was being interrogated by Mrs Lacey. She looked uncomfortable, and I guessed Mrs Lacey was grilling her about her not yet emerged talent.

I unfolded a large sheet of paper. It was an illustrated

overview of the plan. Things were identified by basic symbols, most of which I couldn't follow. It was like Sibéal and Smith had invented an entire coded language. I studied the page, trying to make sense of it. I was especially drawn to the careful sketch of an orchid at the centre of the page.

'That's Calista Harkness,' Sibéal said from behind me. She picked up a brown marker and leaned over the table, quickly sketching something there. She cut a piece of string and glued it down.

'We've thought through everything, Wren,' Maeve said. 'Trust me, nothing can go wrong.'

'Nothing can go wrong,' I repeated. As she moved her hand, I saw what Sibéal had just drawn. Connected by thin string from Carraig Cottage to the Harkness House, then to the nemeta: a small brown wren. Me. I felt tethered by that string.

'Now, don't forget the lucky hairpins.' Maeve held out her hand. Two pewter hair combs with short teeth. Fake vintage with roses twisted into filigree. Not my kind of thing.

Maeve stretched out her hand, insistent, saying, 'You must wear these.'

Hesitating, I cast an eye at the picture of Harkness House. Three months of seeing David and the wrenboys every day. Of doing mundane things, just being there among them.

Three months of deception, of making sure I wasn't caught. Watching that I didn't betray myself with an ordinary word now a potential weapon. Three months of being always, always on guard. Of looking for the right opportunity to find and steal a map from a valuable archive.

Calista's boys roughed them up really bad.

My stomach twisted as Smith caught my eye. Everyone in that room was watching me. I felt a collective intake of breath, a tense beat as they looked at their best hope. Me.

Mrs Lacey took a wet slurp of tea.

'Wren?' Smith said. 'Can you do this?'

Maybe I wouldn't have to be there for three months, I told myself. If I was smart about it, I could get the Lucas map and be out in a week or two. Reaching for the hair combs, I turned to Smith.

'I'll be fine,' I said to him in a loud clear voice, feeling the dull throb where Sibéal's stone had struck. I sounded so calm and assured I almost believed it myself.

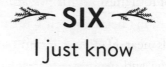

SIX
I just know

I took a bad turn in Lady Catherine's walled garden today.
As I fell, I sliced my arm on the blade of the garden shears.
AdC

I knew the city well. All through my childhood, Smith and I would drive up on Saturdays in his old banger. We'd go to the National Museum and linger in the Treasury. Together, we'd walk down Grafton Street, tramping the red brick smooth. We'd move away from the milling tourists to the quieter residential roads. As we walked, Smith would point out the secret history of the city: there is the Orchard of the Hungry Marys, there the House of the Seven Virgins.

Our walking bound me to the city, as if we trailed invisible threads that became evermore entangled each time we paced through. At some point I realised that marching me through the city and embedding in me its secret stories was Smith's way of making sure that I knew I belonged. That I had a place in the world. That I was not simply the darkling child, the poor motherless girl the villagers loved to gossip about.

But the roads near Harkness House were less familiar. The houses, large and unwelcoming, were hidden behind high walls, and my sense of belonging evaporated. And with it went my confidence.

It took around ninety minutes, two buses and a Luas tram ride, to travel from Kilshamble to Harkness House, but it felt like I'd gone to another world. Early, I stopped at a small café to shake off my bad nerves. Tea to magic myself brave. I ordered at the counter, where a single barista managed the queue. Perched on a high stool at the window ledge, I took out my notes on Calista Harkness, placing the pages like a tarot spread.

I didn't need to look at them. I could hear Maeve's voice whispering small facts: Calista Harkness was fifty-two years old. Born in Kilshamble, she left for Boston aged five. Returned to Dublin for long visits. Came back for good when she inherited the Langstream Crystal empire, now sold. One brief marriage. One son at boarding school. Paranoid about her personal security. A queen among judges, her titles included Grand Magistrate, Hand of Justice, and First Cleave of all Cleaves. She'd backstabbed her older sister to ascend the hierarchy of judges. The lockdown of nemeta happened on her father's watch and she guarded it rigorously. Decades ago, he'd advised judges to buy up land containing the remaining nemeta and keep their locations secret. It was a calculated move to cut us off from the source of our strength. And ensure their own unlimited access. Their hatred for us ran deep, ever since we began to rebel against the law of nature as handed down by the judges.

My ancestors, many centuries ago, realised that the laws as interpreted by the judges favoured their own at the expense of augurs. Laws that insisted judges owned the land and ruled us all. Since the original rebellion, we had rejected the rigid hierarchies of ancient draoithe society. Leaving their brutalities behind, ours was a much fairer community.

Sensing someone approach, I looked up.

'Mind if I sit here?' The stranger gestured to the stool beside mine.

'Not at all.' I gathered the papers and stuffed them into an envelope.

'Let me get that.' My oversized tote bag was precarious on his side of the ledge. As I leaned across, the barista barked, 'Large tea,' and I turned back to see if it was mine.

I heard my bag thud to the ground. Looking down, there they were, my things spilled on the sticky wooden floor.

'Crap.' I hopped off the stool and crouched down. I didn't know where to start: a single lint-covered Mentos, two fake antique lucky hair combs, a knitted hat with an oversized bobble, a letter opener sharpened into a stiletto, and various half-forgotten things that for no good reason I carried around with me every day.

The stranger bent down to help. 'That was my fault. Sorry.'

Glancing up, I noticed his eyes. They were deep sludge. Murky eyes that might have been blue but were darkened to grey. Eyes like the sky on a rainy day.

Marble eyes.

When I was little, I loved Smith's old marbles. Not to play with, but because I'd been transfixed by the swirls of dull colour inside. Even then, I had a thing about colours bleeding into each other. I stared at the stranger's eyes like I wanted to take them out and hold them to the light, as I'd done with Smith's marbles. I grabbed my phone and checked for damage.

The barista hollered, 'Large tea,' while the stranger's hands hovered, then moved to the filigree hair combs. I snatched the tampons, saying, 'I'm not embarrassed.' To convince myself that I wasn't cringing so much that I might shrivel up and die right there. Sibéal would write a grue-some little film about it.

'I didn't see anything embarrassing.' He sounded amused. I picked up the Monopoly cat token. My Lego Wonder Woman key ring with its missing arm and faded mouth.

'Except maybe these.' He held a pair of furry dice that I'd bought for Aisling's car and forgotten to give her. 'Furry dice? Seriously?'

'You never know when you're going to need furry dice. I'd hate to have a furry dice emergency and get caught short.' I stuffed them back in the bag. No wonder it was so bloody full.

The stranger handed me the letter opener, noting the sharpened edge.

'Resourceful,' he murmured, unperturbed by the home-made weapon.

He picked up my knitted hat with its huge bobble and said, 'You look familiar, have we met?'

I studied him. He was attractive, if you liked contradiction: those eyes that were both liquid and stone. Calloused, elegant hands. Sun-kissed in winter. His face was sharp angles with curved lips. The way he spoke was mostly American, but I could hear the Irish beneath.

I liked contradiction.

'No,' I said.

He searched my face. 'Either we've met or you have a doppelgänger. Maybe a sister?'

There was something disconcerting about seeing him absent-mindedly twist my bobble with his rough fingers. It was like the spilled contents of my bag allowed him a glimpse into my soul. And it was all big woollen bobbles with fluffy Mentos mints. And makeshift daggers.

'No sister. I look nothing like my mother. And my father was a con man.'

Grabbing my bobble hat, I shoved it into my bag. 'I'll take it from here,' I said. 'Thanks.'

He picked up a notebook and I caught the edge of a tattoo on his inner forearm. He stood up, placing the notebook on the table.

'I'll bring your tea,' he said. 'It's the least I can do.'

Scooping up crumpled tissues and old sweets for the bin, I sat back on the high stool and the stranger with murky eyes returned with my tea. I tried again to look at his tattoo; it seemed only fair, since he'd seen my stuff all over the floor.

But his attention was on his coffee and his forearm was obscured by the newspaper he was holding.

'You from around here?' I wanted to confirm my directions to Harkness House. But it came out coy. It sounded like I was looking for a reason to talk to him. Maybe I was.

Glancing over, he smiled. 'Yeah, I come here often.'

As if I was trying to pick him up with some tired line. When he'd been the one with the 'Have we met before?'

'So. Do *you* come here often?' he said, and I couldn't tell if I was imagining the flirtatious edge to his voice. And I didn't want to think about how much I was enjoying it. He looked down and said, 'Wren?'

I froze at the sound of my name. I hadn't told him. But then he slid my notebook over. 'Don't forget this.' There was my name, written in silver marker on the black cover. 'Does it mean something, your name?'

As I took the notebook I saw the tattoo on his inner forearm. An intricate snake with its tail coiled as it reared up to strike.

A snake with two heads.

I let go of the notebook and it fell off the ledge, landing again on the sticky floor. But I couldn't take my eyes off the snake. It seemed to rear towards me, as it did on my sixteenth birthday.

'No,' I lied. I was named for the druid bird.

'You OK?'

I barely heard the words.

No.

'Yes,' I said, peeling my eyes from his arm to his eyes.

His grey eyes.

Most of the time, I didn't think about that first vision. Repressed it. Because it marked my failure.

Before, Smith had always said, 'Wren's talent is going to be strong, I just know it.' And afterwards, his sympathetic silence was painful. With that vision, I moved from being the girl with promise to the girl who was worse than blank. It was the moment when I had let Smith down.

I knew those eyes.

I slid off the stool, mesmerised.

'Something wrong?' the stranger persisted.

His grey eyes, the snake eyes from my very first vision, held mine even as he retrieved the notebook. He held it out to me.

'No. I, uh, have to go.' I sounded breathless. My tea untouched, I stuffed the notebook in my bag and left.

It was a bad sign, seeing that tattoo, those eyes, on my first day with the judges. I couldn't understand why a stranger was marked with the snake from my vision. The only vision that had ever physically scarred me. It felt like something was screaming a warning: forget the plan. Back away before it's too late.

But it was already too late. Turning the corner, I could see a large, unfriendly house at the bottom of the cul-de-sac. I had arrived at the Harkness Foundation.

SEVEN
So much fun

My dear friend Elizabeth accompanied me to see
Miss Shackleton's botanical studies. She captures the
essence of the flower and with perfect line and colour.
Her orchids are luminescent.

AdC

The first thing I noticed about Harkness House was the
flowers. There were huge vases of cut flowers in every room,
their scents cloying and close despite the tall windows.

I stood in the marble entrance hall staring at flowers in
water. White lilies floated in a bowl on the table in the
wide, bright hallway. They made such a pretty pattern.
I wanted so badly to fill in the blanks.

'This way,' the housekeeper said, her dark dress always
just ahead of me.

We walked several corridors until we reached the back
of the house, where she swiped a card and entered an open-
plan office suite. A hugely pregnant woman looked up from

her screen, and back down again. A man right next to the door continued writing in a ledger. I stood there like a spare part.

After a long moment, Ledger Man, without taking his eyes from the enormous old-style book, called across the room, 'Someone tell Laney the intern is here.'

I wondered if anyone had told Ledger Man it was the twenty-first century where balance sheets were now computerised. Going by his spotted dicky bow, I couldn't be sure.

No one moved. I stood in the doorway, awkward and spare.

'I'll find Laney.' The housekeeper had kind eyes. She crossed the long room to a door at the other side.

I walked a few steps into the room. The Harkness Foundation was an arts and heritage charity. They took on projects related to art history, listed houses, antiques, and also supported contemporary artists and researchers. Or at least that's what I gleaned from Smith's notes.

Now, what I saw before me was a long room with tall sash windows. Several people at their desks, tapping at computers and looking busy. Framed posters declaring exhibitions, lectures, festivals, retrospectives, walking tours. A small open-kitchen area immediately on my left, a large boardroom table on my right. On the wall was a colour-coded timeline listing different operations and projects, and the duties assigned to each staff member. The panic flared again. I didn't fit with that. I was all mould and moss and random blotches.

Two weeks, I told myself, I'll be gone in two weeks.

'You the intern?' A voice rang from across the room.

I turned to see a young, voluptuous woman striding from the double doors on the opposite side. She wore very high, spiky heels. Her hair was an unusual combination of white and light purple.

'I'm Laney, office manager and assistant to Dr Harkness.' She walked me to the corner, to a wooden desk beside one of the long windows. I looked at her curiously; she couldn't be much older than Aisling.

'This is you,' she said.

On the desk was a bowl-shaped vase of blood-red peony buds curled like fists. Closed like death and secrets.

'You're here to help around the office. Make tea. Run to the post office. Other errands.'

I didn't think she meant to sound imperious. It was just how Laney came across, that thin nose and thin upper lip and posh accent. But I didn't mind. I'd mop the white marble floors if it got us into the archive.

'In order to develop your skillset, you'll also be assisting with two projects.' Laney held up two fingers painted with silver nail polish while I considered whether skillset was an actual word. 'First, the Arabella Project.'

'The Arabella Project?' I hadn't expected this.

'We're doing a massive campaign for the one hundred and fiftieth anniversary of the birth of Arabella de Courcy, nineteenth-century botanical artist.'

Or, Arabella de Courcy, mad tree girl who'd died in Kilshamble woods. I wondered how I'd managed to overlook that one of Calista Harkness's big projects was the Kilshamble tree girl.

'You've heard of her?' Laney was saying.

'Everyone in Kilshamble knows Arabella.' I hadn't meant to make it sound so intimate, like we were all on first-name terms.

Laney nodded. 'That's why this year's internship went to your village.' She made it sound like 'your tribe'. Or 'your planet'. Some distant place she couldn't begin to fathom.

I wondered if Laney knew what the village really thought about Arabella, if she knew the wild stories about the artist and the tree prince. I'd guess not. I'd imagine that wasn't the image of Arabella de Courcy that Calista Harkness was trying to promote. But I realised I was glad, that it seemed redemptive somehow, to rescue Arabella's reputation from lurid village myth.

'The commemoration is our key project these next

twelve months, and we're investing a lot in it,' Laney went on. 'Dr Harkness is very passionate about underappreciated Irish artists. She feels strongly that Arabella de Courcy is one of the most talented artists in Irish history and is determined to raise her profile.'

'I haven't seen any of the paintings.' I searched my brain for nineteenth-century botanical pictures. Nope, none. It occurred to me how woefully inadequate I was for this arts and heritage internship.

'You and everyone else. But that's what we intend to change by the end of this year.'

'What will I be doing?'

'We've a huge amount of media coverage lined up. Dr Harkness gives talks to schools, museums, galleries and historical societies both here and abroad,' Laney said. 'You'll help me with research, some indexing, and you'll organise things like her travel and making reservations, and deal with website queries and create her PowerPoint presentations.'

'Admin.' That sounded doable. 'What's the second project?'

'Organising the Lucas archive. That's a little less glam, I'm afraid. Tedious work, but when it arrives we have to inventory and catalogue everything.' Laney studied me. 'I hope you like dust.'

'When it arrives?' I said. I thought that the archive was ready and waiting for me to snoop through it.

'Yeah, it should get here in the next few weeks. I'd say about three weeks before we're ready to go in.'

'Three weeks?' I parroted, my throat was tight and the words sounded thin. The way Laney was looking at me I realised that she was thinking she'd landed a dud.

I was about to attempt a coherent sentence when from behind me the whistling started. It was a random tune, nothing I recognised but I felt my whole body tense. Beneath the whistling I could hear the coffee machine as water strained through the grounds. The milk frother gurgled and the tune segued into '*The wran, the wran*'. Cups clattered against the granite kitchen counter. Laney was talking to me but I was listening to the footsteps on the marble floor.

'It's the wran.' David was right behind me. He was always closer than I thought.

'Yep, small brown bird. That's me,' I said, finding my voice. Forcing myself to look him in the eye, I was vaguely aware of Cillian and the others crossing the room towards us. Hidden beneath my sleeves, my arms were covered in a raw rash brought on by anxiety. It didn't matter that the last wren hunt had been interrupted, they had time to finish what they'd started.

David seemed even bigger than before. His eyes trailed over my face, lingering on the mostly healed graze at my temple.

'Nice to see you without leaves in your hair.'

My hair. Long, blunt strands wrapped around his hand on Stephen's Day. It had been worrying me. What had he done with it?

Ledger Man looked up briefly, before returning his attention to his writing.

To answer Laney's silent question, David said, 'We're old friends.' He moved closer, brushing his arm against mine. He stood as close as he could get with my overlarge bag between us.

Anger coursed through me. I wanted to say something, but stopped myself. If I spoke now, it would involve four-letter words and the plan would go to the birds. I closed my hands into fists, as if that would help the fighting words stay down, and looked across to the other boys who'd gathered.

But there weren't four of them any more. Behind Cillian's smirks and Ryan's blank stare, I saw him. Eyes like a heavy cloud. Golden skin and dark hair. It was my murky-eyed stranger from the café.

The boy with the snake tattoo was a judge.

'Dr Harkness will see you when she can,' Laney said, walking to her desk.

The boys arranged themselves as they usually did, closing around me and blocking my escape. Big and imposing, they made me feel vulnerable. Cillian leaned against my desk, picking up one of the peony buds and burying his nose in it. I stood in the middle of them, small and angry.

Without warning, the mood among the wrenboys changed. The smirks and smiles faded. Cillian moved away from where he'd been leaning on the desk, his dead little eyes fixed forward. They stood a bit more upright, a lot more guarded.

And then I understood: at the door to her office was Calista Harkness.

I couldn't see much of her from between the boys; I got a glimpse of blonde hair, red lips, a white shirt dress. But we all knew she was there. Without saying anything, she drew our attention.

'Laney,' she called, her voice deeper than I'd have thought.

When the door shut behind Laney and Calista, the boys visibly relaxed.

'I'm Tarc.' My stranger stood a little back from the circle of wrenboys. 'I head up Cassa's security.'

I looked for some recognition that we'd met earlier. For the boy who'd teased me about furry dice. But he gave me nothing.

'Looks like you've met my team already.' The light flirtation from the café was gone and he was all business.

I looked again at the tattoo on his arm. He was Team David. He was not my friend.

Calista's boys roughed them up really bad.

'I've seen them around.' My words were light as I inched away from David. 'Excuse me.' I pushed through the gap between David and Tarc. But David's fingers trailed through the ends of my long hair. I took no small delight in the new scar on his hand.

'Oh, Wran, we're going have so much fun.'

At the cottage, there was a single picture of Sorcha on the wall. My whole sense of her was concentrated in that one photograph. Wearing a blue dress with tiny flower sprigs, she was leaning down, her face tilted up. Her hair was long and sweeping and her mouth wide and generous as she smiled at the camera. But her eyes were sad.

When I was little and still hoped that Sorcha would return, I would stare at the picture, hoping to find something that connected her to me. But I never did. Her pale, freckled skin was unlike mine. Her hair was red and stick straight to my dark waves. Sometimes it seemed impossible that she could be my mother. But the blue of her eyes was exactly the shade of Smith's. The lines of her jaw and nose were the same as his. I would stare at the picture until the fixedness of my gaze inched Sorcha's smile a little wider, made her eyes a little watery. I used to think that if I looked long enough, she would say: *Oh Wren honey, I'm so, so sorry.*

My imaginary Sorcha always sounded just like Maeve.

'Did you talk to her?' Smith's voice came from the kitchen, where he was serving up the one-pot. For a second, I thought he meant Sorcha, who was still smiling down at me.

I wandered into the kitchen.

'What's Calista Harkness like?' He put two steaming plates on the kitchen table and we sat to eat.

Smith had always been intrigued by the enigmatic leader of the judges. He'd call it research, all those Sunday mornings reading the interviews and lifestyle spreads.

'They call her Cassa,' I said, trying to swallow down a bite of meat. 'I didn't speak to her.' Smith's one-pot was always tasty, but the meat was as tough as old boots.

Cassa Harkness had remained shut in her office all day, with only Tarc and Laney going in. My tea-making skills were underappreciated.

Smith didn't say anything but his disdain was evident as he raised an eyebrow and picked up his fork.

'They've run some really cool art projects,' I said, spearing another chunk of meat. My fork met with resistance so I went for a carrot instead. 'And they offer generous scholarships.'

'Judges are very good at appearances,' Smith said, taking another sip from his glass, the red wine staining the cracks in his lips. 'But look at the Abbyvale three. Mick Murphy has pins and metal plates in his arm after what happened. He'll never regain full mobility. Can't be a carpenter with a useless arm.'

'I hadn't realised,' I said, putting down my fork.

'That's *Cassa* Harkness for you. Make no mistake. David and his boys might have got their hands dirty, but they act on her orders.'

And Tarc's, since he was head of security.

'Wren,' Smith said, placing his knife and fork at twenty past four. 'Watch her.'

I wasn't sure what he was saying.

'You want me to spy on Cassa Harkness?'

'I mean she's a manipulative woman. Stay vigilant. Be careful.'

His eyes were locked on mine. Behind him, from the living room, Sorcha in her wooden frame smiled her secret smile.

'But you're right. It makes sense to keep a lookout while you're at Harkness House. We won't have an opportunity like this again.'

'That wasn't what I …' And I gave up. Poised over his plate, alert, I knew he had already considered what I might discover while at Harkness House. 'What do you mean? Am I to find out something in particular?'

Smith didn't respond. He seemed to be choosing his words.

'Like the locations of her nemeta?' I said.

He glanced up sharply.

'What good would that do?' I said. 'It takes six months to forge binds, and we can't have a repeat of what happened in Abbyvale.'

'Just watch her,' Smith said again. 'Find out about judge ways, how their magic works. Observe everything. Especially Cassa. I want to know her weaknesses.'

We knew little about judge ways. They didn't receive talents or follow patterns the way we did. Their magic was nature based: in the old days they'd understood the language of trees, the whispers of water, the howls of the wind and the signs of smoke. And as interpreters of nature, of the divine, they'd laid down the law.

'But how will this help us?' I said.

There was something a little dirty about being a spy. It felt like that smudge of red wine on Smith's lips had somehow seeped into his words and stained the air.

'After we have the Knot, we'll still have to protect

ourselves. What you learn now could be vital to securing our position then. I'm just saying keep your eyes open.'

'OK.' My reluctance was clear. And yet it seemed foolish to object to this when I was already neck-deep, so I added, 'Anything else?'

Smith moved to standing at the sound of voices at the kitchen door. 'Look out for anything about Birchwood.'

'What's Birchwood?'

'Find out.'

With a gust of wind, Maeve came in carrying a large plate of sugar buns while Aisling and Sibéal followed behind.

'Beef and carrot stew, must be a special occasion,' Maeve said and winked at me. Placing the buns on the table, she opened a bottle of Prosecco.

'For Wren's first day,' she said, gathering glasses and grinning at me.

I plastered a smile on my face, but inside I was angry and confused. Hurt. They had me do this big complicated thing and then brought out cake and sparkling wine like it was my birthday. Maeve was still smiling as she poured a small glass of Prosecco for me. Thirsty, I took big gulps, feeling it fizz down.

And then I got it. Bringing cake and wine was the only way she knew. It reminded me of the whiskey and apple bread on Stephen's Day. The biggest problems were treated with sugar and booze.

'How was it, honey?' Maeve said, both hands gently squeezing mine. 'How'd it go? What's she like? Tell us everything.' And then a little quieter, 'Those boys say anything to you? They do anything?'

And I thought about my hair wrapped around David's hand.

'Nothing I can't handle,' I said. 'Must be those lucky hairpins.'

Over Maeve's shoulder, Smith drifted through the wide square arch into the living room. Sorcha's eyes followed him as he settled at the worktable in the corner of the room. He'd built up the miniature war table over the years. Small villages, woods, rivers and fields, trenches and tanks were arranged and rearranged, according to the maps of old battles that he studied.

Smith spent hours working out new strategies and tactics between his endlessly warring sides. The pieces were collected carefully, rescued from obscure fates through online searches, and he often got Sibéal to help him redesign them to fit the different regiments he needed for his battles. She had become increasingly interested in the mechanics of warfare, and the two of them spent many hours with their heads bent over the worktable.

Aisling watched him carefully. There was a slight frown on her face as her eyes ran up and down his body. She was unaware of my gaze on her as she concentrated on him. Read him. I was scratching at my arm again, and it had nothing to do with David or Harkness House.

'Aisling,' I said, and it sounded like a question. She broke away from Smith and turned to me, guilty.

'Wren honey, grab a bun before Ash eats them all,' Maeve called over from the sink as she tipped the Prosecco into her glass.

Aisling was beside me, a slight blush on her cheeks.

'There's nothing wrong with him, Wren, I swear,' she spoke quietly. 'Mam and Smith, they're getting older. I check over them every now and then.'

I understood. Maeve had been dangerously ill last May. We'd all had an awful scare.

'You sure?' I scratched at my arm, feeling the skin tear. The stinging burn was a relief. I looked down and saw a pinprick of blood on my shirt.

There, the third stain I'd been waiting for. It bothered me that it appeared at this moment, as I worried about Smith. He was everything to me. But he'd lived most of his life and, if I survived Harkness House, I'd a lot left of mine. Thinking about Smith becoming ill and frail caused a hundred times the anxiety that David and his wrenboys did. Whenever it happened, it would be too soon.

'That's all, I promise.' Then, dropping her voice, Aisling

said, 'Let's get more of that Prosecco before Mam polishes it off.'

We fed on sugar buns and topped up our glasses when Maeve's back was turned. I wasn't sure if it was the fizzy wine or my imagination or if Aisling really did turn to Smith several times later in the evening, the faintest look of worry in her eyes.

EIGHT
A warning

Since that night in the woods, my art has been transformed.
It is as though there is someone else inside me, directing
my hand as I draw.
AdC

I paused beside the gate of Harkness House. Before, on my wanderings with Smith, I'd felt like the Little Match Girl, always watching from outside. Now I'd been invited in and I realised that, actually, I was an outside kind of girl.

My hand hovered at the old-style latch while I fixated on the stone detail just beneath the roof. A traditional knot design looped around the whole building. The house was cold and elegant, and set on over an acre of garden with mature trees.

'That latch can be tricky.'

I turned to see Tarc. In one hand, he carried a take-away cup from the café. With the other, he reached across me for the latch.

'How old is the house?' I said, staring at the intricate

stonework as he pushed the gate. The twisted detail mirrored the knots in my stomach. I wasn't looking forward to meeting Cassa Harkness.

'It was built by Arabella de Courcy's father but owned by Cassa's family for the last hundred years.' Tarc slipped by me, the cotton of his shirt brushing my coat. He paused in the wide rose-covered archway, studying me. 'C'mon.' The word was lazy, easy. But Tarc standing there, waiting for me, was somehow too much.

I hesitated. The anxiety I'd felt moments before took on a different shape as I looked at the boy beneath the climbing roses. A boy from Team David.

'Nothing to be afraid of.' He was so very wrong.

When I didn't move, he smiled and turned, heading for the door.

'Wait,' I called as I followed beneath the thorny branches. I had to try and get along with them.

'How do they do this?' I pointed to the rose bushes, blathering to hide my discomfort. This morning I felt it acutely, that den-of-lions danger. There was nowhere safe in Harkness House. No one safe. No matter how nicely some of them smiled at me.

'Do what?'

'Train them so perfectly over the arches and yet make them look so wild.'

'Good gardener, I guess.' Tarc seemed wary. Evidently, garden design wasn't scintillating conversation. But I wasn't great with strangers. My circle of friends was small: usually just me and Aisling, maybe Sibéal. Sometimes Simon, with our on-off flirtation. And with Tarc, I was worse than usual.

'Yeah, gardening is cool.' It was like I'd read a book on how not to talk to boys. 'My father was. A gardener, I mean. Not cool.'

'Thought you said he was a con man.' Tarc was looking at me like he was wondering what kind of weirdling they'd let loose among them.

'He moonlighted.'

There were few sure things I knew about my father. I'd heard the grown-ups whisper that he was a cheat and a charmer who could sell a condom to a nun. That with skin as brown as a bear, he came from some hot place far away. And that he was a gardener, and good at it too.

We walked up the front steps, a small frown on Tarc's brow.

'You don't look like a gardener's daughter.'

'What does a gardener's daughter look like, then?'

The way he studied me made me feel like I was going through some sort of security check. Like those eyes could see more than you'd want to share. It made me want to turn and run.

But I was done running from judge boys. So, awkward, we stood at the front door, where he continued to stare. And then he gave a tight, unfunny laugh.

'I don't know.' He shook his head like he was clearing it. 'They have gnarled roots for fingers and toes. Bark for teeth and leaves instead of hair.' Tarc reached a hand to the doorknob. His grin was forced.

'You know about the tuanacul?' I said as he moved into the large entrance hall, still holding the door. I crossed the threshold, brushing past him and stepping on to the white marble. 'About the women with lips of petals, their touch as soft as a leaf, who will kiss you senseless, breathing poison into your veins?'

'You make it sound appealing.' This time the smile was real. His arm dropped and he closed the door, inching closer to where I stood.

'They're meant to be appealing.'

His smile was infectious. Dangerous even. I felt my anxiety dissipating beneath its warmth.

'That's the point,' I went on. 'They lure you, they seduce you with their charm and beauty. And, when you surrender, because surrender is inevitable, they feed on you, drawing your very essence from your body. Then, sucked dry, they cast you out.' I wasn't sure if it was amusement that made his eyes gleam so. 'I grew up half in love with tree men with big strong muscles and half terrified that I'd actually find one.'

'And did you?' he said. 'Find one?' His body angled towards mine.

'It's practically a requirement, living in Kilshamble, to have an encounter with a sexy tree man.' And I heard myself. That light flirtation making my voice soft and words lilt. My stance mimicking his. If Smith could hear me now.

'And what happened with your sexy tree man?' He seemed to loom over me.

'Nothing. It's just stories.' I stepped back and shut it down, whatever it was that had opened up here. 'I didn't realise they were known outside of Kilshamble.'

'That's what you get, hanging out with Cassa.' Tarc sounded disappointed. My gear change had been abrupt.

'She's interested in fairy stories?'

'Only certain fairy stories.' He moved past me, going inside the room behind.

'This is the white room,' Tarc said, all business again. 'For parties and special events. We have a few scheduled over the coming weeks for the Arabella Project.'

The room looked like a magazine photo spread: excessive amounts of marble, uncomfortable antique chairs and strange-looking knick-knacks that were probably worth more than I'd earn in my lifetime. The kind of room where you'd just love to let loose a bunch of muddy, sugar-high children.

As we walked towards the office, Tarc explained security codes and swipe cards. 'It's a very advanced security system.' Most crystal heiresses didn't need security.

'Yep.' We went through the office doors.

'Gallagher, you're late.' David was cheerful.

'And you're skiving,' Tarc said to David, who insisted it didn't matter that he'd finished his training early because he was such a big, strong lump already.

'Looks like you brought the dirt in,' Cillian said, looking at me.

'Don't be a dick, Cillian,' Tarc said, his eyes flashing with irritation. Maybe he was less Team David than I'd thought. But what did it matter if he was marginally less evil than expected? He was a judge.

'Wren,' Laney said. 'Dr Harkness is waiting for you.'

Her face was smooth and polished, her light-blonde hair streaked with silver strands. She wore dark-red lipstick that stood out against the pale thinness of her. Cassa Harkness was delicate with a fine chiselling that shaped her cheekbones and clavicles, that made each bone on her chest visible beneath her skin. She looked breakable.

She didn't say anything, running her eyes over my clothes,

my hair that hung wild. Untidy. I should have remembered Maeve's lucky combs crushed at the bottom of my bag. A light perfume filled the air.

'It's good to meet you, Dr Harkness,' I said. I wasn't sure if it was the lie that made me so nervous or if it was her.

'Everyone calls me Cassa,' she said. She spoke with a vague air, and I couldn't tell whether she'd made a random observation or an invitation to do the same.

Definitely her that made me nervous.

'Cassa.' I struggled beneath her gaze. She was like the sun, and I was wilting.

'You're the Kilshamble girl.'

If they were very talented, I could pick out augurs in a crowd because I felt a pull towards them, like a weak magnetic draw. But there was something else with Cassa. Not a draw, more like a small bite of static. Something that made me want to pull back. Her eyes continued to fix on me and her gaze was greedy.

'David's told me a lot about you.'

Crap.

'Do I need to fact-check what he's said?' My stupid wide smile tried to pass the words as a joke but they fell flat.

'He said he likes your hair.' The look on her face suggested she didn't agree.

I swallowed hard. The silence dragged out, making me uncomfortable.

'We went to school together. Long ago. Before he left and, uh, I ...' I trailed off. Cassa wouldn't want to hear about how Smith began my homeschooling when I was fourteen.

Tapping her pen, Cassa was aggressively bored by my attempt at conversation. I was bricking it. No way could I manage more than a week with this woman.

Her gaze drifted outside and I lost her attention. My sun had clouded over. But I'd been warned about the judges' charm, that strange magnetism that drew people to them and made them such good politicians and lawyers.

'You may go.' She didn't bother to look at me.

Turning away, it felt like I'd disappointed her. And it made me feel odd. She's a manipulative woman, Smith had said, and I began to guess how right he was.

'It's beautiful.' I stopped. On the wall beside the doors was a painting. A watercolour of an orchid.

'That's an Arabella de Courcy.'

I was beginning to understand why Cassa was so passionate about the artist. The picture was simple and elegant. Clean lines and perfect light. The clear, almost scientific precision of it so deeply at odds with the dark stories of the woodland siren creeping along mossy beds.

'Do you have more?' I turned to Cassa, who'd resumed her staring.

'Many more,' she said. 'If you want, I'll show you.'

'I'd like that.'

When she smiled, she drew me to her. I left her office reminding myself of the Abbyvale three.

The wicker man, Aisling's voice in my head added helpfully.

Ignoring the kitchen area, where the security boys were still gathered, I went to my desk. A stack of reports had been dumped there for filing.

A burst of laughter came from the other side of the room. David. I pulled at the neck of my shirt. It was too hot. My skinnies had my knees in a death grip.

Skewering my hair into a loose bun with Maeve's lucky combs, I tried to block out David's voice.

'Got a new one for you,' he said to the boys.

Briefly, I peered up at them. Tarc leaned against the wall, listening. Watching.

'How many augurs does it take to change a light bulb?' David continued.

My whole body stiffened. I willed myself to relax. Keep on reading. Don't let them see that the word means something.

'Thirteen. One to hold the light bulb in place and twelve

to drink enough to make the room spin.' He chuckled at his own joke, Cillian and Brian joining in.

The words on the page blurred while I tried to quell the anger he'd stirred. That's what they thought of us: a bunch of drunk, useless fairground fortune tellers.

My head jerked up without permission and I saw Tarc unsmiling against the wall. He seemed kinder than the others. Or maybe I just didn't want him to be like them because he had nice shoulders and eyes like shiny marbles. Which should have been kinda freaky. But they weren't. Looking at him from beneath my tumbling down hair, I did feel a small prick of guilt that succeeding at my mission would get him in trouble.

I'd do this as fast as possible, I told myself, and soon Harkness House would be a bad memory. As soon as the archive arrived, I'd be all over it like a rash. I'd find the map quickly – how hard could it be?

Tarc peeled himself from the wall. 'Break's over. Get your lazy asses back to work.'

But I suspected that Tarc hadn't been on a break. That he'd spent coffee time sussing out the new girl.

Picking up a pen, I took off the lid. Laney walked by, her heels little dagger stabs to the floor. Flicking through the post, she disappeared into Cassa's office.

'You anxious?'

I knew he was behind me before I heard Tarc speak. I twisted to see him as he leaned over me, placing a shiny laptop on the desk.

'Why do you ask?' Still hovering over me, he opened the laptop.

'I don't know, maybe it's the murderous angle at which you're holding the pen.'

I realised how tightly I'd been clutching it and let go. And with the relief came an inadvertent smile. He straightened up and I felt the loss of his warmth.

Tarc is the snake. Tarc is the snake with two heads, I reminded myself. He would hate me if he knew who I was. He would not hesitate to destroy me if he found me stealing from the archive. He would fight augurs without remorse to protect what they had stolen from us.

He was one of them. He was the head of security, I was the breach. Only trouble lay ahead.

Calista's boys roughed them up really bad.

'This laptop has to stay in Harkness House because it contains confidential information. I'll run through passwords now, if you like.'

'Your tattoo,' I said without thinking. 'Does it mean anything?'

'Don't most tattoos?' he said. 'I kind of want something to have significance if it's in permanent ink. On my skin.'

'What does it mean?'

'It's a warning,' he said.

Right.

'Do you have others?' I couldn't see any, despite his short sleeves. 'I mean, under your clothes?'

What was wrong with me? Was it inappropriate hour or something?

'One more.' He was trying not to smile. 'But I need to know you a little better first.'

If I was the kind to blush, it would have been at his teasing. He grinned and said, 'Your chin. It goes all stiff and pointed when you're awkward.'

Great, a stiff chin. What every girl wants. I stopped myself from grabbing the pen again. Never mind knots, there were snakes writhing in my gut.

'We're not so bad,' Tarc said in such a low voice as he leaned down that I almost didn't hear it. Shoulders close to mine, he powered on the computer. It was how he said it: just a little bit bad. Bad in the right way.

'What kind of a name is Tarc, anyway?' I steered my mind to safer terrain.

'Don't laugh. It's short for Tarquin.'

I laughed: 'You don't look like a Tarquin.'

'What do Tarquins look like, then?' he mimicked my question from earlier.

'Well, their roots are gnarled,' I began and then stopped, awkward. I was flirting again. My chin must have been like a plank of wood.

'Tarc.' Cassa stood at her office door. It was nearly indiscernible, her distress. She smoothed her hair with one hand and blinked a couple of times too quickly, and somehow that gave it away. Tarc stood straight and touched my arm.

'We'll do this later,' he said and ambled over as if there was nothing wrong. But neither of them fooled me. Something had upset Cassa. I wanted to know what could bring such a cold woman to the brink of tears. Just in case.

~ NINE ~
Frog in a pot

A pale, washed-out butcher's wife grabbed my skirt while out today. She said to me: 'You are one of us.' One of us, dreadful words from a toothless drudge.

AdC

I was trying not to cry over spilled milk when Aisling came in through the back door. She stamped her feet, shaking rain on the mat.

'Mam says not to be late for the circle meeting.' She stopped in the doorway, eyes narrowed. 'What are you doing?'

She looked at the wooden table where I sat. Last night's dishes drying on the sink. A pot of tea, porridge. The smear of milk over wood whorls. Of them all, it was hardest to hide from Aisling.

'Having breakfast.' The milk splotch looked like a dragon. I covered it with my sleeve. 'There's more in the pot.'

Aisling cast a glance at Smith's gloopy porridge and pulled a face.

'No thanks.' Putting the kettle on, she said, 'Mam made a loaf.'

Aisling unwrapped the bread from its brown paper and the sweet smell of warm raisins escaped.

Her movements slow and precise as she cut a slice. She sawed through the crust, and then the knife slipped through the flesh of the loaf. She was humming softly, a regular *ti-dee-dum*, *ti-dee-dum*. Gripping the loaf, she cut another, then another. So careful, so deliberate. She turned to the press and reached for a mug, banging it softly on the *dum*, then again and then again.

I tried to stop the smile from forming, but I couldn't. Sometimes, Aisling was so obvious. I looked down at the table, my hair hiding my face while she continued to slice bread, take out plates, pour tea. Every movement slow and exact, following the beat of her wordless tune.

'Are you wickering me?' I said.

She gave a small smile and said with no surprise, 'Ah, you got me.'

But still she tapped a single finger on the table. Every small movement, every sound was rhythmic, like she was forming a web around me. Wickerings were usually benign, most commonly meant to ease and calm the unsuspecting person on whom they were performed. It was almost like hypnosis, capturing a person in the thrall of another, through rhythmic sounds and repeated actions that some augurs could learn with training and practice. Aisling and Maeve were both pretty good at it. I was pretty good at resisting it.

'Did it work?' A big, broad smile, and I wasn't sure if she reminded me of a vampire or a toothpaste advert. That was Aisling, always straddling the line between wholesome and frightening.

'Nope. Still like a frog in a pot.'

'Well, I tried.' She took a sip of tea. 'Want to tell me what's wrong?'

I hadn't spilled the milk deliberately, but when I saw the vague outline of a dragon, I chased it. It didn't come at once. After three minutes of making my eyes glaze over, I got a short, sharp flash. I hoped I was wrong.

Aisling picked up a slice of bread and thickened it with butter.

'A little bread with your butter?' I grabbed mine before she could give me a heart attack. Not for the first time, it occurred to me that despite her talent, Aisling would make a terrible nurse.

We sat for a few moments in comfortable silence. Ten minutes before the circle meeting where I'd talk about my first week at Harkness House. But the milk dragon had left me unsettled.

'Ash,' I said. 'What if the plan doesn't work?'

'How could that happen?' She spoke carefully. 'Once you get the map, Mam will track down the stones and fix the nemeta.' She took a huge bite of her bread.

'And find Sorcha.'

Aisling nodded, her mouth full.

'But what if it's worse to find her than to have her lost?'

'Ah,' she said, her face relaxing with the sudden understanding. 'It's your mother you're worried about.'

'Sorcha,' I corrected.

'A mother never forgets her child,' Maeve's voice interrupted from the kitchen door. Sibéal appeared behind her. 'They can cut the baby's cord, but never the tie that binds.'

Aisling rolled her eyes. I studied the butter on my bread. I wasn't sure I wanted to hear this. I was ambivalent about Sorcha. Part of me wanted to believe Maeve's talk of enduring connections, but it was hard to get over the whole abandoning me as a baby thing.

Maeve wrapped her arms around me, folding me into her snapdragon dress. She loved bold, exotic prints. Dresses with biting flowers and sharp, pointed vines. I could spend days in those dresses. I could find whole worlds between Maeve's bosom and her lap.

Sometimes I tried to direct my visions. I would focus on a specific question. With the milk dragon, I'd asked where Sorcha was. And I was disturbed by the answer: Sorcha wearing a yellow oilskin and huddled on a grey bed in a grey room, arms around her legs. She lifted her head, her eyes sad and vacant. Her skin was dull, her hair lank.

Maeve sat at the table. 'You are like my very own daughter. I first held you when you were a tiny baby. All sallow and scrawny.'

'Aw,' Sibéal smirked.

'Not much has changed.' Aisling laughed into her tea.

'You were frighteningly silent,' said Maeve. 'So miserable, and yet you never cried.'

And again, I wondered what Sorcha was thinking that night she left. I wondered whether she passed by the cot with a sickly baby between taking the watch and the earrings. And even now, I wished I knew if she regretted anything of that night.

'That's because Wren always soldiers on.' I thought there was a sharpness to her words, but Aisling was laughing.

Maeve looked at her watch. 'Here, we'd better head off.'

'Come and see my new storyboard, Wren?' Sibéal said. 'After the meeting?'

With her dark hair and dark eyes, Sibéal looked nothing like the others. Aisling called her a changeling. Sibéal claimed that nothing would have made her happier, but really, she was all about family.

'I don't know. Does it have a PG rating?'

'There's blood.'

'A romance, then. Does it involve falling in love with something human, animal or plant?' I said.

'They're here.' Maeve was looking out of the living-room window. 'Hurry, Wren.'

Downing the bitter dregs of tea, I followed Maeve next door, to Cairn House.

I'd never been to a circle meeting before. They were usually closed to the rest of us who weren't in the circle of seven, the higher-ranking draoithe who advised Maeve and made decisions for the grove. But today I was a special guest.

The meeting was in Maeve's good sitting room. As I entered, I kissed Smith and Simon on the cheek. Old Cormac O'Reilly grabbed my hand with his dry, scaly paw. Fidelma Walsh, a pharmacist with a fine sense of pattern, pulled me into a squashy hug. Her son, Dermot, smiled, his eyes bright behind his glasses. Colm Wood, a history teacher who lived two villages over, raised a hand in greeting.

As I sat, I cast a glance at Simon. It was generally agreed that he'd be ard-draoi when Maeve eventually stepped down. He was young, but his talent was strong and he was passionate about the grove. A little serious, a little too tough guy, but a good friend. Sometimes, a little more. Simon caught me looking and winked. For the first time, his attention felt heavy, not entirely welcome. But I wouldn't examine this unexpected change. Wouldn't question whether it had anything to do with a certain stormy-eyed boy with a snake tattoo.

'The Lucas archive hasn't arrived,' I said, once everyone was seated. 'It will be a few weeks before I can get in.'

I told them about my first meeting with Cassa, how intense she was.

'Talk us through her security.' Maeve was different here, leading a circle meeting. Sharper, more decisive.

'A state-of-the-art alarm system was installed recently. The security boys are all judges, rather than an outside professional company. But they take it very seriously. They patrol the house and gardens regularly. Cassa never leaves without at least one of them with her. They're strong.' Though we knew that from what happened with the Abbyvale three. 'They train every morning between seven thirty and ten.'

'Mick Murphy said there were two of them that night in Abbyvale. That sound right?' said Maeve.

'Only two?' I said, hoping that Tarc wasn't one of them.

'Who's in charge?' Simon asked.

'Tarc Gallagher.'

'Gallagher?' Smith said, his brow creasing. 'One of Theo Gallagher's boys? I didn't realise they were around.'

Tarc was unexpected then. I should tell them about his tattoo, that I'd seen it years ago in a vision. But what if I told them and I wasn't allowed back? Aisling would replace me without hesitation.

'And the office staff?' Fidelma said. 'How involved are they?'

'A lot of the work is contracted to freelancers, but there are four full-time office staff.' I described the staff members. I told them about David's light-bulb joke, and how it wasn't hidden from anyone, which made me think that Cassa's office was staffed only with judges.

'But they said it in front of you too,' Simon said. 'So either they see you as invisible, which is good, or they were baiting you.'

'What about Tarc Gallagher?' Dermot said.

Simon was looking at me intently. He watched me fidget with my hair and I hastily brought my hand down. Simon knew I was uncomfortable. He knew I was hiding something. Perhaps he could sense the inexplicable guilt that made me unable to look Dermot in the eye.

'What about him?'

'Is he suspicious of you?' Simon said.

'No more than he should be.' I remembered Tarc watching me from the other side of the room.

'Have you noticed anything unusual about him?'

'Unusual in what way?'

'Does he have any strange markings?' Colm spoke up from where he sat, sunk into Maeve's large armchair. 'Has he said anything that struck you as odd?'

'There is something. About David,' I said, mostly because I wanted them to stop asking me about Tarc. I looked over to Simon, offering him this truth. 'On Stephen's Day, he took strands of my hair.'

And I'd triggered the first explosive.

Smith was out of his seat, Simon's face was like a stone. Maeve's mouth froze in a silent 'Oh'. Colm scribbled frantically in his notebook.

'Can they trace me through my hair?' I said, my hands curling over the edges of the chair.

'No,' Maeve said, but she sounded grim.

'Taking hair,' Colm said. 'For judges, it's an assertion of domination developed by their warrior unit centuries ago. It's, well, a kill mark. David has marked you for the kill.'

My anger was a tight furled thing. A blood-red peony bud. David had put a kill mark on me. I barely listened to Dermot explain how in the old days warriors would cut a lock of hair to indicate an intent to kill. It was a form of torture, the sure knowledge that the judge warrior would punish, slowly and painfully, when least expected. I was too busy thinking of ways I could punish David. I would be methodical. I would be measured.

Dermot tried to reassure me that most likely David didn't mean to kill me, just dominate, subdue, defeat. At that point, the meeting descended into a discussion about the judges' first ré órga, the golden era when they developed superior military strength through a brutal system of warrior training. But really, all I wanted to know was how to get through the next weeks, not history lessons of defunct warrior units.

'I think the kill mark is a test,' Smith said as I stood to leave the meeting. 'To see if you react to its significance.'

He touched a hand to my cheek. 'Don't let David see that you understand what it means.'

And with that I was dismissed.

'We need to talk about Abbyvale.' Maeve brought the meeting back to order.

As I left the room, I heard Simon say, 'And we need to talk about retaliation.'

I closed the door, glad to be out of that room. I couldn't wait to get to the woods, to feel my feet pound against the ground as I ran through my anger. But I'd promised Sibéal

I'd look at her storyboard.

She was at the desk in her bedroom, scribbling desperate words, as if by racing across the page she could escape her birthday that was fast approaching. Aisling lay on Sibéal's bed, reading a book. She glanced up at me, and seeing my face, wisely returned to her book.

On the desk was a clay figure of a girl with the head of a deer. Long, branched antlers. In the legend, Sadhbh was turned into a deer by Fer Doirich, a druid with dark powers. Sadhbh wore skinny jeans, a messenger bag slung across her chest.

I picked up the clay Sadhbh, feeling the antlers branching from her long hair. I wanted to get the circle meeting out of my head. The kill mark. Snitching on Harkness House. Yes, I understood it was for the greater good. But I'd never liked tattling.

Sibéal handed me her storyboard. 'My film is based on the real history of the Tuatha na Coille.' The people of the woods. Sibéal was an Irish-language purist and bristled when the village people conflated the Irish words to 'tuanacul'.

The first picture was of a wide-eyed, Manga-style girl running through the trees. 'A beautiful girl is hunted by bad boys.'

'Glad my annual hunt trauma feeds your creative process.'

'The girl runs through the forest,' Sibéal continued, ignoring my comment. 'But the boys gain on her. Desperate, she begs the forest to hide her. The trees have mercy and they turn her into a weeping silver pear tree.'

On the storyboard, the weeping silver pear bore delicate white flowers. Boys stood frustrated beside it.

'But a ragwort sees everything,' Sibéal said. 'When it hears what the boys have to offer, the little ragwort blabs. The boys capture the girl and reverse the spell. But they botch it, so she is now half human, half weeping silver pear. At first, this is kind of awkward. She loves to feel ants walk down her face. She loves to bury her feet deep in the soil, feel it rich and fresh on her skin. But becoming part tree has given her magic powers. So she smites her enemies.'

'Smite,' interrupted Aisling from the bed. 'I love that word.'

'She curses the ragwort,' Sibéal glared at Aisling, 'making it a poisonous, unwanted pest.'

'Sounds like your kind of gruesome,' I said, picking up a small wooden box on the desk. Beneath the box was a sticky note where Sibéal had doodled a smiling flower declaring: *If friends were flowers I'd pick you!*

'But that poor weed,' I said. 'The girl wouldn't have had magic powers if it hadn't blabbed. She would have been stuck as a tree.'

I turned the box in my hand. An augur's puzzle box, its secrets long told.

'The necessary betrayal,' Aisling said. 'Like Judas. Without the betrayal, there's no salvation.'

'Weeds are cool.' Sibéal reached for the puzzle box in my hand and moved the slats to lock it. 'They'd be the best spies. They'd listen in and whisper secrets on to their little weedy friends.'

'You know that the Tuatha na Coille are just stories, right?'

Sibéal looked down at her notes but the set of her shoulders made it clear. *I know things,* her shoulders said.

Looking at Sibéal's box, now locked and out of reach, I had this elusive sense of another puzzle. One I didn't hold all the pieces to. One I couldn't entirely understand.

✦ TEN ✦
What are you hiding?

I have been quite unable to convey the sadness I always
perceive in daisies. They suggest to me that particular
loneliness one feels when in a crowd.

AdC

A man's watch with a leather strap. Two rose-gold ladybird earrings, wings aflutter. A worn gold necklace with an unpolished stone.

Without realising it, I inventoried everyone. Catching the bus on a wet Wednesday, my eye swept over hands, wrists, ears. Searching for the jewellery that marked Sorcha's absence. Seeing a leather watch strap, both brown and worn, I held my breath as I checked for a thin freckled wrist. It never was her. Still, I couldn't stop myself from imagining it: the sweep of red hair, the wide smile, a blue flower-sprig dress.

At Harkness House, a truck was near the garden door. Tarc emerged from the back. Jumping down, he pulled at a huge box, loading it on a hand truck. Cassa watched, oblivious to the rain that was now so soft it was almost invisible.

Inside, the boxes had been stacked beside the broad, curved staircase. One flight led upstairs to Cassa's private rooms and another down to the basement library. The boxes were stamped 'Confidential' and marked as property of the Harkness Foundation. I touched my hand to the wet cardboard.

'Wren,' Tarc said, wheeling in the next load. He was soaked, his dark hair wet and his charcoal top plastered to his skin.

'Is this the Lucas archive?' I tried to hide my excitement.

'That's the last of it.' He lifted the top box and stacked it with the others before wheeling the hand truck outside. I peered down the basement stairs, only to see David's staring face framed by the banister below. His laughter travelled up and followed me down the wide hallway to the office.

After lunch, I grabbed a few books and went in search of the cosy chairs in the basement library. Harkness House was still cold and unfamiliar, like it knew I was an intruder. But it felt different in the library.

Sunlight streamed in from high, horizontal windows. Only partly beneath ground, it was a huge open room with hardwood floors, rows of tall bookshelves and a large oak table. From their rosebud vases, solitary poppies peered out of the narrow windows like sentries. Near the staircase was a wide, thick door with a keypad attached to the wall.

The archive.

I stood at the door and examined the keypad. My face against the wood. The muted sound of voices from inside.

Settling on the couch directly across from the archive, I opened a compilation of letters. My eyes kept darting to the oak door. I was working on the Arabella Index, a detailed table of references to her life and art. It meant searching art books for mention of her and then categorising it. I wasn't sure how trawling through a million old books on nineteenth-century art was going to develop my skillset. I'd rather carry on making tea.

After an hour of dull details that really had no business in any letter, the thick archive door opened. David emerged. Tarc held the door for the wrenboys. I fixed my eyes on the page until they'd passed.

'Little bird.' I might have imagined the whisper.

Through the open archive door I caught a glimpse of shelves, a reading desk and chaos. Boxes had been opened and papers were strewn across the room, as if someone had rummaged through the priceless archive without care.

At the desk sat Cassa. She was motionless, her arms

stretched out in front of her as she looked straight at me. There was an eternity in that gaze. She just stared, not smiling nor acknowledging me. A white potted orchid on the desk, a large wooden box and a pile of books in front of her. I could just make out the title of the fat one on top: *Lady Catherine's Garden Journal.*

The door started to swing shut. Still Cassa stared.

Watch her.

But, caught in her gaze, it felt like the tables had been turned. That it wasn't me with the secret agenda, with the bag of tricks and deceit. That instead of watching, I was being watched. Again I felt that repel, like we were two magnets facing the wrong way.

She looked at me as if she could see some hidden thing. I didn't worry that she could tell I was an augur. Rather, it seemed her all-knowing gaze saw more than just a girl in a library. Self-conscious, I touched my hair that had half unravelled from its loose bun. Maeve's lucky hair combs hung precariously near my shoulders. The door eased shut. The boys with their heavy boots had already disappeared up the stairs. And still I felt the heat of Cassa's stare.

I was late leaving Harkness House that Friday and missed my bus. Thirty minutes before the next one and I was ready to eat a scabby child off the floor. I went to the Tesco

Express, where I skulked the aisles looking for food. But staring at the ready-to-go shelf, it felt like there was lead in my gut. On my way to the checkout, I grabbed a drink and a banana. Texting Smith, I bit into the banana, wondering at the strange taste and texture in my mouth. Looking down, I saw that I'd bitten into it, skin and all.

'Wren?'

I turned to see Tarc waiting behind me, holding an energy drink, and I swallowed the peel. It wasn't too bad.

'Your go', Tarc said, and somehow his words seemed a challenge. I wondered if he knew about the kill mark. Would David tell him?

I turned away but Tarc stayed a step behind. Distracted, I put the banana in the bagging area and the machine beeped with a bland anger.

'You need a hand there?' He raised an eyebrow at my inept checking-out. 'Not your talent, huh?'

My spine went rod straight. But Tarc was smiling and it seemed he meant no innuendo.

'Hitting town?' I gestured to the energy drink while an attendant placated the machine.

'More like hitting the road.' We walked out of the shop. His big black car was parked on the street.

'I can bring you to Kilshamble,' he said. 'I'm headed that way.'

Nothing was in the direction of Kilshamble. Except judges. Too many judges.

'If it's no bother.'

Tarc turned the ignition and the thick idling of the diesel engine highlighted the silence. Across the road, something caught my eye but was lost in the steady stream of people.

Tarc pulled out. And a little way down, there it was. The thing that had resonated: a lone figure wearing a yellow raincoat. Sorcha. In my milk dragon vision, I'd seen Sorcha wear a coat just like it. As we drove by, I craned my neck to see a face, but it was dark, and she had the hood up.

Tarc negotiated a large roundabout with impatient commuters who creatively interpreted the rules of the road. Then we were out of the city and on the motorway.

'So, you've known David a long time,' he said. 'You hang out much?'

'Well, you know, I've never been to visit him,' I said, curious how David and Tarc fitted together. 'Have you?'

'Visited David? Not exactly.' He was one of those drivers who happily took their eyes off the road, chatting easily. One languid arm reaching forward. His fingers tapping on the bottom of the steering wheel, as if he were half listening to some inaudible tune.

'But you're friends, right?'

'We went to school together,' Tarc said.

'You were at the same boarding school?' I turned to face him. 'In New York?'

'Boston.'

Of course. It was generally agreed that following their lean years in the 1800s, before the second ré órga, the judges had been saved by the wave of emigration to the States. With that characteristic charm, they sometimes popped up as politicians or celebrities. But not all judges were schmoozy charmers. Some were quiet, almost taciturn. Like the boy beside me.

'The same year as David?' I had a weird image of Tarc and David confined by school desks, discussing poetry.

He nodded. Tarc wasn't exactly chatty about school.

'Is he always that smug after exams?' I remembered how particularly insufferable David was on Stephen's Day.

'Exams?' Tarc glanced over. 'David tell you about that?'

'Back in December.' I looked at my hands. 'Told me all about how he'd celebrate with a new tattoo.' Which made me think about Tarc's hidden tattoo. The one he didn't want to show me. I wondered where it was.

'You get yours too?' I hadn't meant to say that. Just as I didn't mean to check him out so thoroughly, running my eyes from his arms, his chest, down to his legs.

My eyes up again, I saw he was watching me, amused at my scrutiny.

'Do you have one?' He smiled, keeping his eyes on mine.

'What, you'll show me yours if I show you mine?' I really needed to shut it.

Tarc laughed. It was so easy to be with him. Except that it wasn't.

'No tattoos,' I said. Just mottled skin from imaginary snake venom. 'But I did get myself a little reward after finishing my Leaving Cert.' I'd sat the national exams the previous year thanks to Smith's homeschooling.

'What kind of reward?'

'I'll let you know all about it if you answer a question.' I smiled at him from under my lashes.

'A question?' His eyes met mine.

'One question.'

'Then you better make it good.' He looked in the mirror as he indicated to overtake.

'When you said your tattoo was a warning, what did you mean?'

We whooshed by an eighteen-wheeler. Tarc didn't answer.

'It's nothing,' he said eventually. 'It's just a Birchwood thing. Calling it a warning is an in-joke, I guess.'

Tarc wasn't a good liar. But I couldn't focus on that now.

'Birchwood?' I didn't sound as casual as I'd hoped.

'Yeah, our school.' Tarc's finger hovered above the radio power switch, then jabbed it on right in the middle of some inane jingle. His words had lost that flirtatious edge. Guess he didn't like this game any more.

'How is Birchwood a school?' Why would a school interest Smith?

'It's a nickname. And that's two questions.' He was looking at me quizzically.

'Sounds more like an isolated asylum from a Gothic horror.' I shrugged, trying too late to affect nonchalance. 'But I guess that works for David.'

'Birchwood isn't like most schools.' He pinned me with those steady marble eyes. I'd been too obvious. 'The curriculum isn't exactly standard.'

I was dying to ask about the non-standard curriculum. Maybe they studied things like the Judge History of Wickerwork (modules include weaving of baskets and men; augur derivation of 'wickering' as pattern-based hypnosis abso-fucking-lutely not covered). Or Nemeton Acquisitions: 'as long as they're ours.' Or How to Hunt and Pursue Girls Through Woods. But I knew Tarc was baiting me. He was gauging my interest in Birchwood. Assessing whether it rang odd. So I dropped it. Pulling out my phone, I called Smith.

'I'm getting a ride home,' I said, glancing at Tarc, who

was focused on the road. I suspected he wasn't appeased. 'From Tarc.'

There was a pause while Smith considered this. 'OK,' he dragged out the word. 'We have to be at Sibéal's concert.' There was no concert. Sibéal didn't do concerts, unless they involved beheadings or public flogging.

'But you have your key,' Smith continued. 'And we'll be back shortly.' Which translated as, 'We'll be home as soon as the bad guy leaves.' He rang off.

A signpost emerged from the darkness, lit up in the headlights, and then disappeared.

'So I guess I'll have to confess,' I said.

'Confess?'

'My reward after Leaving Cert.'

'Yeah?'

I lifted my shirt to reveal my belly button. The rose-gold stud was delicate and small.

'It's …' He was looking down at my skin. 'Quaint.'

He smirked, and then snuck another peek before I covered it up. He liked it all right. And just like that, the prickly mood changed into something else.

'You like working for Cassa?' I said, to fill the silence.

'Sure,' he said. 'When I start university in September, I'll stay on part-time.'

'Why does Cassa need five big strong bodyguards?' I knew the First Cleave of Ireland would have personal security. But even so, that was some excess of testosterone at Harkness House.

'There's been a bit of trouble.'

'Trouble?'

'Harassment. A few threats. There was damage to her place in Connemara,' he said. 'And before the security was updated at Harkness House, there was a break-in in the middle of the night.'

I suspected that this trouble was exaggerated. That Cassa rather liked having a bunch of big, strong boys to protect her delicate little self. I was pretty certain that 'security' was a euphemism for judge-boy gap year. The thing to do after axe-throwing at Birchwood.

Tarc turned into the main street of Kilshamble. 'Which way?'

I gave directions and after a few quiet minutes, we arrived outside the cottage. Smith had left a light burning. Maeve's house was in darkness.

'Thanks,' I said, getting out of the car. But before I'd shut my door, Tarc was out and striding towards me.

'I'll see you in.' There was mischief in the way he said it. Like he'd put up with all my nosy-parker questions and now it was his turn.

'It's fine,' I said. 'You're not *my* bodyguard.' I didn't want him in the cottage.

'Sure, but since you have one handy, you may as well use me.' He smiled.

'Really, I'm OK.'

'What are you hiding, Wren?' Tarc opened the gate. 'Are your childhood photos that bad?'

'Terrifying.' I walked down the path, my mind checking over the living room to see if there was anything in the house that could give us away.

Opening the door, I saw the room through Tarc's eyes. It was tidy enough, but clearly hadn't been hoovered since I last ran through it two weeks ago. The war table covered by an old canvas. Clutter on the overstacked bookshelves. The unfashionable rug and the shabby couch. I could see his eyes running over the titles of the books. The empty plate and coffee mug. I felt defensive. There was something meagre, something so thin about it all. Not the cheap fabrics and the worn patches on the couch, but the idea of it as home. It looked like a gentleman's quarters in a retirement village, not the place where a child grew up.

Tarc stepped over the threshold and I watched in quiet horror. The first time a draoi entered another draoi's home was significant. There was an implicit offering by both, an exchange between the two. Probably out of habit, Tarc touched the door frame as he entered, just missing the small hand-drawn spider that marked this as the house of an augur. An unconscious gesture, but one that reminded me how similar and how different we were. Eyes on me, he didn't see the spider. Touching the door frame of a house you visited was meant to bring luck to that household. I couldn't count the number of times Simon had done the same thing. It jolted me to see Tarc doing something so ordinary. I hadn't realised that judges did it too.

'Wren?' he dipped his head so I would look at him.

'Right.' I breathed out. 'Everything's fine. I want to get to bed.'

It was half eight on a Friday night.

'Yeah?' He seemed to find it funny that I was so eager to get rid of him. There was a smile playing about his lips. Which were pretty nice lips. And it lit up his marble eyes. Which were staring at me too intently.

He stepped closer. 'No wild night out for you?'

'Wild in Kilshamble is a little different from how you might understand it.'

'How is that?' And closer. He put his hands on my shoulders.

'It's ...' I trailed off as Tarc bent his head in front of mine. This close I could see the detail of the swirling colours in his eyes.

'Unbridled. Dangerous,' I sounded breathless. 'You should be careful here. It's not like other places.'

In that moment I could almost believe that tree men prowled the woods. That they looked for girls to lure to them. To kiss, to touch. I could almost hear them whispering to me.

Tarc drew closer.

'The rules are different here.' My words were barely audible.

He leaned into me and I couldn't move. Gently, sweetly, he kissed my cheek. A barely there brush of his lips on my skin. Then he stepped back.

'Night, Wren.'

And Tarc was gone. I could feel the echo of his kiss. The call of the woods. I stood in the living room, still rooted to the worn rug. The room exactly as it was before, yet something had changed. Something unnameable. It felt almost like Tarc's sweet kiss was the opposite of a kill mark. A promise of something. But with the same power to destroy.

When Smith returned to the cottage, I was pulling my hi-vis raincoat over my running clothes.

'He came inside.'

Smith wasn't happy.

'Just to the door.'

He eyed the living room, checking that everything was in place. That Tarc hadn't nicked the silverware. Even though we didn't have any silverware.

'I found out what Birchwood is,' I said, while Smith sniffed around suspiciously. 'It's the school David and Tarc went to.'

Smith was at the war table, pulling the canvas from it.

'David's school? Wasn't that called St Barnaby's?' He absent-mindedly picked up a soldier.

I shrugged. I hadn't a clue.

He closed his fist over the soldier. Smith was deep in thought.

'Tarc said Birchwood is a nickname.' I went over to the war table and stood beside him. 'Why's it so important?'

Smith exhaled. 'Of course it is. Of course, you clever girl. Good work.'

He slung an arm around me in a sideways hug. So slight, that extra pressure, that tightness with which he held me. As a child, my clothes were often a little grubby, my bed never made. I'd gone to school with greasy hair, and sometimes made myself peanut butter bread for dinner.

But I'd never wanted for attention. I'd learned maths at Smith's war table as he explained equations using soldiers, and geometry through battle trajectories. I'd learned history as we analysed myths. And I learned geography by walking outside with him. I didn't have parents who cared for me with hot meals and clean-washed clothes. But Smith showed his love by teaching me his passion, and in this we had forged a deep bond.

I released myself from his hold. Strapping on my reflectors, I ran out into the rain, into the night. While I ran, I wondered why Smith hadn't answered my question. Birchwood meant something, but he was reluctant to tell me.

ELEVEN
Romeo and Juliet

Elizabeth made her brother show me his secret mark.
AdC

We were in a meadow down on the Lacey farm, three miles from Kilshamble. Once a month, I went with Smith to check our nemeta. Sometimes they prickled with new energy, perhaps after a storm or else an inexplicable gift from nature. But we hadn't had one of these surges in a long time.

'Smith, why did you want to know about Birchwood?'

He continued walking. 'Thought it meant something. But it doesn't matter.'

I hung back, lost in thought, while he continued ahead. I wasn't convinced by his answer. It reeked of that mindless mollification he dished out whenever he didn't want me worried.

'Bastards,' Smith said, stopping suddenly. He didn't have a quota. He didn't need one. For a man who loved stories of war, he was exceptionally mild-mannered and rarely moved to curse.

From his stiff shoulders, it was clear he wasn't happy. On the other side of him, just out of my line of vision, was a standing stone, the tall, narrow rock we used for seasonal rituals. Only last Samhain, after the autumn rites, I'd kissed Simon, pressed up against the red rosehips entwined in the whitethorn hedge. It seemed like a lifetime ago.

I looked up, not seeing the problem. Only as he stepped aside did I see the large smiley face drawn with black spray-paint.

He went up to the stone, tracing his hand over the desecrated surface. I couldn't tell whether it was sadness or anger that filled Smith's eyes.

'We'll wash it out,' I said.

That was the trouble with small villages. Kids got bored. Kids found spray-paint. The black eyes stared out at me, the inane grin an offence.

'Come on.' I steered him away. 'We'll fix it.'

But I knew why he was upset: when nemeta were vandalised, they didn't work as well.

We'd walked a few steps when Smith stopped and looked back. His usually sharp blue eyes were clouded with worry.

'What is it?' I said, still holding on to his arm.

He frowned. 'I'm probably overthinking this.'

'Tell me anyway,' I said.

'What if it isn't local kids? What if this is the work of Cassa's boys? David and Tarc and the others?'

I looked at the smiley face. It seemed to say, 'Gotcha.' Just like David. But I couldn't see why Cassa's security would be on a small unproductive farm near Kilshamble. This wasn't judge territory.

'How would they know to come here?' I said. 'I just can't see it.'

'You're right,' Smith said, and we walked together. But he'd paused, and in that pause, my own worry crept in. Tarc had driven this way the previous night. Did he, after leaving me at the cottage, come here with black spray-paint to desecrate an augur nemeton?

We left the Lacey farm, then checked the hill above the quarry before heading to the woods. Hidden between the trees were two burial stones, both of them marked with weathered carvings. All three nemeta were weaker than last time.

Leaving the burial stones, Smith and I walked through the woods. When we reached Arabella's cottage, I went in.

This was where Arabella was loved by her tuanacul prince, if you believed the Kilshamble stories. Where she painted her flowers, slowly killed by every kiss she shared until only a husk of a girl remained. I thought of Tarc kissing my cheek and I knew for sure how a kiss could ruin a girl.

Running my eye over the moss-covered grey, I saw the broken cottage in a new light. The internship had given me a glimpse of the real Arabella, one whose talent had gone ignored.

My mind on talents, I said to Smith, 'Was Arabella de Courcy an augur?'

He took out a flask and poured coffee into the small cup.

'Yes and no.'

'How is that possible?'

'Her mother was an augur, but her father was a judge.'

'Oh,' I said. 'How unfortunate. Was it all Romeo and Juliet?'

'Only to the point where her mother fell pregnant. Then his undying love died a quick and horrible death. She didn't survive childbirth, and Arabella was taken from her augur family and raised by distant cousins. She was brought up as a judge and forbidden any contact.'

'So her art was a talent, like ours?'

Smith nodded.

'Arabella de Courcy is the reason the judges claimed Kilshamble. When she came to live in the woods, the judges wanted to be sure that her augur family wouldn't get to her.

So they moved in here, put a kill mark on any augur who settled. And until us, no augur has.'

'But why would they go to so much trouble for one girl?' A girl who was pretty unstable, by the looks of it. And at a time when the judges had been weak.

'There've been other children who are half judge, half augur. Rarely, because the animosity between us runs too deep, but it has happened. Those children have always been either firmly augur with a talent, or else clearly judge with an affinity to a natural object.'

'Arabella was clearly augur, so why did the judges want her?'

'Because Arabella was both. She was truly both augur and judge. With her combined magic, she could have been a very powerful woman. And you know how the judges are drawn to power.'

I felt an unwelcome kinship with Arabella. She'd grown up without a mother, had been abandoned by her father before she was even born. I knew what that was like.

Smith downed his coffee and reached for the flask. As he moved, my eye fell on a bunch of lilies in the corner of the ruin. They looked fresh.

I took a deep breath. 'Did you ever meet my father? Was he an augur?'

'I saw him once from a distance. And no, he wasn't an

augur.' Smith twisted the flask stopper open, and then twisted it closed again. 'When Sorcha fell for him, it was like she had been infected.' Twisted it open. 'She was feverish, lost to the rest of us the moment she met him. I knew she would pick him.' He twisted the flask shut. 'I just hadn't realised that she wouldn't pick you too.'

I stared at the moss on the tree, thinking about Smith's words. About my mother's passion. I hadn't known that I was born from such wildness. But it was a sour, curdling ardour that killed rather than kindled. A passion that had left no room for me. I had a secret fantasy where instead of stealing Smith's watch, my mother chose me. Picked up the quiet, hungry baby and left.

I was glad for the noise and madness at Maeve's house. Aisling was squabbling with her mother while they half watched TV. Through the open door, Simon was beneath the kitchen sink, fixing Maeve's leaky pipes. Sibéal, talking to no one in particular, explained the newest clay statues she'd made. She was sculpting figures for her film about a stupid prince and a dandelion woman who bled milk sap. It was not going to end well. Not for the stupid prince.

'I'll never marry her off,' Maeve, in a sepulchral voice, told a Kardashian.

'I don't want to get married,' Sibéal said. 'But I wouldn't mind a liaison with a tree man. As long as he's ripped.'

Maeve looked up from the TV. 'Don't say things like that, Sibéal.'

I wasn't sure if she was objecting to the liaison or the tree man.

'It's just talk, Mam,' Aisling said, reaching for the bag of Doritos and stuffing a handful in her mouth.

Maeve's attention was back on the screen. 'What is your one wearing?' she said with gleeful horror. 'She'll be awful cold.'

'But, Shibs,' I said, 'won't he suck the life out of you? Steal your oxygen when you sleep? Slowly petrify you? First your feet turn to roots, and then your calves. Your thighs go all barky, and then one day you see your hair has become branches waving ever so slightly in the breeze.'

Sibéal was smiling at me like I was mad, so I continued.

'Rooted to the ground, you'll cry resin tears of the most beautiful amber and no one will hear you scream.'

'Yeah? But they'll be screams of pleasure.'

'Sibéal!' Maeve reprimanded her.

'Can you imagine how big his –'

'Sibéal!'

'His muscles, Ma, his muscles. Get your mind out of the gutter.'

Shaking her head, Maeve disappeared into the kitchen.

Sibéal's sixteenth birthday was looming and her talent hadn't wakened. I knew that behind the glib talk, the manic clay modelling and ideas for film scripts, she was anxious. She was running out of time, and I knew what it was like. I remembered too well the weeks before I got my talent, dreading that I would be blank. Then, afterwards, wishing I was.

I wanted to reach out to her and say, it's OK to be blank. There are worse things. But I knew that she would see only my broken glimpses of the future and wouldn't understand. Instead, I followed Maeve into the kitchen.

'I can't help thinking that we're missing something,' Maeve was saying to Simon. 'That there must be a faster way to bind to the nemeta. Imagine if it took less than six months.'

'What good is that when we don't know where the judges' nemeta are?' I said as I walked into the room. Simon peered out from under the sink.

'The Abbyvale three found one. It's always possible.' Maeve grabbed my arm. 'Have you seen anything recently?'

And I wasn't sure what the right answer was. I wasn't supposed to encourage the visions, but something about the way Maeve looked at me made me think she hoped I had.

'I'm not supposed to,' I said.

'Oh.' She dropped her hand. Definitely disappointed. Simon stood up, dropping tools into his box.

'Should be fine now, Maeve.'

'Great,' she said. 'Thanks, Simon.' But her words lacked her usual vigour. She looked towards me again, biting her bottom lip.

There was always this push and pull: did you or didn't you. Don't chase the vision, don't stare at your soup, but maybe just a small glance. It was like they couldn't decide. They couldn't encourage me to develop my talent the way that they had insisted Aisling study nursing. But they couldn't forbid me either; it went against their nature.

'Not a bother.' Simon hesitated, looking towards me.

I busied myself with filling the dishwasher. I didn't want to go for a walk with him.

'See ya, Wren,' he said, also disappointed.

After Simon shut the door behind him, Maeve turned to me again. What she wanted was clear in her face.

'I haven't seen anything for a while now,' she blurted. She wasn't able to tell the future, but the clouds revealed things about the present that she couldn't otherwise know.

'It's been pretty wet,' I said.

But I knew it was because our nemeta were running dry. Performing only the barest minimum of the old rites and ceremonies weakened our talents. If this continued, the old ways would fade to a handful of stories whispered beneath the trees.

'Even on good days,' she stepped closer, lowering her voice, 'when I try to read the positions of clouds, divide the sky into different spheres, it just throws up garbage.'

'How long, Maeve?' I asked. Through the open door, Aisling was still absorbed in the TV. Sibéal had disappeared.

'A while,' she sighed. 'Since I was sick.'

'Last May?' I was incredulous that Maeve had gone so long without seeing anything in the clouds.

'I'm worried about Sibéal.' She wiped her hands on her printed flowers. 'Her birthday is in March.'

'You need me to take a look?'

'No blood,' she said. 'And please don't tell Smith I asked. I know it's dangerous, but if you do it only once or twice, surely that can't hurt?'

Maeve was like a child stealing sweets from the candy jar. *Just a small one,* not realising how quickly they added up.

'Sure,' I said.

As I reached the back door I turned. 'Maeve? Why did Smith ask about Birchwood? What's that about?'

'Nothing to fret over. Just a rumour that a bunch of judges from Birchwood are coming here.'

'So, schoolkids?' I said, pulling the door open. 'A bunch of posh thugs like David?'

'Exactly. No problem there.'

I stepped outside, relieved. Smith had been right, it was nothing.

'Wren,' Maeve called before I shut the door.

'Yes?'

'Thank you.'

I nodded and went home. We were spoiled by our talents. We could question the present and search the past for what we missed the first time. If our talents were like maps, mine was one where some intrepid traveller had forged ahead and found the lay of the land disappointing. So he had embellished it. Added caves and secret passages. And extra dangers. Here be dragons. Mine would be an acid trip kind of map. But sometimes it would trick you and other times it would guide you home. You just never knew which.

TWELVE
Handle carefully

*I stayed down at the lake, watching the lilies among the
water weeds. They seemed to call to me in an echoing song.
'Do they not get lonely?' I asked Lady Catherine. I would
hate it if they were lonely.*

AdC

Another week had passed and I was nowhere close to
getting into the archive. I wanted to scream with frustration. Nearly a month at Harkness House and I was still
indexing diaries and compiling guest lists for endless parties.
Nearly a month, and I was still looking over my shoulder.
That dreadful anticipation of when David would don an
invisible mummer's mask and finish what he'd started on
Stephen's Day. Complete the promise he'd made when he
took my hair.

'Handle carefully, some of these are very old.' Laney
carried a pile of books to my desk. She made an excellent
torturer. She had an impressive ability to know when I was

at breaking point, and how to tighten the screw ever so sweetly.

'You need to be especially thorough with these.' She handed over two fat volumes. 'Lady Catherine's garden journals. They're from the archive. Even Cassa hasn't had a chance to read them. You're the first.'

'Lucky me.'

From the window, I saw Tarc emerge from the garden and head towards the office.

Grabbing *Lady Catherine's Garden Journal: Volume I*, I escaped to the library. I didn't know if he'd vandalised the standing stone at the Laceys' farm; just being in the same area that night wasn't exactly evidence. I didn't want to think about it.

The garden book was a whole new level of dull. Lady Catherine meticulously documented her planting and weeding habits, as well as regular updates on the general health of her plants. Seems the roses had an awful time with aphids in the summer of 1870.

'Just kill me already,' I whimpered, banging my head against the table. My face turned to the side, the cool wood against my skin, I stared at the archive door.

'Pretty.'

I heard Cassa's voice just as her hand reached out and touched Maeve's combs in my hair. I sat up hastily, searching for an excuse. But really there was none. I'd seen Cassa berate Cillian for sloppy posture, I'd seen her make Laney squirm for work slightly less than perfect. And there I was, sleeping on the job. I waited for the harsh words.

But she smiled. 'I haven't forgotten my promise.'

She spoke sweetly, but I couldn't shake the sense of a honeyed threat.

'Promise?'

'To show you more of Arabella's paintings.'

'Now?'

'They're in storage.' As she moved, I caught sight of her hands. Long and elegant, with a diamond and moonstone ring. Soil stains in the creases of her fingers.

'But we'll exhibit them at an Arabella de Courcy Retrospective next month. At the Huntsman. I want you there when we open.'

As she walked away I said, 'Cassa?'

At the foot of the staircase, she turned her head.

'What really happened to Arabella? Why did she leave her family to live in the woods?'

I felt some empathy with Arabella, maybe because we'd both lost our parents. And because we were both drawn to the woods. It bothered me that she'd been disloyal to augurs, that her actions led to more mistreatment of us by judges, when she was one of us herself.

Standing there in the shafts of light from the high basement windows, Cassa looked almost ethereal.

'This story,' she said, 'the truth about Arabella ... When I tell it, I ask for something in return.'

She turned her face to mine, searching. I got the sense of a taut line that stretched from her to me, as if she was reeling me in.

'What do you ask for?' I said.

'Do you really want me to tell you?'

Blank promises were dangerous. And to make one to a woman like Cassa was insane. And yet I badly wanted to know.

My hesitation broke the moment. It was too late. The line had slackened. She was already going up the stairs.

Cassa was gone but the delicate top notes of her perfume lingered. I had the strangest feeling of having had a conversation with a ghost or a dream. Like it hadn't really happened.

It was later in the afternoon, after hours of Lady Catherine's garden and the many people who had admired it, and all the bloody weeds, when I realised that I knew the code to the door.

Laney had been in and out of the archive all day. I'd tried watching her pin in the number, but I only managed to see that it started with three, the rest of the numbers obscured by her sharp silver talons.

Made of shiny chrome, the keypad was sleek and stylish. But as a security device it was daft. Every time a number was entered it emitted a different key tone. It was only after I'd heard it for the tenth time that I realised I could work out the sequence by figuring out the sounds the different keys made.

I waited until Laney was bossing the caterers in the kitchen. Certain I was alone, I hummed the tune while I played the keypad. After a few minutes, the door clicked open.

I'd always felt the odd one out in our grove, my sense of pattern a distorted, discordant thing. I'd once seen a picture of a crazy spiderweb after the spider had been fed caffeine. That was me, a wonky spinner, like a caffeine-addled spider.

But here, I'd done it. I'd discerned the code through the pattern of the key tones. Maybe I wasn't as rogue as I'd feared.

I pulled the door shut without going in. Instead, I went back upstairs to the office. Restless and fidgety, I waited at my desk until Laney was ready to lock the office.

'I'm going to push on with the indexing for an hour or two,' I said. 'That OK?'

'Sure,' she said. 'But stay in the library, I'm turning on the alarm here.' I was leaving the room when she called after me. 'There's an Arabella fundraiser in the white room this evening. Don't get underfoot.'

The house felt different outside of office hours. The constant stream of people in the daytime seemed to shrink it. And now, resettled to full size, it felt cavernous. After checking the staircase, I entered the code and slipped inside the archive.

Laney had been busy. Books, document boxes and folders were stacked on the shelves in no discernible order. I felt a sudden panic at the volume of stuff. How was I meant to find a single map in that clutter? I felt annoyed with Basil Lucas: was all that paper really necessary? Wouldn't someone think of the trees?

Frustrated, I leaned against the table. I picked up the carved wooden box beside me. Like the one on Sibéal's desk, it was an augur's puzzle box, something my ancestors crafted to amuse themselves. This one was much larger, with a more complex puzzle. To open the box, wooden slats were moved around to complete a pattern.

I turned the box over. It was open, which meant that the code had been cracked. I turned the box over again, examining the pattern. For an augur, it was laughably easy, a child could do it, but those easy puzzle boxes could be deceptive. I shut the box and pushed the lever that locked it, unravelling its code. Then I looked for the real pattern, the hidden one. The less obvious pattern that would open the bottom cavity that Cassa might not know about.

It took a few minutes to push the small squares and circles into position. Moving the last slats, I hesitated. In the archive, with its damp and dusty books, I felt a sense of foreboding. It always turned out badly when nosy girls opened secret boxes. Look at Pandora, that didn't work so well for her.

I heard a bump against the library wall and I started. And then another, like a small animal was trying to break in. Then another, against the archive door. My heart wild, I stared at the door, half expecting David or Cillian to kick it down.

Then I registered the low hum of the vacuum cleaner. Angela, the housekeeper. My legs jellied in relief.

I'd been in the archive for nearly an hour. Security monitored the house. I was being reckless. I lifted the lid, now locked to the top cavity. Inside the small bottom compartment was a square of paper.

'How's things?' I heard David call over the Hoover. Angela turned it off, but I couldn't hear her soft voice through the thick wall.

'Here, I'll carry that up the stairs for you.' I could just about make out David's words as my unsteady fingers unfolded what I'd found.

Returning the box as it had been, I left the archive a few minutes later, the page tucked into my pocket.

At the top of the basement stairs, I paused at the sound of laughter and music coming from the white room. The Arabella fundraiser.

I stopped for a moment. To my right was the garden door, I could slip out quietly and steal away with my prize. To my left, the house was crawling with judges.

I should go home. I'd found something new, something that might help us. But that night, I had a rare opportunity to watch Cassa outside of our normal workday.

I hesitated. Then turned left.

THIRTEEN
Watching you

*In the garden, I had the most extraordinary desire to put
my tongue to the wet mulched leaves. I was surprised
by their cool, refreshing tang.*

AdC

I slipped into the small alcove beside the white room,
probably the old servers' entrance. Cracking open the door,
I looked inside.

The white room was glorious. Giant flower arrange-
ments stood on huge pedestals. There were easily fifty
people, and I was surprised to see so many girls my age; not
the usual crowd for a fundraiser. The girls were so polished
in their expensive dresses, perfect make-up and swishy hair
as they stood beneath the sparkling crystal chandeliers
with their champagne flutes. I watched from my corner,
probably grey with a faint layer of dust from the archive.

Near the string quartet, Tarc also watched. He was dressed
in black, and seemed to be working, but that didn't stop a

group of girls from swaying over to him. They chatted easily, the girls laughing. Their bodies were soft and leaning towards him. Something bitter as beer churned inside me.

And it occurred to me that if there was any truth to the stories of the tuanacul, they would not be the wild tales that Sibéal loved but something quieter and more essential. Something infinitely more frightening. They wouldn't throttle you with their roots and vines. They would observe you furtively, the way a forest watched a girl running helter-skelter. They would be detached and knowing. They would be strong and sure. In this way, I could understand how Arabella might love a tree prince.

Something at the main entrance to the room drew Tarc's attention. I followed his line of vision and saw Cillian gesturing to him with the hand signals he'd used in the woods. Tarc left, and my gaze drifted across the other guests.

Cassa was in the centre of the room. A line of girls, each waiting their turn to speak to her. Pretty maids all in a row. I stared for a moment, trying to figure out what was going on.

Then I saw her. She was wearing a white dress that set off her dirty-blonde hair. She was beside Laney, laughing. I couldn't move.

There was no reason for Aisling to be at Cassa's party.

Yet there she was in white tulle. She turned, looking in my direction like she knew I was there. She was different in that room. She looked like the other girls, glamorous, confident. She stared at the darkened doorway and I shrunk back. Aisling stepped towards me, her arm stretched out, but I turned away and fled.

I was turned inside out. Had Maeve sent Aisling? Why would they hide this from me? What else had they not told me?

In my haste, I'd headed for the main door. But as I neared it, I heard the sound of laughter from the other side. Not wanting to encounter Cassa's guests, I quickly turned round and made for the side door near the drive.

I was almost at the glass door when I heard the boys coming. Panicked, I ducked into a dim room and watched as Tarc and Cillian passed by. They moved with such quiet intent, and again I wondered if it was Tarc who'd hopped over the Laceys' fence and run through the fields towards the standing stone.

Some seconds after they'd left, I slipped out of the door. Keeping to the wall, I followed them. It was beyond foolish. I couldn't think what they'd do if they caught me. Something rustled behind me. I turned but saw no one. I scanned the garden, the door, checking the shadows for movement, but there was nothing.

At the corner of the house, the boys were out of sight. I searched the paved drive, the trees along the perimeter wall. Ahead was the garage where Tarc and David kept their cars. My heart thudding, I crossed the open space between the house and garage and crept towards the driveway. Peering around the wall, the boys were at Tarc's car parked in front of the garage.

'What time are we meeting Canty?' Cillian said, then lit a cigarette, cupping his hands around the flame.

'Nine.' Tarc checked the time.

'What's he got?'

'Says he knows something.'

'You trust him?'

'Not in the slightest.'

'Want me to ring David?' Cillian took a leisurely drag. 'He's probably getting his pretty frock on.' Cillian had one of those slow voices that always sounded like he was a little bored.

'Nah.' Tarc looked towards the garage, and I pressed my shoulder against the wall.

More silence. They didn't strike me as bosom buddies, those two. Tarc was restless, moving aimlessly.

'What's the deal with David and Wren?' Tarc said.

'No deal,' Cillian said and looked at the glowing tip of his cigarette.

'So why does David always look like she just peed in his cornflakes? She dump him or something?'

'Not a chance,' Cillian said. 'David wouldn't tap that. I mean, she's not bad, but she looks like she'd scratch your eyes out.'

Yuck, did he just say 'tap'? Of course boys talked about girls like that, and girls did the same with boys. I wasn't exactly innocent of it, but I didn't like hearing it. Not about me.

'Something not right about her, don't you think?' Cillian was looking at Tarc.

'I guess she's a little jumpy maybe.' Tarc sounded cautious. Reluctant. 'Seems nice.'

Nice. How lame.

'If you're looking for a nice girl, go back inside,' Cillian said. 'There's a load of them, girls like us, and wearing their pretty dresses and heels. I'm sure they'd love to get to know you.'

'Not tonight, thanks,' Tarc said.

I leaned back into the wall, feeling the rough surface soothe the ache in the palms of my hands. The boys fell quiet. Time to go.

I peered out for a last look, only to see Cillian shaking his head, staring at Tarc with a broad smile. Then he laughed. 'Oh man, this is hilarious. Wait until I tell David.'

I frowned, wondering what I'd missed.

'He took her hair, you know.' I could hear the smirk in his words.

'David took Wren's hair?' Tarc was incredulous. 'Why would he do that?'

Cillian stared at him for a moment. I wondered if he'd tell him about the chase. About their game. But then Cillian laughed. 'David thinks she's hiding something. Wanted to draw her out.'

'She's just a girl.' Tarc sounded moody. Distracted.

'You hear she stabbed him after Christmas?' Cillian went on. 'Just like that. Right through the hand.'

'Wren?' Tarc whipped round to face him. 'Stabbed David? Why?'

Cillian shrugged, saying, 'Who knows what drives crazy. Just watch your back with that one.'

His elbow was around my neck before I knew he was there. I knew the smell of him, the feel of him. I struggled against his choke, scrabbling at his arms.

'You spying on us, Wren?' David said, pulling tighter.

I tried to break out of the hold but I was no match for him.

'I knew you were up to something,' he said as I pushed against him. Maybe I could slam him into the wall. Bash his head or stick his ear with my trusty letter opener.

As I struggled, my bag fell, thumping to the ground. There went my letter opener. David shifted slightly, enough for his hold to loosen. I inched forward. But I'd barely taken a step when he grabbed me again, tighter this time.

'Jesus, David. Let her go.'

Tarc stood there, features cold and knife drawn, and still I'd never been more glad to see him.

'I caught her spying,' David said. He was triumphant. 'She was right here, watching you.'

'Let her go.'

David released me and I bent to pick up my bag, hiding how badly shook up I was. My throat was tight from where David had gripped it. When I looked at the boys, Tarc was watching us with an inscrutable expression on his face.

'Oh, would you ever get over yourself, David,' I said loud and cross, hoping they couldn't see my nervous hands.

'What are you doing here?' Tarc finally spoke, sheathing his knife.

'I was working late. Ask Laney,' I said folding my arms. 'I arranged with a friend to pick me up. I figured it would be easier getting out of the garage gate because of the fundraiser.'

The boys stood around me, all three of them, unsmiling.

'I reckon we search her,' David said, pushing an unlit

cigarette into his mouth. 'I bet we find her phone's on record.'

'Oh, for God's sake. You're not going to search me. I was working late, and now I'm wondering what the hell is wrong with you. I didn't realise listening to boy gossip was the crime of the century.'

All bluster, trying to hide how afraid I was. The folded square of paper I'd stolen from the archive was in my pocket. It wouldn't be hard to find.

'Where's your friend?' Tarc said.

'Probably outside,' I waved a hand at the gate. 'So if David's done trying to kill me, it's been a long day.'

Before I turned, I caught it. That glint in David's eye.

'Kill you, Wren? Now where would you get a crazy idea like that?'

'Perhaps from that excellent demonstration of a choke-hold you just did?' The words sounded reasonable enough, but if David had been suspicious before, it was doubled when he reached for the ends of my hair and I jolted like a frisky pony.

'Really?' he said, and I could hear the smile in his words. 'That all?'

'I don't know what you're talking about,' I lied.

Tarc was still looking at us, his face giving nothing away. 'Let's see if your friend is here.' He clicked a button and the electric gates swung open. Of course, there was no one waiting for me in the road.

'Must be running late.' I hoped I didn't sound as desperate as I felt.

'Why don't you call?' Tarc spoke easily, deceptively casual.

I couldn't call Aisling, because she was inside doing whatever the hell she was doing. I wasn't sure if I was more hurt or cross about that. My only other option was Simon. He wasn't likely to be in the city, but he might link me up with a friend who'd oblige. I rang him, terrified he wouldn't pick up.

'It's me,' I said, my knees wobbly with relief when Simon answered. 'You were supposed to meet me five minutes ago. Where are you?'

He paused. Then, 'Sorry.' He played along. 'Got held up. Where did you say you were again?'

I rattled off the address, praying that by some wild stroke of luck he was in the city.

'There in ten.' Simon rang off.

'He was delayed. So thanks for the concern. You boys can go off and play with your knives or whatever.' I ran an eye over their dark clothes, the waistband where Tarc had sheathed his knife. My distaste was real and obvious.

'We'll wait for your friend,' Cillian said. And smiled. 'Just to be sure you're safe.'

'You haven't explained why you were hiding behind the garage,' David said. He was still looking at me with that fixed gaze.

'I wasn't hiding,' I said, looking at Tarc. 'I heard my name. I was embarrassed.'

And for the first time he couldn't meet my eye. He shifted, checking the muck in the gutter.

When Simon came barrelling down the road in a borrowed car, I felt a whole different kind of anxiety. He pulled over on the opposite side of the road, and I started walking.

'Aren't you going to introduce your friend?' Tarc said, checking out Simon.

'It's late.' My words were abrupt. 'Got to go.'

I saw through the car window that Simon was wearing a baseball cap pulled low. He wasn't taking any chances. Already, Tarc was noting the registration.

I got inside and leaned back against the headrest, letting out a three-monthly allowance of dirty words.

And then Simon started laughing and I fell in with him, the relief bringing huge gulping laughs and tears to my eyes.

'What the hell did you get up to?' he said.

'Wren.' It was nearly midnight when Aisling, in that white dress, stood in the doorway to my bedroom.

I looked up from my desk, where I'd been staring at the page I'd stolen from the puzzle box. It wasn't the map Smith was looking for, but a different secret. The beautiful slanted markings that spoke to something deep inside me. The page was old and worn along the folds. It was coded in Ogham and I needed to know what it said.

'I know you saw me at the party.' She sounded contrite as she stepped into my room. Only Aisling could pull off white tulle and not look like an oversized flower girl at a wedding. She still had that layer of gloss around her. It was easy to forget that she was one of us. One of the imperfect girls who'd carelessly lost a parent or two, struggling along.

'Why didn't you tell me you were going?' I put the pen down on the desk. Then picked it up again. I was sore and annoyed and worried about what else she'd kept from me.

Aisling sat on the bed, her dress spreading daintily. 'I wanted to tell you.'

'But you didn't.'

'I'm sorry.'

'Why where you there?'

'Simon asked me.'

'Simon asked you?' I couldn't keep that sense of betrayal from my voice. He'd said nothing when he'd driven me home. I'd never known Simon and Aisling to keep secrets before. And certainly not from me. It hurt more than I let on.

'He's worried about what happens afterwards.' Aisling looked down at her hands. 'He wants to gather more information. So we agreed that I'd befriend Laney. Ask a few questions.'

'Did the circle decide this?'

'Not the circle. Just Simon.'

'It's reckless. What if David had recognised you?' My voice was rising.

'There were other girls from the village there,' she said quietly, pleading. Don't wake Smith. 'And Simon stayed close in case I needed help.'

'Let's just stick to the plan.' I was bone weary.

I couldn't articulate this feeling, this sense of wrong at deviating from the plan. We had a map, I didn't want to veer off course. It seemed that if we did, I'd somehow get lost and never find my way home from Harkness House.

Something must have shown in my face, perhaps I wasn't as good at hiding my feelings as I thought. But her voice was urgent, begging me to understand. 'I have to do something. I want to help you.'

Aisling was perched at the edge of the bed, anxious. She hated for anyone to be cross with her. Part of me, the hurt part, wanted to let her stew in it.

'Then don't hide things from me.'

The silence was tense as I sat at my desk. In front of me was the page I'd taken from the archive, teasing me with its secrets.

'I'm sorry I hurt you,' she said.

I went over to Aisling and sat beside her.

'Is there anything else you haven't told me, Ash?' The weight of the stolen page felt heavy in my heart. I too was keeping things from her.

'No.' She placed her hand, fingers splayed, beside mine. 'Nothing at all.'

But I wasn't sure I believed her.

I didn't know when it was that Aisling and I had stopped touching, other than a cautious hand on the shoulder, a brush against each other as we cleaned the kitchen. As children, we'd often curled up together in the same bed. Her arms, legs and face had been as comfortable and familiar as my own. And then we didn't seem to do it any more. Any move to hug or kiss was awkward and unpractised. It might have started when our bodies changed with puberty, when what was once known became mysterious. And then she got her talent and I feared that Aisling could read my secrets by touching me. But that night as we sat on my bed she twined her fingers in mine and gripped them tightly. I held on to her as if it would save me from being swept away.

FOURTEEN
For you

Today a woman from the village presented me with a doll.
It is an odd specimen, made of cloth, leaves and dried
flowers. Elizabeth has named it Bláithín.
AdC

The next morning, I faced death by historical art journals.

It was the beginning of February and the midpoint between the winter solstice and the spring equinox. Groves would spend the morning watching burrowing animals emerge from their holes, and so forecast the weather for spring.

And there I was, alone at Harkness House. I figured Cassa and her gang were marking the cross quarter with the Rose Gairdín, plotting world domination or something.

Alone, bored and in serious danger of bleeding eyeballs. I hated missing out.

My phone chimed with an incoming text from Aisling.

Got the FOMO really bad?

That girl could read my mind.

She sent another text, this time a picture of Maeve and a few others staring at an animal hole. It looked uncharacteristically dull, the women staring with exaggerated tedium. Usually, the grown-ups staved off the cold with whiskey, and it was very cold up there in the hills. The result was that everyone behaved a little badly.

A few minutes later, my phone chimed again and it showed all the older ladies of the grove, skirts lifted, cleavage exposed, even a flash of knickers. Now my eyeballs really were going to bleed.

A little show from the ladies of Whitethorn Grove. We miss you darling. Spring's going to be shite. I'll bring you Annie's boxty cakes. XOXO

Annie's boxty cakes were vile.

Sighing, I opened the second volume of Lady Catherine's garden book. I wished for a paragraph where Lady Catherine grew faint while watching a hot gardener dig all those flower beds. Why didn't the good Lady write about that?

But, paging through the journal, something else caught my attention:

The child has become fixed on these fantasies. She believes that she is being hunted. I have seen her emerge scratched and bruised from the woods beside the house. She must inflict these injuries upon herself.

Maybe my interests were too narrow, but frightened girls in the woods always got me. I skimmed the next pages, looking for more.

The girl is much subdued. She spends hours down at the lake watching the water. 'Do they get lonely?' she asked me, pointing to the lilies between the water weeds.

I shut the book. It made me feel odd. Fidgety, but with my hands fitted wrong to my body. On my desk was a fresh bowl of pink peonies. The flowers were open and beckoning.

I pulled the bowl closer, burying my nose in the scent of petal and leaf. Drawing back, I stared at the crowded flowers until I couldn't see them any more.

And then – Cassa in a shallow grave. Dirt covering most of her face. A pale white hand half hidden, half visible. Her eyes shut, her hair matted. She was wearing a white dress, an old one of Sorcha's that now hung in my wardrobe. A satisfied smile. And then, just like my vision of Sorcha being eaten, it fuzzed over and I saw myself. Just the briefest second, it was me there in Sorcha's dress, in the grave. And as quick as a flash, there was Cassa, smiling in the earth again.

I pulled back. It felt like my head had been underwater. Like I'd been drowning. It was wrong, I told myself. People didn't smile in their graves. And even though I could rationalise that it was because I felt vulnerable, I hated that I was seeing myself in these horrible visions.

'Where did you go just now?'

Cassa appeared at the edge of my desk. Not in a grave. Not smiling. She was very much alive and almost predatory. Still wearing her coat, she leaned towards me with undisguised interest.

I shook my head. I never could speak immediately after.

Cassa watched me, and the intensity of her stare reminded me of the day she'd watched me from the archive. It was a searching gaze, like she could find answers just by looking. I felt a burst of terror that she'd figured it out. What I'd done just now. And what I was.

'Just smelling the flowers,' I managed. Innocent as a daisy. Almost believable, but for that slight breathlessness.

Flowers. It wasn't a grave. It was a flower bed. I'd seen Cassa planted in the earth.

'Cassa?' David sidled up to her. 'Can we talk?'

My heart pounded. If Cassa was suspicious, David was the worst person to show up right now. He'd feed her uncertainty, and delight in it.

'What did you see just now?' Cassa's voice was low.

'Pink peonies?' I kept my face neutral. Sibéal and Aisling had both coached me in 'How to tell lies so it looks like the truth', and excess body language was a giveaway. Too bad about my twitchy eye.

Cassa drew back, still staring at me. She peeled a dark-green leather glove from one hand, then the other, fixing her eyes on mine. David hovered behind.

'What is it, David?' She didn't bother to look at him.

'Could we go to your office? I don't think it's a good idea to –'

'Do you have knowledge of an imminent security threat?' She sounded almost bored. Like they'd had this conversation before.

'Not imminent, but I think you should hear this.' David's cheeks were slightly pink.

'I'm listening.' She touched the peonies, her fingertips brushing the petals.

David cast me a surly look and said, 'There're rumours …'

'Rumours?' Cassa's soft murmur was designed to slay.

'… about the crowd giving us trouble.' He meant augurs,

obviously. 'They have a long-term plan to annex, uh,' he glanced at me and finished lamely, 'the property we value most.'

Nemeta. Which meant David was talking rubbish. We had no plans to take judge nemeta. We didn't even know where they were. Anger flared and I wondered how often he fed Cassa bad information. Was he trying to heighten the tensions between us? Was David so bloodthirsty that he wanted a war?

'And that's not all.' He turned to me and I knew he was going to tell her about the kill mark and that he suspected I knew what it meant.

Cassa finally looked from the peonies to David.

'Last December –' he started.

'Where did you hear these rumours?' Cassa cut him off. 'Your contact? Or are you going to repeat village gossip and pretend it's fact?'

'Sometimes valuable information comes from unlikely sources.' He sounded wooden.

'Perhaps. But every time you've come to me with village mumblings,' she looked pointedly at me, 'you've been wrong.'

She stepped towards him. And even though he towered over her, it was clear who had the power.

'I'm getting tired, David.'

'Tired?' He swallowed.

'Of you.' Her voice was cold as ice. 'Sort yourself out. If you suspect a problem, bring me evidence. Don't be a whiner.'

Cassa walked away from him, but halfway to her office, she stopped.

'David,' she said, finally bringing sweetness to her voice.

'Yes, Cassa?'

'Does it bother you?'

'What do you mean?'

'That you'll never measure up to your brother?' She went on to her office, not bothering to check the damage.

From the look on his face, she couldn't have hurt him more. I hated David, but I almost I felt sorry for him as he withered beneath her words.

'Don't you fucking dare,' he hissed at me and walked away, slamming his hand against the door as he left.

And I realised that in pitying David I'd gained a small victory. But it felt dirty. I sat there, conflicted with this shameful pleasure that his humiliation had made me feel better about myself.

Later in the afternoon, I was making tea when the courier brought a parcel.

'I'll take that,' Tarc said as he entered the office. I hadn't seen him since the previous night's awkwardness.

He signed for the parcel and took out his knife to rip open the plastic covering. I caught a brief glimpse of carvings on the handle.

He couldn't quite meet my eye, and I felt ill at ease with him. Did he see me differently now? Crazy stabbing weird girl. But *nice*.

Tarc opened the box and inside was a handmade doll put together with cloth, twigs and leaves. Her face was blank, no eyes, mouth or nose, and she wore a grey headscarf. The red floral cloth of her dress fell around her in layers, reminding me of an old-style farmer's wife. Two branches shot out of the sleeves and ended in leaves. Her legs and feet were a bunch of dried flowers.

Tarc glanced at the card.

'A brídeog,' I said. A little Brigid. The making of dolls and Brigid's crosses were common activities for children at the beginning of February. The dolls were meant to welcome St Brigid into the home. Or the goddess Brigid, if you were one of us.

'Why would someone send Cassa a brídeog?'

'It's not for Cassa,' Tarc said, handing me the box and a card with my name on it. 'It's for you.'

I was leaving by the rose archway when Tarc called after me.

'Wren, wait.'

He was framed by the tall lines of the grand front door. The way he stood there, breathing deeply and less composed than usual, sparked something inside me. As he strode towards me, the skin on my hands felt pricked by small pins. I was hyper alert, as in those moments before falling into a vision.

In another life, another time, he could be an ordinary boy walking towards me beneath the tangled branches of a climbing rose.

'I want to apologise. For last night.'

My eye fell on the fine cords of muscle in his forearms. The bones in his hands.

'What exactly are you apologising for, Tarc? That charming conversation you had with Cillian? Or pulling a knife while David had me in a chokehold?'

'All of that, I guess.' He seemed miserable.

Those veins that ran down through his hands. Part of me wanted to stretch out the tip of my finger and trace the blue thread as it disappeared beneath the muscle and bone. The more sensible half just wanted to be on the bus with the city lights fading behind me.

'What were you doing last night?' I said. 'Where were you going?'

He just looked at me.

'Something was off,' I went on. I knew I should walk away, stop poking at this, but my feet had rooted themselves to the paved path. 'The way David was creeping around. That knife. Do you always carry it?'

'Well, it is handy for opening parcels.' Then he relented. 'I work in security, Wren.'

I wasn't asking the right questions. But I couldn't say what I wanted: how far would judge boys go to ensure they maintained the upper hand in the struggle with us? I wanted to know if he'd been there that night in Abbyvale when the augurs were beaten up.

'Do you damage ...' the standing stone with its spray-painted smiley face, '... other people's things? Their property?'

'Property? What do you mean?' And the way he looked at me, it felt like Simon reading my smallest fidgets.

'Are you one of those boys?' I tried again. 'The kind that hurts and breaks and doesn't care?' Boys like David. Who'd just come out of the front door.

David waited on the top step, a rectangular blot on my vision. He stood there behind Tarc, not saying anything.

He was suspicious. But he had no proof. And after hearing his conversation with Cassa, I knew he'd need evidence before he could say anything about the kill mark to her. I had to make sure he didn't get any.

Tarc touched a hand to the creeping rose. 'I don't mean to be.'

'But your friends are.' I jerked my head towards David.

Tarc turned and saw him.

'Why did you go to Kilshamble, that night you gave me a lift home?'

He hesitated. I started walking away.

'Wait.' Three steps and he was right behind me. 'I took flowers to Arabella's cottage.' He shrugged. 'Cassa asked me to.'

'That's all?' The fresh lilies in the corner of the ruin.

'That's all.'

I nodded and walked out into the late afternoon, going beyond my bus stop to the next. I passed the Orchard of the Hungry Marys – once a field of apple trees, now a fancy hotel – where shamed women who'd been cast from their families would gather.

How relieved I was that Tarc hadn't damaged the Laceys' stone. And also annoyed, because I shouldn't have cared.

But I did care. I cared more than I wanted to. If I'd trailed a ribbon each time I travelled to and from Harkness House, I would have left an intricate pattern over these last weeks. The endless repetition of coming into the city, to the house, and then leaving again at the end of each day. The slight variations when I stopped for a tea or walked to the next bus stop. This pattern was an oversight in the plan. Or perhaps a risk Smith decided to take, that this repeated moving between two destinations would set up a relationship between them and me, not unlike a wickering.

And there I was, caught somewhere in the middle.

☙ FIFTEEN ❧
Everything that is wrong with us

There must be something wrong in the kitchen. Our meals
taste as though they have been seasoned with sawdust.
AdC

The page was filled with neat ink scratches, the regular lines
and shapes that made up the Ogham alphabet. The markings had been made on thick paper that had been folded
along the same grooves many times.

I was in Maeve's kitchen, the stolen page in front of me.
With the help of Maeve's Ogham reference book, I was
decoding the script and translating to English. The page had
sparked a burning curiosity in me and I had to know what
it meant before handing it over. So far, I had the title: *The*
Definitive Traits of the ... But I was stuck on a symbol. It
looked like a quinquetra, a five-fold knot, and resembled a
flower. Not Ogham; I'd never seen it before.

Aisling sat across from me, murdering a bowl of ice
cream. Beside her, Sibéal wore large white-framed sunglasses.

She'd been shading a figure of a girl running. But she'd stopped minutes ago, the storyboard and selection of pencils abandoned. Listless, she looked out of the large windows, face turned to the sky.

I knew what she was doing. I'd done the same thing in the weeks before I turned sixteen: gazing at the clouds, chasing the flight patterns of birds, frowning at bodies, staring unblinkingly at flames, trying to trigger a talent.

'I heard there's going to be an Arabella de Courcy Retrospective down at the hotel. Big party planned in two weeks,' Aisling said.

'Yeah, Cassa told me.' I was only half listening as I decoded the marks on the sheet of paper.

'Why didn't you tell us?' Aisling sounded annoyed, but I wasn't sure. I peered across at her. She was such an advert, creamy-skinned girl with spoon between luscious lips.

One of the slanted lines was obscured by a fold. The paper had worn thin there and I raised the page, tilting it to get a better view.

'Wren.' Definitely peeved at me.

'What?' I looked up at her. 'I didn't think it mattered.'

'The village will be crawling with judges.' She stood up, her chair scraping the tiles.

'Newsflash, the village *is* crawling with them.'

I'd figured out the next section: *Almost an orphan.*

How was someone almost an orphan?

'You should have told us.'

Actually, thinking about it, I was almost an orphan. Hadn't a clue about my father. And, frankly, the dead/alive status of my parents hadn't really mattered these last seventeen years. They were as good as dead for all the parenting they'd done.

'I forgot.' I glanced up again.

Sibéal held a snowdrop to her eyes. Through her sunglasses, she was squinting at the green and white heart. Aisling was beside her, just standing there and staring at me, empty bowl in hand. I covered the stolen sheet with another page, an old poem in Ogham.

'What else have you forgotten?' Aisling said.

'I don't know,' I said, my hand feeling the stolen page I was hiding beneath the old poem. 'I try to give an account of what I see at Harkness House. Sometimes I make mistakes.'

But Aisling was right to question me. There were things I was withholding. Like Tarc's tattoo. His lips on my cheek. The page under my hand. Again, I felt that mix of shame and exasperation. I wanted them to stop at me. I felt guilty for keeping my secrets.

'Why are you so interested?' I diverted the conversation. 'Is it because of Simon?'

'What do you mean?' Aisling's attempt to dissemble was a dead giveaway. Any doubts she and Simon were hiding something from me vanished.

'Are you and Simon still trying to do my job for me?'

'Simon and I are … just getting to know each other better.' The way she looked at me made me wonder if I'd totally misunderstood. I couldn't be sure whether Aisling and Simon were investigating on their own or if it was something else. All I knew was that Aisling and I used to tell each other everything. Now we didn't. And it sucked.

Aisling leaned over my shoulder, and my breath caught. I'd covered the stolen page, but not the words I'd translated.

'Poems about orphans? In Ogham? Seriously,' she said, taking her bowl to the sink. 'That's just weird.'

She left the kitchen and it still didn't feel right between us. Perhaps it was because of the night she'd appeared at Cassa's party, in white tulle. The night I realised that there were limits to what she shared with me.

Sibéal was now looking into a kaleidoscope, her left eye screwed shut and her mouth a little open as she turned it round and round. My sleeve had furrowed up my arm, and I could see the raised, bumpy skin from my almost imaginary snakebite.

I pulled the Ogham sheet from beneath the poem. After thirty minutes, I had a list.

The Definitive Traits of the ✸:
Almost an orphan.
Grows where the last ✸ trod.
Steals the love [lost to the fold of the page] *from the garden.*
Marked by the garden.
Wakens the doll.
Sees what isn't [lost to the fold of the page].
From the line of the judges.
Brings the golden time.

While I puzzled over the list, Sibéal pushed back her chair and moved to the window. She opened it, letting in a rush of cold air. Climbing on to the window ledge, she leaned out. She looked like the figurehead on a ship. Or a girl about to jump.

'Shibs,' I said. 'You know some of the stories and traditions of the judges, right? Tell me about the second golden era.'

Sibéal didn't answer. She seemed so unlike herself. The kitchen was freezing but still she leaned out of the window, her body a line of steel.

'The second ré órga,' she spoke eventually, 'was in the late nineteenth century, and it was all about making money. It wasn't enough to physically outclass us, they had to be richer too.'

She finally looked at me, her large sunglasses covering nearly half her face. Outside, a fat cloud blotted the sun.

'I don't think you can blame them for that,' I said mildly. 'I doubt being better than augurs was their main motivation.'

Sibéal jumped down from the window ledge.

'I blame them for everything that is wrong with us,' she spat. 'They've destroyed our nemeta by putting in roads and fugly shopping centres.'

She stood there like a vengeful angel.

'Isn't that in the hands of the county council, not the judges?' I tried to placate her.

'And who do you think owns the county council?' she snapped. 'In the last seventy years they've ensured that they either own it or destroy it. Leaving us with the dregs. That's your Cassa Harkness. Remember that when you make her tea.'

'I understand you're upset,' I said. Sibéal's simmering anger about her not-yet-emerged talent found an easy target with the judges. 'I've been there. But –'

179

'But what, Wren?' She pulled off her sunglasses. I was astonished at how wretched she looked. Her eyes were puffy from crying and there were dark half-moons beneath them. 'You going to tell me they're not all like that? Because, really, you've been eating cake with them and oh look, they're all cute fluffy teddies underneath.'

'Oh, Sibéal,' I said. 'I wish I could help.'

'You *can* help.' She pushed the sunglasses back on and picked up her pencil. 'Stop being so afraid. Get what we need from Cassa Harkness. Don't let your fear screw this up.'

'I'm not afraid,' I said, stung.

'Yes you are. You're a big scaredy cat, and that's going to be our undoing.'

'I have to tread carefully with Cassa. She's no fool.'

'You're asking me about the judges but you're the one who's with them every day. Why haven't you opened doors that you're not supposed to open? Why haven't you stolen documents or uncovered secrets?'

'It's not that easy to snoop when –' And I stopped. I couldn't explain it. That push and pull. She was right. I was holding back. And it was because I wasn't sure of anything any more. I felt the draw of Harkness House. I felt loyalty to my grove. It left me confused.

'When you're scared,' she finished for me. 'I wish it had

been me. I wouldn't be checking over my shoulder every minute. I would have owned this.'

'It's freezing in here.' Maeve came in, immediately sensing the odd mood.

She pulled the window shut and Sibéal turned away, hiding her obvious anger. 'You girls OK?'

'Grand, Maeve,' I said. 'Just heading home.' Sibéal wouldn't look at me and I was peeved because she'd hit a nerve.

Gathering my things, I paused at the list. Now that it was translated, I had no reason to keep it. I should hand it over to Maeve. Prove Sibéal wrong.

But I didn't want to. Translating the list hadn't eased my curiosity. If anything, it was stronger now. I wanted to know what it meant. If I handed the list to Maeve, she'd give it to the circle and I'd hear nothing more.

'Wren,' Maeve said in a low voice, glancing at Sibéal, who took no notice of us. I pressed the folder against my stomach.

'Did you get an answer for me?' She tilted her head towards Sibéal.

'I tried once, but nothing.'

'Once?' Maeve said.

'I'll give it another shot.'

With a last glance at Sibéal, who was now holding a

pencil and glaring at her storyboard, I went next door to Carraig Cottage and found Smith out in the back garden. He was peering into a large cardboard box. Something moved angrily inside.

'What's that?' I said.

'Ruth Lacey got word of a divining hen down in Carlow.'

'For ooscopy?' None of us had that talent.

'With a divining hen,' Smith pre-empted my objection, 'any talented augur can read its egg. You'll be guided in the interpretation by how the yolk spreads. The egg does the work, not the augur.'

'Me?'

'Your talent is the best suited to this. You're the only one who sees beyond the present.'

I went over and looked inside the box and stared down at the furious black hen. Smith already kept hens, it wouldn't put him out to have another.

'Why?'

'Maeve is convinced there must be a faster way to bind to a nemeton. She's really excited. It's not easy sourcing a divining hen, you know.'

'I'm sure.'

Smith lifted the box into the hen enclosure and tilted it.

She came out like a dark wave, wings flapping wildly, and

squawking at us in a volley of clucks. Taking two cautious steps, she looked around her new home, unimpressed.

'So I have to collect an egg?' I said. 'Then what?'

'Maeve has the instructions,' Smith said, bending down to pick up a hurley stick that was half hidden in the grass. 'She lays blue eggs, so we'll know which are hers.'

He positioned the long wooden hurley in his hands. I picked up the sliotar, the leather ball, and threw it to him.

'Have you been in the shed lately?' he said, tossing the sliotar up and whacking it with the flat end of the hurley. It zipped right over my head before bouncing against the wall.

'No.'

When he was young and jobs were scarce, Smith had worked as a bricklayer in Manchester. Beneath the sag, the hard muscle from years of physical labour was still there. He'd always loved sports, especially hurling, and he'd tried to hide his disappointment that I could barely tell one end of the stick from the other.

'Something's got inside.' He struck the sliotar. 'A magpie.'

It bounced back and he caught it, glancing briefly at me before striking again.

'Built a nest up in the beams.' Catching the sliotar, he turned to the shed wall beyond the hen enclosure and aimed there. 'She's messing my floor.'

'Sure she's just looking for shelter,' I said. 'It's been a hard winter.'

'Not in my shed.'

Smith hit too high and the sliotar went into the field next door. I scaled the high stone wall to retrieve it. The horses looked at me curiously. Finding the ball, I climbed up again. Balancing at the top of the wall, I called, 'Smith!' as I poised to throw the sliotar to him.

But he was already mid-swing. He twisted his body and the broad, flat end of the hurley hit an object with a powerful thud. A strike like that should have sent the sliotar over the roof, but instead I saw an explosion of feathers. Red and feathers spattered over the grass. The hen clucked, either in excitement or disapproval.

'Keep clear of the shed,' Smith said. 'Unless you want to clean it out.'

'What was that?' I climbed too fast down the wall, banging my knee hard against the stone. I scrambled over to Smith, ignoring the dull throb in my leg.

'Magpie,' he said, stepping over the mess of feathers and blood. I looked at him, incredulous. I wasn't sure if the sick feeling came from the pain shooting up my leg or from looking at the remains of the bird Smith had killed.

'Ah, Wren,' he said, looking at my face. 'Magpies are pests. You should see the state of the shed.'

He threw the sliotar at me and, off guard, I only just caught it.

'Come on, let's get the tea.' Smith examined the flat edge of the hurley as we walked back inside, his arm draped lightly across my shoulders.

✦ SIXTEEN ✦
Not a virgin sacrifice

I saw the meat hooks strung with red flesh.
AdC

'I'll be there with you,' Aisling said, but it wasn't true. She'd be at the Arabella de Courcy exhibition party, but she wouldn't be with me.

In the mirror, I could see her skin was glowing, her eyes bright. She wore a black dress that made her hair shine like a halo.

'You aren't wearing that, are you?' Aisling turned from her reflection and looked at my jeans.

I wasn't feeling it. Excitement had been growing in the village these last days. Not because people wanted to see Arabella's art, but because they'd heard the rumours about Cassa's lavish parties. If I could skip it, I would. But Cassa had invited me herself, and she was a hard woman to refuse.

'It's a judge party. You can't wear jeans.' Aisling was at my wardrobe. She drew out a long white dress. Sorcha's. The only thing of hers I owned.

'It's a party,' I rolled my eyes, 'not a virgin sacrifice.' We didn't do those any more.

'This one then.' She pulled out another dress. 'Demon green. Just like your eyes.'

It was a slinky pale-green thing. Too short. Aisling was ferreting about with the shoes she'd brought. I grimaced at the heels. Too high.

'It's cold.' My objections were dismissed. But I let her do it anyway. I let her change my clothes. I let her do my hair, make-up. Maybe I wanted her to.

'Isn't this a bad idea?' I said. 'The two of us at the same party? David knows we're friends. He watches me too carefully.'

'So, we're friends. That doesn't tell him anything.'

But I couldn't explain to Aisling the way David watched.

'We'll keep a distance. Won't draw attention to us.' She circled a finger between our faces, a simple gesture for a rich, complex, beautiful thing. Us. 'Laney invited me anyway.'

I was possibly a little jealous of Laney. Aisling and I hadn't had much fun lately. The plan seemed to creep into everything, like colours running in the washing machine.

'How did you meet Laney?' I said. They ran in such different circles.

'A teeny tiny bit of online stalking,' she said, and held up her thumb and forefinger to show a small gap. 'It's surprising how easy it is to manufacture connections, to know where people like to hang out. The things they're interested in.'

We stood side by side in the mirror, delighting in the differences brought on by pretty dresses and make-up. Then we walked down to the village.

As we neared the main street, I hung back and let Aisling go ahead. It wasn't a good idea to arrive together.

Outside the Huntsman, the dying winter sun fell on the stone paving. On the far side of the hotel were the Straying Steps, where Ned Healy, haruspex and butcher, had left the severed hand of his cheating wife. When her lover arrived at the steps at the arranged time, he found only her outstretched hand, the bloodied wedding ring proof of the vows she'd broken. But that was from the secret history. The stories that only we knew.

It seemed like the entire village had come to the first night of the Arabella de Courcy Retrospective. The function room was lively with fiddles and flutes, while villagers in their Sunday best clutched their drinks. Craning their necks to get a looky-loo at the American heiress and her big, strong boys. Who, admittedly, didn't look half bad in their suits. Only their boots gave them away. Like cloven hooves peering out from their dress pants.

And on the walls, the Arabella de Courcy paintings. I went a little closer. There were about twenty of them in total, all from Cassa's private collection. The picture closest to me was a study of a daisy. I looked at the picture carefully, wondering why it bothered me.

'If you were a flower, which would you be?' Laney stood beside me with a glass of champagne.

'Never really thought about it,' I said. 'Probably a daisy.' I gestured to the painting in front of me.

'You're no daisy,' Laney said. 'I'm lisianthus. Purple. That's a daisy.' She pointed to Aisling, who was scrutinising a painting on the other side. I knew what she meant.

'Does something strike you as odd about this picture?' I said to Laney.

'Odd? No. It's just a flower.'

I moved on to the next one. Again, there was something not right. I studied the picture, trying to figure out what it was.

'You're something different,' Laney continued. 'Maybe a rose.' She tilted her head to examine me. 'No, too classic. A poppy? Marigold?' She paused. 'Of course, a peony. White.'

Like the flowers on my desk. It felt like Laney was trying to tell me something and I wished she would just say it.

Excusing myself, I moved towards the bar. But someone stepped in front of me. I looked up and saw David. I edged to the left, and he did the same. I stepped to the right, and he did the same. Left again and he blocked me, all the while backing me towards the wall. I felt it against my back and tried to scoot around him, but his arms caged me in. He'd chucked his suit jacket and his tie looked like it wanted to strangle him. I knew the feeling.

'What do you want, David?' I said.

'Security check.' He relaxed his arms down to his side, but I still felt caged.

Behind him was another man, one I didn't recognise. He had a narrow frame and a thick moleskin jacket with a scraggly yellow flower on one lapel.

'Go home,' David said. 'No one wants you here.'

'Cassa does. She asked me herself.'

And without meaning to, I'd managed to rattle him. It was fleeting but I saw it bothered him. That Cassa seemed to like me more than she did him.

'Why, David?' I said, pushing away from the wall. 'Are you this bitter because, much as you despise me, you're just a small village kid? Like me.'

'I'm nothing like you.'

It was then that I caught the ink creeping out of his rolled-up sleeve. He saw me looking and pulled it up further. A two-headed snake.

'For passing my exams.'

'Well, that's not very original,' I said. Nodding to his friend, who was still staring at me, I walked away.

'You disappointed I didn't get a wren?' David called out. 'Am I breaking your heart, Little Bird?'

'Wait,' Moleskin said.

I turned. 'For you.' He took the flower from his lapel and bowed as he gave it to me.

'I insist,' he said when he saw me hesitating. He pushed it into my hands. Creeper.

I strode across the room, anywhere to get away from them, then I looked at the flower. Ragwort. A poison flower. Sure, less so for me than a cow, but really, what kind of man gives a girl poison flowers? I dropped it to the ground.

Not looking where I was going, I nearly walked straight into Tarc. Cillian was close behind him.

'You look, uh, nice,' he said, running an eye over my dress.

'Nice?' I smiled at him, ignoring that traitorous flair of delight. 'Seriously. Stop with the nice.'

He laughed and suddenly it wasn't so awful, him there in Kilshamble.

191

'You don't look too bad yourself.' Understatement. 'That what you wear when you work evenings?'

'Sometimes,' Cillian answered for him. 'But we're really here to look for girls, right? I've been telling Tarc all about the Kilshamble girls.'

'I won't get in your way so,' I said, supressing that sudden awful bitterness. I had no business being jealous.

I slipped through the glass doors to the wide veranda. Then down the steps into the garden. I could breathe a bit easier here, away from everyone.

But I wasn't alone. On the other side of the lawn, Cassa stared at the fountain. If I didn't know any better, I'd think she was trying to read the water as it gushed from the stone fish mouths to the pool below. She seemed lost in memory, lost in something from long ago as she stood there.

I only registered the soft music when Cassa looked up, tilting her head to the side. It was almost inaudible, the faint sound of long, sad notes. She stared at the darkened hedge. Then, as if drawn by the music, she set off towards it.

I hurried across the grass. Reaching the fountain, I realised I'd heard the tune before. I didn't know it, just enough to appreciate the disconcerting familiarity. The strangeness of it coming from the hazel hedge.

Cassa's high heels had been placed in a neat pair. As if she'd slipped them off before going into a temple.

The ground was rough and uneven, so I placed mine beside hers.

The music called to me. Like behind the hedge was a pied piper who stole girls from gardens. Like the tree prince who'd lured Arabella to the woods. Barefoot, I pushed through the thick foliage, feeling the stones and twigs and roots under my feet. The music stopped abruptly.

When I emerged in the lane on the other side, whatever whimsy I'd felt was rudely dispelled. Cassa wasn't alone.

Lit only by the streetlights from the next road were several men wearing ski masks. Cassa was slung over a shoulder, her pale arms hanging down a broad back.

'Hey!' I shouted.

One of them turned to look at me, and I felt a draw, a magnetic pull. He was an augur, a strong one. He ran on, catching up to the others. It didn't take a genius to figure out they were Abbyvale augurs intent on revenge. I counted six of them as I ran behind, shouting at them.

It was futile. I couldn't stop them. I'd left my phone in my coat pocket. My best bet was to go back through the hedge and scream for Tarc and the wrenboys.

Then he was there, as if I'd somehow summoned him. Tarc pushed through the hazel hedge. He ran hard, passing where I dithered, following the men down the lane. Realising they were pursued, they picked up speed.

But Tarc was fast. He'd nearly caught up with them, when one stopped. Something sharp glinted in his hand. His face, like the others, was hidden. Tarc charged at the man and they locked into each other. Ahead, the other five ran down the tree-lined lane, one of them carrying Cassa. I sprinted after them.

The men were nearing the end of the lane. On the other side of a cattle gate was a blue van.

'They're getting away,' I yelled at Tarc as he dealt a blow to the man, sending him reeling. I felt it in my gut, that punch from judge to augur.

Ahead, the men were a few feet from the gate.

I turned to see Tarc looking at the trees with fierce concentration. Just a few seconds he stood there, I might almost have imagined it.

Then he was barrelling forward, with no heed that he was outnumbered. As he charged, the man carrying Cassa tripped over one of the thick roots. Cassa went skidding on the dirt. Quick to his feet, the man was already in a fighting stance as Tarc approached. The others stood ready, holding knives and clubs.

It was that moment before. Laden, like a cloud about to break. Within seconds, things were going to get really ugly. I didn't know where I stood; I didn't want Tarc overpowered, nor did I want him hurting augurs. Again, I felt it, the tug of the pattern I'd made between Harkness House and Carraig Cottage, that pull in both directions.

The men began to move on Tarc. As he fought them off, it became clear that, unlike the men he was fighting, he was no casual brawler. Every movement revealed a grace and efficiency that came with years of training. It sickened me to hear the crunch of his fists, his boots on the bodies of augurs. He was alert to every man, wherever they stood, anticipating their moves.

Several augurs were down. One man's ski mask had come off, revealing a soft-cheeked face streaked with eye black. These were just ordinary young men. It was so wrong.

I went to Cassa. If I could get her away, the fight would stop.

'Can you stand?' I said to her.

Looking up, I saw an augur charge Tarc from the side as another holding a club ran at him from behind. He blocked the first, just missing the second. It was a brutal blow by the heaviest man, bringing him to his knees. Seizing the advantage, two augurs grabbed him by the arms. Another landed a hard fist in his gut. Then another. The blows kept coming, until a loud crack sounded. Tarc reared back, exploiting the distraction to pull free.

A tree had split down its length. Part of the trunk came

crashing down, the branches hitting two of the men. It missed Tarc by inches. I stood there, gaping.

The tree had fallen directly between him and the augurs, blocking them off.

Tarc was in front of Cassa, his knife out.

But the men were up and jumping the gate. Car doors slammed and they sped away.

'Tarc,' Cassa said.

He was breathing heavily, and even in the dim light I could see he'd been hurt.

Tarc helped Cassa up while I gawked at the split tree. It had been so quick and so unlikely, my brain was frantically trying to rationalise what I'd seen. Tarc staring intently. The tree that had looked perfectly healthy suddenly dividing in two. That was one well-timed coincidence. Except, as Smith always said, there was no such thing as coincidence, only partially formed patterns.

Laney was at the hazel hedge, her face pale and worried. She reached for Cassa, soothing her hair and checking her face.

'Wait,' Cassa said. She turned Tarc towards her, inventorying the damage. She took in the scrapes and grazes, the soil and blood on his white dress shirt.

'I will make them pay for every drop of blood they spilled tonight. They will regret laying a hand on one of mine.' Her awful words were at odds with her soft murmuring tone. A mother singing a terrible lullaby to her children. I made myself watch. This was how judges were nurtured. With whispers of war and retribution.

I was grateful for the dim garden lights. No way could I hide how her words affected me.

'Wren?' Tarc came to me. 'You OK?'

He steered me along the hedge, into the corner. He walked carefully, trying to hide his pain. I heard Laney's low, anxious voice as she tended to Cassa.

'Is this what you meant when you said the curriculum at Birchwood was non-standard?' I said, as Tarc ran a hand over his face.

'What do you mean?'

'What just happened?' I moved closer to him. 'That tree?'

Across the garden, on the veranda, stood David and Cillian. Cassa was striding towards them.

'Got lucky,' Tarc said.

'That wasn't luck,' I pushed.

'We should go in,' he said. 'You're freezing.'

With the adrenalin comedown, the cold was fierce. But I wasn't going to let this go.

'I know that there are some strange things in the village,' I said. 'I've heard that some families are a little … different.'

He looked so tired. His shirt, smeared with dirt and blood, hung loose and several buttons were missing. His head was bent and the gingerly touch to his ribs told me he was in pain. But if we went back in, I'd never know. If he didn't tell me here, now, he never would.

Eventually he spoke. 'And if some of us were different, how would that work?'

'They say some families are descendants of the ancient druids. That magic runs in their blood.'

I stopped and tried to discern his features. 'Is that what happened with the tree?'

'Magic.' He exhaled. 'I'm not sure I even know what that is. I think my idea of magic is different to the usual understanding.'

His eyes held mine as he acknowledged what he was. I felt so guilty I couldn't be honest with him too.

I waited. I wanted to hear him describe it, this sense of magic that was both pervasive and limited. And I wanted to hear how it worked for judges.

'You have to keep this between us, Wren.' He moved closer so that the space between us became tight. He paused, as if trying to find the words. 'There are particular natural objects that we're drawn to. That we're agitated without. Our totems. And it feels like this thing, maybe plant or rock or flame or some other natural element, gives us strength. That they could almost speak to us. Except, they never do really. Not in any kind of obvious way.'

'A tree cracked down the middle is pretty obvious.'

He looked back to the lane, as if he could see the damaged tree. He seemed almost as perplexed as I was.

'I don't know how,' he said. 'But sometimes, when I really need it, it is.' His words were a confession. Quiet and closed. Words to be whispered in the dark.

'Promise me you won't tell?' Tarc leaned towards me, his voice urgent.

I stood stupidly. How could I make a promise like that?

'You have to promise, Wren.'

'I won't tell anyone about the tree.' And the words were like poison. It was a promise I couldn't keep.

He nodded. 'I need to get back there.'

I thought he meant Cassa, but then realised he was speaking about the injured tree. Great. The boy I was crushing on against my will was off to talk to a tree.

'To retrieve their knives.' He almost smiled. 'It could help us identify them. And also, the tree.'

Then he was gone.

On the veranda, Cassa, her dress creased and mucky, was annihilating David and Cillian in her cold, controlled way. I waited until she and Laney were inside before I went up the steps. David glared at me, his misery and fury loaded into that one look.

Back in the event room, I found Aisling talking to her schoolfriends. She was bright and feverish, like she'd been drinking. Brian and Ryan were at the entrance, looking a little dazed. Cassa must have torn a strip off them too.

I viewed the paintings again before I left. Making a slow circle around the room, I examined each one in careful detail.

Arabella's flowers were exquisite. More than simply a reproduction or a scientific document, the watercolours conveyed personality. The coy seductiveness of a cherry blossom, the innocuous toxicity of oleander. But, as I made my way around, I began to understand what had unnerved me earlier. Not unlike my spinny eye, hidden in the pictures was something a little human. The form of a girl, the line of a nose and mouth below the barest hint of an eye. The curve of hip and breast. Not only had Arabella de Courcy painted the flowers with personality, she'd hidden a girl inside them.

SEVENTEEN
But false

The Girl of Leaf and Petal is but a game and yet, in our preparation, there are moments when I glimpse an almost ancient truth. At times I feel that Elizabeth and I have stumbled upon something uncommon, whose power we cannot begin to fathom.

AdC

'Wren,' Laney said. 'There you are. You're getting started on the archive today.' She smiled at me, dimples showing. Apparently, hanging out at a hazel hedge after an attempted kidnapping was a bonding ritual with Laney.

'No more journals?' I was almost disappointed. I wanted to know more about the troubled girl in Lady Catherine's garden books.

'Don't be silly. There are always journals. Now,' she talked at me, 'loads to do.'

She gave instructions while ushering me down the hallway to the basement. We found Tarc along the way and she gathered him too. She talked fast as she moved us to the staircase, explaining what needed to be done. I didn't hear half of what she said.

Too quickly, Laney ended with, 'So I'm sending in the muscle.'

She tilted her head at Tarc and turned away, her high heels loud on the marble.

'Did you get any of that?' I said to Tarc. His face was grazed, the skin on his temple a rich shade of mottled purple. So beautifully textured, it called to me, saying, *Read me.*

'No.'

We went downstairs and he entered the code for the archive, the clicks beeping a little tune.

'You know that it's daft to have a keypad with key clicks that make different sounds, right? It's like the keypad sings a tune.'

'That would be daft,' Tarc agreed amiably. 'But this keypad doesn't sing a tune. The key clicks are completely tuneless.'

'It totally sings a tune.'

Tarc looked at me with exaggerated patience. He pulled the door shut and entered the code again.

'See,' he said, completely satisfied, as if there hadn't been a distinct little tune to the clicks. I looked at him carefully to see if he was having me on.

'I'll do it.' I pressed out the first line to 'Mary Had a little Lamb'. Smug, I stepped back. 'See?' I mimicked him. Then looking at him sideways, 'Unless, of course, you're tone deaf?'

Tarc's lips were twitching into a smile and he shook his head, the laugh escaping.

'Is this your party trick? Do you hear voices beneath the microwave hum? The washing machine?'

'You know, I haven't tried them,' I said, wondering. 'But you heard this tune, right?'

'You're funny,' he said, and I realised that he thought I was being playful. He hadn't heard the tune. He couldn't.

'Right. Funny,' I said, backtracking. I'd heard a tune as plain as day. 'I'm hilarious.'

But I felt unexpectedly crushed. Just another wonky spiderweb. The key clicks all made exactly the same sound. Except to me. It was my spinny eye, but in audio.

'So we change the code every week,' Tarc was saying as we went inside.

Working in silence, I inventoried the unsealed boxes while Tarc stacked the high shelves. I wanted to ask him about totems. About magic and trees behaving strangely. But I knew he was avoiding that.

'Are you here because I don't have security clearance for the archive?' I watched him wince as he reached up.

'I think you might be getting upgraded soon.' He laughed. 'Cassa likes you. Here, let me get that.'

Wouldn't that be nice, I thought. Upgrade to Wren 2.01. Eliminate the wonky.

He reached for the box I was pulling down but I swatted him away. As much as he was trying to hide it, he'd been hurt at the Huntsman.

'I can manage,' I said.

'I know.'

How? I wanted to say. *You barely know me at all.* And then I realised that I had said it aloud. Just the last part: you barely know me at all.

He looked up from the table where he stood. He seemed so unsure of himself.

'Sometimes you get to know people in small, quiet ways. Like when they fidget with their hair. From the things they don't say.'

And his words made me stop, my hands half opening the cardboard box. He looked back at the shelves he'd been stacking and continued. 'If you watch, listen carefully. If you're still enough. Then the sense of them is there.'

I didn't know what to say to that. So, keeping my hands busy, I went for glib: 'Well, that sounds just a teeny bit creepy. Bet you say that to all the girls.' I picked up a large hardback book and opened it.

'Not all the girls, no.'

His gaze was intense and I wanted to turn away. But I made myself accept it, the something that was being offered in that look. It went on longer than it should, until I noticed the word just beyond his head. The label on the box: *Maps*.

Could it be that simple? That the document we were searching for was neatly packed and labelled in this otherwise unholy mess? But I doubted I had the right security clearance to start pulling down boxes and rummaging through them just yet.

'So.' Girls. 'Was Cillian right? About the Kilshamble girls?' I wanted it to be true. 'Were you at the Huntsman looking for girls?'

I wanted him as callous as Cillian, so I would like him less.

I wasn't sure if my heart was thudding away because of the maps, or because of what was lurking beneath our conversation. Smith was right; sometimes questions mattered more than answers. Because by saying those words, I'd admitted that I cared.

'Yes.' He fidgeted. 'No. It's not what you think.'

'It's not exactly a multiple-choice question. A, yes. B, maybe. C, only if they were redheads. It's more like true or false.'

A long-settled dust clung to the covers of the book I was holding and in between the pages. It sat thick on my fingers, in my throat, and it felt like sadness.

'True or false?' I said.

'True.'

I shut the book, dust billowing up to my face.

'But false.'

Over the next days, I continued to spend mornings in the archive. Usually Laney accompanied me, occasionally Tarc. I was never alone. The box of maps remained untouched.

I'd tried a few times to resume the conversation from the hazel hedge, but Tarc always, gently, firmly closed down all talk of judges and their totems. So I was surprised when one morning, on a page, I saw the symbol for the Daragishka Knot, the rearranged trefoil that Sibéal had drawn on Smith's roadmap of the plan.

I must have stared at it longer than I thought, because Tarc was behind me, looking at what had caught my attention.

'That's the Daragishka Knot,' he said.

'What does it mean?' As if I didn't know.

'Legend says that each of these loops,' he traced the outline of the knot, 'was once filled with a power stone. And of course, Basil Lucas was obsessed with anything to do with stone.'

'Lucas obsessed with stone?' I gestured to the room filled with containers of stones, geodes, rocks, gems. 'I had no idea.'

'His totem was rock.' Tarc smiled.

'Where are they?' I said. 'The stones that belong in the knot?'

'That's a slightly tricky question.'

'Why?'

'There's a story about a girl whose lover had been fatally wounded in a battle. Desperate, she took three stones and placed them inside the Knot. She named the stones, marking each with a promise.'

'She'd have been better off learning basic first aid.'

Tarc pointed to the empty space in the top loop. 'She named the first stone Betrayal.' Then he moved his finger down to the second space. 'The second Sacrifice.' And with his finger on the third: 'Surrender.'

'Seriously?' I turned to look at him. 'She played with stones while her lover died?' Judges were weird.

Tarc laughed. 'It's a story. Legends are deliberately deceptive. I've heard at least three variations. Lucas was fascinated by the Daragishka Knot because of how the stones were infused with an intent and acquired power.'

'Did she get help? That desperate girl?'

'Open up, Gallagher,' David shouted, pounding on the archive door.

'So the story goes.' Tarc was moving to the door. 'But the price was high.'

He opened the door and I heard David, low and fraught. Listening in, I heard him say something about a breach in the south garden wall.

'I've got to run,' Tarc said. He was tense.

Heading to the door, he paused and turned. 'Laney doesn't trust anyone,' he said. 'So she'll most likely be down soon.'

'And you do? Trust me?' Reckless, Wren.

'Of course not,' he said. But as he walked through the door he added, 'Except perhaps at night. Beneath the trees.'

Then he was gone. I was finally alone in the archive.

I lined up the ladder to the shelf and climbed until I could reach the box. Opening it, I saw a heap of maps. I searched through them. Most of the maps were old; Smith would go mad for them. There were maps of Hy-Breasil, and detailed descriptions of the island's terrain. But I didn't have time to study them. I flicked faster.

Then I found something. It wasn't labelled, no words of description. Just a printout of a map of the country across several A3 pages dotted with red Sharpie. It might be something else entirely, but it looked like the map Smith had described. Lucas's map of the locations of the Daragishka stones. I grabbed my phone and took photographs, then returned the box as I found it.

Laney strolled in several minutes later, and I realised that Tarc was wrong. She did trust me. And that made me feel a hundred times worse. It would have been easier if she hadn't. But it was disloyal to feel guilty about helping my grove.

'It's a gorgeous day out,' she said. 'You've been doing a brilliant job. Take the afternoon off. Sunshine pass.'

On the way back to the office, I sent the photos to Smith. My mission was complete. I'd found the map. But instead of the elation I'd expected, I felt a strange kind of numb.

Aisling skipped class and we went back to Kilshamble, where the grove was gathering in the old abandoned quarry in the almost warm sunshine. It was an impromptu celebration of my success, and spirits were high. Smith played Texas Hold 'Em on a card table, chipping in with the banter. We weren't a large grove, but we'd known each other forever and we were like family. Maeve and four other women sat on deck-chairs, sharing a bottle of Baileys and coleslaw cheese sand-wiches. Someone attached their phone to a small portable speaker and music blasted through the large space.

'Wren, come on, have a game,' called Maeve, holding up a Scrabble box.

'Not a chance. You girls are way too good.' It was true. They were vicious women and won by inserting words like 'qat' in unlikely places.

'You did it,' Smith said, his eyes shining with pride.

'It makes sense to you?'

'Of course,' he said, showing me the picture. 'See, connecting all these red dots forms several triangles all over the country. The exact locations will be at the core of three equilateral triangles. It will take a day or two to get these and match them to GPS coordinates.'

'When do I resign?'

'When we know what the three locations are. Say, three days, just to be sure.'

'Three days.'

I felt relief, huge relief. But also something else. Before I could identify it, Sibéal approached and slipped her arm through mine. Whatever it was, the awkwardness that had stewed between us was gone, and it was just like before.

We walked further into the quarry, towards the deep pools, talking a load of nonsense. We repeated 'echo' over and over, and laughed at our voices bouncing across the high stone walls. We found Simon and the other boys and tried to persuade them it was manly to take a swim. In the freezing water. In their jocks.

Simon stood at the edge of the pool, lost in thought.

'So you and Ash can stop all the secret service stuff now that we have the map, right?' I said.

'I wish it were that simple,' he said.

'It *is* that simple.' I smiled at him.

We stood at one of the dark pools, aiming stones at the mouth of a large, rusted fuel container in the middle of the water. We listened for the loud clanks of the stones hitting the metal, ten points if we got one inside. Simon usually scored the highest, but not this time. When I teased him about losing his touch, he grimaced, holding his shoulder.

'You hurt it?' I said. 'Rough game again?'

I reached for his shoulder, squeezing it gently. Simon was mad into sports and it wouldn't be the first time he'd hurt himself playing.

'It's fine.' He was looking at me strangely, and it made me feel uncomfortable. He could tell, of course, and sighed. I pulled my hand back and turned away.

'Wren, we need to talk.'

I really didn't want to. Simon had always been fun, it was never anything more. Talking sounded like not fun.

'Sure.' My reluctance was more than obvious. He wouldn't need his talent to see it. 'But not now, not here.'

I left him to join a game of hide-and-seek with Aisling and the smaller children, hiding behind inexplicable leftover walls, a dumped fridge and broken equipment whose purpose we couldn't begin to fathom. Aisling won. She'd always been good at hiding.

I loved the quarry. It was a guilty love, because my grove mourned the green mound, the powerful nemeton it had once been. But I saw beauty in its sharp face and hidden pools, its brown desolation.

Just before we left, I stood beneath the irregular rock face of the high quarry wall, black and grey with streaks of brown and topaz running through it. And I let a vision come, strong and hard.

Something close, something private.

Something that I both dreamed about and feared.

Around me, everyone laughed, unaware that I'd taken another step in the wrong direction.

EIGHTEEN
Call them by name

I find myself rather liking the taste of dirt.
AdC

In my last days at the Harkness Foundation I wanted to set something right.

Cassa was at her desk, looking at photographs from the Arabella de Courcy retrospective. In her hand was a picture of Aisling and her schoolfriends.

She dropped it on the desk and, upside down, I studied it. Aisling was a little off from her friends, talking to David, Ryan, Brian and Cillian. They were looking at her, their faces stupid and utterly riveted. It was nothing new, Aisling did that to boys. I just never thought I'd see it with *those* boys.

Cassa looked peeved, and I guess she'd just confirmed that her security team had been flirting while the enemy tried to run off with her.

'I found something,' I said. 'In the garden book.'

I held out the folded Ogham sheet that I'd stolen from the archive.

'What is it, Wren?' she said, and her kind tone made me feel ashamed. But I couldn't confess that I'd broken into the archive and found it in the puzzle box.

Cassa took the sheet from me, keeping curious eyes on my face. Only once the creased page was unfolded did she look down at it. One quick glance and a sharp intake of breath.

The Definitive Traits of the ✸:
Almost an orphan.
Grows where the last ✸ trod.
Steals the love [lost to the fold of the page] *from the garden.*
Marked by the garden.
Wakens the doll.
Sees what isn't [lost to the fold of the page].
From the line of the judges.
Brings the golden time.

'Where did you find this?' Cassa sounded almost breathless. Her mouth was round with surprise. 'I've been looking everywhere.'

Her careful guard had fallen, reminding me of the day I'd seen her rummaging through the archive.

'Lady Catherine's garden journal. Volume two, I think. Laney said that you hadn't had a chance to read it?' The lie burned my cheeks.

She stared at the sheet. Her pale face was now so white that I thought she'd faint. From the way she looked at it I could tell she didn't need help interpreting the marks.

'Cassa, you're due at Trinity in thirty minutes,' Laney came into the room, followed by David. 'There's awful traffic …'

'Wren found it,' Cassa said. 'The list was in the archive.'

'Wren found it?' Laney frowned. 'And removed it from the archive?'

'It was in one of Lady Catherine's garden books.'

'Really?' Laney's frown deepened. 'I looked through those.'

David leaned forward, his interest piqued.

'You must have missed it.'

I was hot beneath Laney's gaze.

'Seems like it,' Laney said doubtfully, but her face said, *I never miss things*.

'I was right,' Cassa said, holding up the page. 'The list is real.' She looked at me. 'And *Wren* found it.'

The third time those words were uttered, and this time I heard the strange emphasis.

All three of them examined me like I'd grown an extra head.

Laney was still looking pensive; she just wasn't convinced.

'Those journals aren't going to index themselves, Wren,' she spoke sharply. She seemed troubled. But from the way she watched Cassa, I suspected she was more worried about her than me.

Leaving the room, I heard Cassa saying, '… find the girl, I'll be the one who brings on the third.'

I leaned against the wall outside her office. I'd been careless. I'd made Laney question me.

'I can confirm the identity of three of the Huntsman assailants.' I heard David through the open sliver between the double doors.

It was lunchtime, and the office was empty but for Ledger Man, who sat at the kitchen table with his sandwich. Immersed in his book, he was oblivious to me eavesdropping at Cassa's door.

'And?'

'They're from Abbyvale.'

'You tell me this like it's news, David.' Cassa sounded irritated.

Laney murmured, 'Your coat.' Silence, and a small snapping sound.

'Why are you still here?' Cassa said a few seconds later.

'I'm requesting permission to retaliate.'

'Remember your place, David.' The bite in her words should have warned him to back off.

'These men tried to kidnap you.' He spoke too fast when he was upset. 'They stole a nemeton. They hurt my brother, *your* nephew.'

'You had your chance to fix this at Abbyvale months ago. You should have taken care of them then. Now you do it my way.'

'Cassa, we have to act before —'

'Enough,' Cassa almost shouted. She paused, then said with acid calm, 'There will be penalties for insubordination.'

I heard her move around the desk, most likely to stand in front of him.

'David Creagh, you have attempted to act beyond your rank and status. You have spoken inappropriately. You failed in your duty at the Huntsman, allowing yourself to be distracted. Your failure to secure the situation in Abbyvale with adequate action against rogue augurs has endangered your Cleave and Magistrate. How do you plead?'

'Guilty.' David's voice was barely audible.

'You'll be fined. I give you the choice to pay in blood or coin.'

'Blood.' The word was a whisper.

'A blood fine it is.' Her coat rustled. 'Look at me, David. There is honour in a blood punishment. You chose right.'

If he responded, I didn't hear it.

'Reparation is set for seven thirty tonight. You're dismissed.'

I hightailed away from the doors, nearly running to the bathroom. Once inside, I put my back to the wall, trying to stop the trembling.

Had Cassa meant that David should have killed the Abbyvale augurs? Isn't that what 'taken care of them' meant? And a blood fine? Working at the Foundation, with all its emphasis on art and beauty, had made me forget how brutal the judges could be. We loved to whisper stories about the judges and their punishments. But I hadn't fully believed them. I'd thought the stories were exaggerated. It sickened me to hear Cassa demand punishment in blood.

And even though it was David's blood on the line, I couldn't shake the fear of retribution if they discovered how I'd deceived them.

Going home that evening I was filled with anxiety. Because of the conversation I'd overheard. Because of my recklessness with the Ogham sheet. I should have known Laney would have checked the journals before handing them to me.

At home, Smith and Maeve were in the kitchen, reading the newspaper.

'You're late,' Maeve said, her attention on the paper. 'Dinner's in the oven.'

I thought about the rearranged trefoil, the coiled knot of stones, and it felt like there was a similar tangle inside my head. Inside my heart.

'The stones are named.'

I just stood there, still in my coat. It wasn't what I'd meant to say. But I couldn't tell them about the Ogham sheet, it was too late for that. And I was afraid to tell them about the conversation I'd overheard about offing augurs and blood punishments. What if they took it as a threat and acted first?

It was bloody hard work trying to prevent a war.

'What was that, honey?' Maeve didn't look up from the paper.

'Tarc told me the stones are named. Sacrifice, Betrayal and Surrender. What does that mean?'

'Hy-Breasil is not easily found. And when it is, there's always a cost.' Smith took my coat and hung it on a hook. 'When Ruairí Ó Cróinín landed on its shores after being shipwrecked, he lost everything. One stone marks this sacrifice, given through the seven years he lived there.'

Smith tipped the teapot, hot brown liquid filling the mug. 'Another stone for the betrayal he suffered, by his wife and family. The third, the strength stone, is his surrender to the island and its treasures.'

He slid the mug to the edge of the table.

'You're cold,' he said. 'Come over to the stove.'

'Tarc told me some story about a girl who needed help.'

'It's natural that we have different myths attached to draoi practice. How you understand the Daragishka Knot depends on who you are. If you're a judge, it's something potentially dark and dangerous. If you're one of us, it's redemptive.'

'Because what could be more redemptive than sacrifice?' Maeve said. 'What can prove love more than giving someone up for a greater good?'

And still I stood there with my fists clenched at my sides. It was all too much.

Who bloody cares, I wanted to shout. I might have blown my cover by trying to do the right thing, if I knew what that was any more. What about the woman in the yellow raincoat? And what does a blood fine even mean? Was it a small, symbolic gesture or something more sinister? And why the hell was I so worried? I didn't like David. It shouldn't bother me. I didn't want it to bother me.

At that moment, the weight of the last weeks was unbearable.

Smith reached his hand out to me, his long, strong fingers on my arms. 'I know we've put you in a difficult position, I know you're struggling against the pull of the pattern you're forming by coming and going between the two houses. But you're strong enough to resist it. You've always managed to fight off wickerings. This is the same thing.'

I'd always managed to fight off benign wickerings. I wasn't sure this was the same thing.

'Tomorrow is my last day,' I said. 'So it doesn't matter any more.'

But that wasn't true. Harkness House would still draw me to it. It would be a long time before I wouldn't feel its pull.

'There's been a new development,' Smith said. He sounded reluctant. 'I've got locations for the stones. One is Cassa's place in Connemara. Another is somewhere in Kerry, and it's likely that's Sorcha's stone.'

He hesitated and I knew I wasn't going to like what came next.

'The third stone is at Harkness House,' he said.

I hadn't realised how much I needed to get out of that place. How much I wanted things to return to normal. To immerse myself in augur life. How I feared that continuing to move between the two houses would make it impossible to extract myself.

'I have to search the house?' I said, thinking how impossibly big it was.

'We can get a location by finding specific things around it,' Smith said. 'Maeve will consult the clouds, and we should be able get you close. Just a few more days. A week at most.'

'Why on earth could we not have just done that in the first place?'

'Because objects like a desk or chest of drawers or a hairbrush mean nothing if you don't know where they are.'

I hesitated. If Maeve still hadn't seen anything since last May, this wouldn't work. But I wasn't sure what she'd told Smith and I didn't want to betray her confidence.

'I can do it, Wren.' Maeve spoke gently from where she sat at the kitchen table. 'Go wash your hands. Let's get a hot meal into you.'

I hadn't realised I'd been shivering. But I was glad to hear Maeve's dry patch was over.

Up in the attic, I stopped in the doorway. The brídeog was sitting on my desk. For a brief second I was overwhelmed by an awful, unsettled feeling, that cold pricking. There was an earworm in my head, a song that I didn't realise I knew: *Beneath the oak my love does lie. A sword through his heart, an arrow in his eye.*

And as I washed my hands I remembered. It was the tune that had drawn Cassa out of the garden at the Huntsman. It must have stuck in my mind, and my warped unconscious provided the lyrics.

While Smith heated my dinner I wolfed down two bananas. I'd developed a taste for the skins, must be some kind of deficiency. Zinc, probably. Or magnesium.

'Ah, Wren,' Maeve said, 'you'll ruin your appetite.'

I picked up the folded newspaper. I'd caught a glimpse of something earlier and I wanted a second look.

I flicked through, ignoring the plate that Smith set beside me. And there it was, a small article with a picture. A three-hundred-year-old beech tree in Wicklow had been partially chopped. Looking at the picture of the damaged tree, I knew it was a nemeton.

'I told you you'd wreck your appetite,' Maeve scolded, looking at my untouched food. And then she saw the news article.

'Who did this?' I said.

'I didn't want you seeing that,' Maeve said.

'Is someone damaging nemeta?' I said, remembering the smiley face on the standing stone in the meadow.

'This doesn't look good.' She sat beside me.

'Is it our nemeton or theirs?' I dreaded asking the question. There was no grove of augurs who could afford to lose a nemeton.

'I don't know,' Maeve said.

But I saw the look that passed between her and Smith, the look that made me certain she was lying. It had to be an augur tree.

Which meant that the likely culprits were judges. Not Tarc; my gut told me he couldn't do that to a tree. Not hacking it with an axe.

It must have been David. David who was so keen for retaliation. David who wanted blood.

Blood.

I noticed the time. Seven thirty-five. The broken tree a desecrated temple.

Maybe he deserved to be punished.

Smith was quiet, standing in the square arch. He turned to the living room and went to his war table. His silence and the set of his shoulders spoke volumes.

'I'm going for a run,' I said.

I needed to work away the knot inside. The thought of even a few more days at Harkness House made me sick. I hated what had happened to the tree. I hated that for a few seconds I'd entertained the idea that a blood punishment was deserved.

I went to Smith and put my arms around him, when really I wanted him to put his around me.

But Smith was distracted. Briefly squeezing my hand, he went back to positioning his soldiers in their endless war.

NINETEEN
Trees are just not sexy

Another injury to my arm today. Lady Catherine says
I need to be watched carefully while outdoors.

AdC

'Wren.' Aisling's voice drew my attention from my soup. From the restaurant wall behind her, two ugly stone faces stared down at me.

'What?' I said, squirming beneath her fierce gaze. She looked at me so intently I wanted to cover my face with the paper napkin.

'Don't play with your soup.'

'You know it's rude to read your friends without permission.' I took another slurp but it was disgusting.

'You're right,' Aisling said. 'So rude.'

But she didn't avert her gaze. She seemed most fascinated with my head, as if it were circled by a halo of stars.

'What's the verdict?' I said, crunching something gross. 'Healthy, sickly or bonkers?'

She hesitated. 'Go easy with the spinny eyes.'

I shouldn't tell her that Maeve had asked me to look, then.

'Don't think I haven't noticed,' she added.

'What?' That now too familiar low-grade anxiety rose.

'You didn't greet them,' Aisling said, tilting her head to the gargoyles behind her.

'Do I have to?'

Looking at her face, the answer was clear.

'All right,' I sighed, facing the gargoyles on the wall. 'Hello venerable stone faces, you look dour and pissed off as always.'

'Wren!' Aisling admonished me. 'She doesn't mean it.' She placated her stone-faced friends.

Aisling always insisted on greeting the gargoyles that snarled above us. She said it guaranteed they'd keep our secrets. That whatever we spoke about beneath them wouldn't be whispered to the other gargoyles in the county and beyond.

'Now, what's the story with what's-his-name?'

'Who?' I played dumb.

'Cassa's right-hand man. Dreamboat.'

I pulled a face at her ridiculous terminology. Aisling's knowledge of boys was mostly informed by a five-year addiction to old romance novels.

'Tarc?' I said.

'Well, I wouldn't kick him out of bed for eating crackers.'

'Aisling, he's the enemy,' I protested. 'He has horns hidden in his hair and his feet are cloven hooves.'

'Sounds like you're trying to convince yourself.' Her eyes were sparkling. She was enjoying playing with me. 'Anyway, villainy adds a certain frisson, don't you think?'

'No one under forty says "frisson".'

I looked down at my soup, trying to determine what flavour it was meant to be. But it was impossible to tell from the reddish-brown murk; I'd more easily tell the future than what it was made of. I half-heartedly dipped my spoon, avoiding the bits and pieces floating in it. An eyeball here, a toenail there.

'You'd tell me if there was something, Wren?' She was observing me carefully. 'The way you talk about him, I wonder sometimes.'

'I don't talk about him.'

'Exactly.' She was triumphant. 'If he didn't affect you, you would. So, talk.'

I hesitated. Even as she sat there I could still see the other Aisling, the glossy girl at Cassa's party. The girl with bright eyes at the hotel exhibition, surrounded by judge boys. But I remembered us sitting on the bed, our hands entwined. I needed Aisling.

'You know those stories that Sibéal goes on about?' I said.

'The numpty prince and the evil, devious, beautiful plant lady who devours him? That kind of thing?'

'Do you ever wonder if they're true?'

She raised an eyebrow. 'I never, never thought I'd hear that from you.'

'Not in the way that Sibéal tells them,' I said quickly. 'Not with all the drama and gore. But something almost like it.' Something like Tarc's intent gaze before the tree split in two.

'Are you saying you think Tarc is a tree?' She shook her head. 'Why?'

'No, I don't think he's a tree.' I took a deep breath, wondering where to begin with that night at the hotel.

'You think he's a sexy tree man?' Aisling leaned forward. 'Like Groot?' She preferred Hulk. She liked them green, large and not particularly verbal.

'I wouldn't put it like that.'

'I hate to tell you, but trees are just not sexy. They're rough and scratchy and you could get your hair all tangled in their branches.'

'Hmmm,' I said thinking that, actually, trees *were* kind of sexy.

'Oh my God, Wren Silke, you have a crush. On a man you think is a tree. Only you would get a crush on a tree

229

man.' Then she amended: 'And Sibéal. God, what are ye like?'

'No,' I objected too fiercely. 'He'd hate me if he knew what I really was.'

'Keep your guard up.' Her warning was gentle. 'Remember who he works for. Who he is. And who his friends are.'

'How could I forget?'

'You and Tarc, you're the fundamental collision between art and nature. It could never work.'

Speaking of art: 'Ash,' I said and pushed my soup to the side. 'That night at the hotel. Did you wicker the security boys?'

'Why do you ask?'

'The way you were when I came in, all bright and electric. And I saw a photo in Cassa's office. They were utterly transfixed.'

Aisling paused, like she needed to form her answer carefully. But just as she was about to speak she looked at the door and said, 'There he is.'

I turned round and saw Simon walking through the doorway. The restaurant was empty, just us, and suddenly I wished for noise and bustle.

He came to our table, standing there uncertain. For once, it was easier for me to read his body language, he was so obviously uncomfortable.

'You've been avoiding me,' he said.

Wary, I glanced at Aisling, who'd clearly set this up. She was studying the dessert menu, even though she always had the sticky toffee pudding.

'It's been busy.' Lame. But he was right, I had been avoiding him. I raised an eyebrow. 'Is this an intervention?'

Simon slipped into the booth beside Aisling, holding his hands together as if in prayer.

'Wren, there's something you need to know.'

Nothing good ever started with 'there's something you need to know.'

I didn't miss the look between them. But I didn't need to be sat down and mollycoddled; it had never been like that between Simon and me.

'You're right,' Aisling said. 'I wickered the security boys at the hotel exhibition.'

'I was there that night, Wren.' Simon looked unhappy. 'Outside the hotel.'

'You were?' I was confused.

'With the augurs from Abbyvale. I thought we could make a deal with the judges if we took Cassa.'

'You?' My mouth fell open. 'That was you?'

Horrified, I stared at him. I couldn't imagine him doing something that awful.

'You could have gone to jail.' I shut my eyes. 'And what you did to Cassa … She was traumatised.'

And David. I had no love for that boy, but I was still troubled about his blood punishment. I'd seen him the next day, his face tight and unhappy. He did his training as usual, but he was pale and stiff and, as much as he'd tried to hide it, his pain was obvious.

'I'm sorry it had to come to that,' Simon said. 'But we're worried.' His hands were near mine, the tips of our fingers inches apart. 'Something doesn't sit right.'

Across from me, his eyes looked so gentle, the shape of him so painfully familiar.

'Ash and I, we want to find another way.' He struggled for words. 'It's wrong that you're the only one sticking your neck out.'

'Just trust the plan,' I said through gritted teeth.

'That's the problem. I don't. Sometimes Maeve gets stuck in rigid, outdated ways of thinking and overlooks more innovative answers.'

'Innovative? You kidnapped Cassa because you think this isn't innovative enough?' I hissed.

'No,' Simon burst out. 'I think they're making mistakes. I think they're missing something, because I can't see how ...' He stopped, rubbing a hand over his jaw.

'So you thought you'd ransom Cassa? What for? What could be worth resorting to kidnapping?' I was too loud.

Aisling glanced at the waitresses, but they were too busy gossiping to mind us.

'Nemeta. We wanted them to give us nemeta. Listen, Wren, they're going about this all wrong. What if the Daragishka Knot doesn't work? What if it's just a myth? We need to take more decisive action.'

'And you thought they wouldn't retaliate?' I was shaking. 'You thought ransoming Cassa wouldn't start an all-out war?' I couldn't believe what Simon and Aisling had done. 'So that's why you wickered the security boys? So that they couldn't respond to Tarc's call for backup?'

Aisling nodded.

'And that's how you hurt your shoulder?' I asked Simon. I wasn't sure what he knew about the tree. He hadn't seen Tarc's intense stare. 'When the tree fell?'

'We got unlucky,' he said.

'Was it you? Did you beat Tarc while his arms were held?' He nodded, ashamed.

'We need to find another way. Together,' Aisling said and put out her hands, palms up, pleading. 'No more secrets.'

'It's nearly over. Trust the plan.'

'Listen, Wren. I have an idea,' Simon said. 'We have to target Cassa where she's weakest …'

'Will you listen to yourselves?' I exploded, and the waitresses turned to stare. 'Just stop. Maeve will get me an exact location of the stone by the end of the week. Please just stop whatever it is that you're doing before someone gets hurt.'

'Don't think that people won't get hurt if we do it Maeve's way.'

I threw my napkin on my plate. 'Please, don't try to tell the future. Leave that to those of us who can.'

I stood and left them there, their faces as grim as the gargoyles above. I remembered the day of the Ask, when Aisling had hoped it would be her. Had I misread her? Was it that she really wanted the internship, the adventure that it brought? Was Simon's ambition to become ard-draoi greater than I'd realised? I couldn't understand why she and Simon were potentially jeopardising the plan and blowing my cover. I couldn't reconcile the two friends I'd known all my life with the two people who'd colluded to kidnap a woman. It made no sense at all.

TWENTY

It's you

I hear rustling through my dreams. The faintest notes
of a song.
AdC

I sat on Cassa's garden bench, eating an apple. Overhead, a murmuration of starlings rose from the roof, flying towards a cluster of trees. Their small bodies speckled against the grey sky, swirling from one intricate pattern into another. I tried to break it up the way we always had, dividing the sky into different spheres and reading the movement of the birds, but it was no good.

The past ten days had been awful. Aisling and I weren't talking. Maeve, despite assuring me that she was close, still couldn't tell me where to find the stone.

The chattering of starlings filled the air. A few latecomers moved to the high branches, their wings flapping frantically. Hearing a crunch on the gravel path, I turned swiftly, hoping it wasn't David or Cillian on their regular patrols.

'It's you,' I said as Tarc stepped from the tall shrubs. I wondered how long he'd been watching me watching the birds. I felt a skip of anxiety: what if he knew I was trying to read them?

We sat quietly, listening to the starlings. When they lifted off again, their wings like heartbeats, they moved as one. My face turned to the sky, all I could see were the things I couldn't see. The patterns I couldn't decipher, the messages I couldn't read. I closed my eyes.

'Maybe you should take a few days off.'

I opened my eyes and looked at him. 'Why?' There was a bitter taste in my mouth, and it had nothing to do with the apple pips I'd chewed. Just beyond him, a clump of bushes caught my attention.

'You seem tired. When you started here you were bursting with energy. And now, well, I just think you could do with a rest.' He had something in his hand, a small round object that he was twisting and turning between his fingers.

It bothered me that he thought I didn't look well. It caused my little vain heart some distress. Sleep was elusive. If I hadn't lived in the cottage most of my life, I would have thought it haunted. I'd wake from fleeting, manic dreams with the stuttering stop-start of rustles and scratches.

'Sometimes Cassa,' he started, then stopped, worrying

the object in his hand. 'Sometimes she doesn't realise when she's asking for too much.' He looked up at the birds as he spoke, and it seemed he meant more than journals and tea. 'Even when she makes it hard to say no, there are times when it's necessary. Maybe …'

But whatever he was about to say was lost in the ringing of his phone.

My eye returned to the bush behind him. It reminded me of the whitethorn tree on the day of the Ask, where I imagined the figure of a woman. Only this time it felt like the tree was watching me.

'She's here with me,' he said. 'All right.'

There was the slightest movement from the bush, like it was stretching out a leafy arm.

'Cassa wants you to come to a party on Saturday night.'

'What is that?' I said, distracted. 'The thing you have in your hand?'

He opened his fingers and at the centre of his palm was an acorn.

'Lucky acorn,' he said, closing his hand again.

I hesitated. 'Will you be there?'

Suddenly it felt too much, the nearness of him. It wasn't in the plan. I thought of those charts, notes and diagrams on which Maeve and Smith had worked through possible permutations. Nowhere had there been a box diagram offering an alternative, should I find that Tarc's proximity affected me so deeply. Nothing had prepared me for this hyper alertness to him. I was aware of every part of his body: his long, muscular legs, those arms, that chest. I felt myself drawing closer.

'I'll be there.' He didn't sound enthusiastic.

For all the wrong reasons, I said, 'I'll come.'

He nodded. But he didn't seem happy about it.

'Then you're taking tomorrow off. I'll tell Laney.' And he stayed on the bench, his arm against mine as he shifted to return his phone to his pocket.

'What's bothering you, Wren?' he said, his voice so gentle.

But I was taken by the figure in the bushes. I could only make out the slight shape of a head, like there was someone enclosed within.

Tarc seemed closer than before, the weight of his arm against mine, and part of me liked it, while part of me wanted to leap up from the bench. He turned towards me, his face nearer to me than I'd expected.

I jumped up.

'I need a minute. Alone.' I sounded like I'd been running.

'Sure,' he said easily, and I held my breath as he crossed the courtyard towards the house.

'Wren,' he said, turning.

'Yes?'

'You look like you need this more than I do.' He tossed the acorn to me and I caught it.

He hesitated, then repeated, 'Lucky.' He paused. 'Look after it. And remember, you can say no to Cassa.'

I watched him go inside the glass door and then I went to the bush. As I drew nearer, I began to see familiar features. Hair, hands. Red Converse.

'Are you insane?' I said, peering between the leaves.

Sibéal was there, curled into a small hollow. I wasn't sure if I was relieved or more afraid that it was her and not something … other.

'You have to get out of here.' It wasn't easy, shouting in a whisper. 'They check the garden. A lot. How did you even get in?'

Sibéal gave a little smile. 'What's bothering you, Wren?' She spoke in a mocking, high-pitched voice. Then she put a finger to her lips and, like a cat, slipped beneath the branches and out of sight.

I turned from the bush to the bench, wondering how bad my conversation with Tarc had looked to Sibéal.

The next morning, I was snug in my childhood bed tucked under the eaves. My desk looked wrong but, half asleep, I couldn't say why.

Then I realised: the brídeog. Her red floral skirt and

outstretched leaf arms were the last things I remembered before turning out the light. Seeing the gap on the desk, I felt a weird lightness. I had a fleeting sense of strange dreams that pulled me in and out of sleep. A light brushing noise on the stairs. A slow whispering song: *Beneath the oak my love does lie.*

Scrambling out of bed, I stood in the centre of my bedroom, as if it were possible to launch a stealth attack on a doll of leaf and cloth. I quartered the room with my eye, carefully examining every part.

And there she was. Down the side of the desk. She must have tumbled over. I picked up the doll and tried to shove her in an overstuffed drawer.

And then I looked again. The doll had landed too far from the desk to have simply fallen because of a banging door. To land in that spot, she would have had to jump. Staring at the floor, I tried to remember exactly where she had been before I picked her up. I was sure it was near the cracked floorboard. Except I wasn't.

I just didn't know. I examined the doll as if she were going to disappear in my hands.

Sighing, I tossed her on to the desk.

In the bathroom, I got a scare when I saw my face. My eyes were bloodshot and slightly yellow where they were meant to be white and clear. The yellow blended unflatteringly with the green, like some kind of diseased feline. A bruise had formed along my jaw. I'd had a spinny-eyed moment with mildew the previous night. Before falling asleep, I lost myself in the stained ceiling. And saw, then felt, a fist looking for my face. It was the second time that a vision had physically marked me.

Downstairs was quiet. I knocked at Smith's door and peered in to find his bed in the same state of disarray as yesterday. Sometimes he stayed at Maeve's. Not a thing I wanted to dwell on.

Pulling a ratty cardigan over my pyjamas, I slipped my bare feet into old wellies beside the kitchen door. Outside, the frost in the long grass seeped through the cracks in the soles.

Smith had complained that the black hen rarely laid. And that she ate the eggs before he could collect them. She'd pecked the other birds and had closed her horrible little beak around Smith's finger. She was not a very impressive magic bird.

I couldn't see her with the other hens pecking around the grass. I went into the henhouse, stepping between the dried droppings. No hen. No eggs.

The brídeog had unsettled me, and I half expected the hen to have vanished. That morning, everything felt that bit more unstable, less rooted to the world.

Rounding the cottage, I spotted fresh chicken poop on the front drive. Squawking sounded from the opposite hedge and I went out into the road, thinking up bad chicken jokes.

It didn't bother me when I heard the car approach. The village already found me a little odd, so out and about looking like the dog's breakfast wouldn't cause any loss of esteem.

But the car slowed down and the driver called out, 'Hey, Wren.'

There were few people who could be that ra-ra up-and-at-'em so early in the morning. He was also one of the last people I wanted to see outside the cottage.

'Hey,' I said. 'Nice morning isn't it?' Which translated loosely as 'What the hell are you doing here?'

'It's grand,' Tarc said in the way that only Irish people mean grand. Not majestic and opulent but fine yeah good OK all right let's get on with things.

'So, why are you here outside the family homestead?' I gestured to the cottage. Which was not grand, in the usual sense of the word.

'I'm heading to the village. Hop in, I'll buy you tea. You know you can't resist tea.'

My confusion was evident. I looked down at my broken spotty wellies and pyjama bottoms dotted with grey hearts that Maeve had given me a few Christmases back. My hair straggly over my bruised jaw.

'I'm not dressed.'

He gave me a onceover. 'Looks good to me.'

'Five minutes.' I glared at him. 'You're not coming inside. You're staying right here. And I'll have a large tea. With a pastry.'

As an afterthought, I turned back. 'If you see a hen, catch it.'

Pulling on my jeans, I entertained myself with the thought of Tarc being pecked by that devil bird.

Smith had come home and lit a fire while I'd been out tracking the hen. The woodstove needed cleaning, judging by the smell of smoke in the house.

I found him in the kitchen.

'Tarc's outside,' I said as I popped my head in. 'He's on his way into the village. I'm going with him.'

Smith was making something that involved extensive use of all the surfaces. Probably toast. He raised an eyebrow.

'Since when did you become his assistant?'

'He probably just needs a local to interpret the natives. Won't be long.' I kissed his cheek. 'Be good.'

Back at the car, Tarc was standing next to it.

'Where's my hen?'

'You mean the one I saw walking towards the house? She seems like a very nice pet. Docile.'

'She went back in? Where was she?'

Tarc pointed to a hole in the hedge. I went over, squatted down and saw a large blue egg. Very large. That must have hurt. That explained the infernal shrieking. No wonder she went into the hedge for some privacy. I covered it with grass.

'So you happened to be driving past my house?' A quiet lane that led to an abandoned quarry.

'I have absolutely no excuse.' His lips curled into an almost smile. 'I was passing through the village. I wanted company. Just ended up coming this way. Guess I hoped you'd be out looking for hens.'

His words sat uncomfortably.

'You mean you wanted protection.' I crossed my arms. 'You don't trust the natives. And I make a good human shield.'

He laughed. 'Your knowledge of the locals is a draw card.'

'Why are you here?'

'Been working. Now I'm suffering a severe caffeine deficit. I figured you could tag along.'

He got into the car and started the engine.

'Tag along?' I climbed in beside him, wondering what part of running an arts and heritage charity involved the security trawling small villages early in the morning. 'I think you meant to say you wanted me for my expertise.'

'You're right, Wren. I'm interested in your skills.'

His words were casual. Light. Still, I wondered if he meant my talent. He couldn't know I was an augur, there was nothing that told. Even if he had caught me staring at birds. Sure, normal people watched birds all the time.

'Hey, what happened here?' he said, running a finger down my jaw.

'Hit it off the bedside table. Bad dreams.'

'Dreams?'

'Just dreams.'

In the village, I showed Tarc the main tourist attraction in Kilshamble: the village green where the bleating of animals could still be heard when the wind blew right. He admired it dutifully.

'There's a paint colour called Kilshamble Green that's the exact shade of slaughterhouse grass,' I said as we passed the newsagent's. 'Very stylish.'

But Tarc had stopped, his attention taken by something just inside the newsagent's door. The morning papers. The headline screamed: 'Fire at Newton Grange.'

'What's Newton Grange?' I said.

He skimmed the article, turning to page five, where it continued. The fire had been contained to the barn and apple orchard. One dead, and two in hospital for smoke inhalation and second-degree burns.

Mrs Forde gave a loud cough from behind the counter, but Tarc didn't seem to hear.

'I think she wants you to buy it,' I whispered loudly.

He returned the paper to the stack, and we walked out of the shop. A dark mood had settled on him.

'Gallagher,' said a voice from beneath the awning.

'What the hell happened last night, Canty?' Tarc's fury was unexpected. 'You sent me on a wild goose chase.'

'Got the wrong information.' He shrugged. 'It happens.'

Then he stepped in front of us, hand outstretched with something yellow in his palm.

'For you.' He looked at me.

So fast that I barely saw him move, Tarc had the man up against the wall. He held him by his moleskin jacket collar.

'I don't believe you.'

Moleskin, who'd been at the Huntsman with David, struggled against Tarc, but was pinned firmly against the wall. Tarc spoke in a low angry voice. And then Moleskin said something that caused a rush of anger in Tarc, who shoved him harder against the wall.

'Out of my hands, man. It was out of my hands.'

'Oh no, boys, none of that here.' Mrs Forde came out of the newsagent's and glared at them. 'Go on. Take it somewhere else.'

For good measure, she glared at me too.

With a final, disgusted shove, Tarc let Moleskin go. He walked ahead, visibly trying to rein in his anger. Moleskin lit a cigarette, keeping his eyes on mine while I muttered an apology to Mrs Forde.

Moleskin strolled off in the opposite direction.

I started after Tarc, but was held up by Mrs Forde, who asked after Roibeárd, which always confused me until I remembered she meant Smith; he went by his middle name in Kilshamble. He was an awful flirt and popular with ladies of a certain age.

I caught up with Tarc, who was standing rigid ahead.

'This what happens when you don't get enough caffeine?'

'What?' He was stiff and distracted. Then he seemed to notice me, to remember where we were.

'We're in frontier land,' I touched his elbow. 'The sheriff will hound you out for unnecessary violence.'

Though really, in Kilshamble, our one-man uniformed presence was David's uncle, who would likely pat him on the back and invite him in for a whiskey.

But Tarc was visibly upset. More than anger, something else was running through him, agitating him. His struggle for control was clear in the hard line of his body, his clenched jaw.

I pulled him down the small lane between the tea room and the credit union. He stared furiously at the scratchy grey wall. Then he hit out, pounding it several times, cursing with each fist as it landed.

'Hey,' I said. 'Want to talk?'

He said nothing.

'Is it the fire at Newton Grange?' I pushed.

But he stood there, the ugly grey wall behind him as he breathed deeply, trying to settle his agitation.

I took his hand, folding it in mine. His skin was grazed and I wiped the blood with a tissue from my pocket. He watched me.

'Wren,' he breathed.

Just behind his head, I saw that someone had sprayed *Wickd bad!* on the wall in black paint. Then I realised I was tracing patterns on his hand with my thumb. Ogham letters. R–E–N. But he was too preoccupied, too miserable to notice. I'd never seen him like this, lost and sad and angry.

So I put my arms around him, trying to give him comfort. I pulled him towards me, my body making sense of this new thing: the wide shoulders, the smell of laundry detergent and night, the hard back beneath my hands. The unfamiliar feel of him, fleeting and forbidden.

I drew back from the awkward hug. But Tarc caught my hands, holding them to his chest. My fingernails with their scrappy black nail polish against his jacket. There was a brief hesitation.

Again, everything that bit more unstable, less rooted to the world.

And then he was all in. His mouth on mine, his hands now firm on my lower back while mine snaked around his neck. He held me close and his agitation morphed into something else.

It felt every bit as good as I thought it would. His kiss, his touch quieted something I didn't realise was unsettled. Fed a hunger I'd only half acknowledged. The way he held me, kissed me, it seemed he felt it too. I leaned into him, the rough surface of the wall scraping my hands.

It went on for too long before I realised where we were. What we were doing. I broke away. Where was my sense? Getting hot and heavy with Tarc in a Kilshamble side alley. Beneath *Wickd bad!* in black on grey.

It wasn't supposed to be like this, with the ugly wall, the slaughter grounds in my peripheral vision. Tarc gripped by some unknown darkness. The real fear of being caught.

It wasn't supposed to *be* at all.

My unease must have been evident. Because his soft smile faded and he bumped his head against the wall.

'I'm sorry.' He looked away, pre-empting my response. 'I shouldn't have.'

'Tarc,' I said. 'I can't.'

I wished I could explain. Two words was all it would take: judge, augur.

'My grandfather,' I said, trying to find the right words. 'He'd be after you with a shotgun if he saw us.'

'He's protective?'

'Not exactly.' I shuffled. 'He's particular. And I don't think he'd … He's a hard man to please.'

I didn't want to say it: I don't think he'd like you. I knew he wouldn't.

'It's like that, huh?' Tarc pushed away from the wall. 'Is that why you're so tough?'

'We're from different worlds, Tarquin.' I said, cutting through the half-truths, the evasions. 'You wear your privilege so easily, even while you're playing security guards.'

What is it like, I wanted to ask him. *What is it like being one of them?*

'I should go home,' I said.

I knew the path that had been laid out for him. He would study law, get his degree. Probably move back to the States, where he'd be stuffed into a suit and he'd forget about the girl who lived in the village beneath the clouds.

And I would stay in Kilshamble, where you could smell blood on the grass and hear the ghostly bleating of dead animals. I would wander the forest, finding secret pictures, until eventually I would lose myself entirely.

I turned away.

The lane was quiet. The world went on, oblivious to the deviation that we'd just taken. A blip in the pattern that would get smoothed out in the bigger picture, but there'd always be that small tell. An anomaly, that's what it was. Our kiss against the grey wall with its misspelled *Wickd bad!* was a beautiful incongruity in an otherwise regular design. Momentary, and never to be repeated.

'I'm not like that,' Tarc said.

But he was like that. I had allowed myself to forget where he came from. Who his people were and what they were capable of.

'Who did it?' I said, forcing myself to face it as we left the lane.

'Did what?'

'David's punishment.'

His eyes widened.

'I overheard Cassa. Was it you?'

Tarc exhaled. 'I can't talk about this.'

An old woman dressed in black walked by, fixing her beady eyes on mine. Across the way, big brawny Ryan stood on the pavement with his mam as she looked at her lottery ticket. There was something hangdog about the way Ryan stood there, holding the bag-for-life with its milk and bog rolls while his mam talked at him.

'Who did it?' I said.

'Cassa.' He'd gone all rigid again. 'Cassa does it herself. Unless ...'

But he wasn't saying any more.

'What did she do to him?'

'Wren, stop. I can't tell you.' His voice was bleak. 'You don't want to know.'

We walked back across the slaughter grounds, the easy mood from earlier gone.

'We're ruled by an old code. This is how it is. How it's always been.'

'How often does Cassa punish people? Has she hurt you?'

I wanted to see how far he'd take this.

'She only does what's necessary.' But he didn't sound convinced.

I couldn't see how punishing your nephew or his amateur security friends was ever necessary. I looked askance at Tarc. His job kinda sucked. Always having to fix things, sort stuff out. Spin the PR. Chase the bad guys. No, the good guys. If he was chasing augurs, then he was chasing the good guys.

I was getting a headache.

Tarc picked up his pace. He said nothing more. The conversation was done.

Just before we crossed to the car, he turned abruptly. 'You can't tell anyone.'

His anger had returned. I couldn't believe that I'd confused the line between good and bad, right and wrong. He was so obviously wrong. He exuded wrong, just standing there, his mouth a tight line, the tension in the way he held himself as he waited for my answer. Wrong.

'You have to promise.'

'I won't tell.' Wrong. Wrong.

He gave a curt nod and strode across to the car. I didn't want to be on the bad side of Tarc. I realised, not for the first time, how hard it would be later, when he knew what I'd done. When we were openly enemies.

Approaching Tarc's car, I noticed someone standing on the green. Someone wearing a blue dress with a yellow coat. I registered the presence like a fly at the corner of my eye. It was the persistent stillness that drew my attention.

I turned and there was Sorcha in a yellow raincoat. She stood on the old slaughter grounds, facing us. Lank hair, dull skin.

A petrifying jolt shot through me.

'What's wrong?' Tarc said.

I looked at him but didn't answer. Then I looked back at the green, but she'd moved away, towards the church. My hands were shaking. It couldn't be her.

'I thought I saw someone. But I was mistaken.'

'Who was it, Wren?' Tarc was leaning towards me. 'Why did they scare you so much?'

'It's nothing.' I forced a smile. 'I must go.'

'Don't go.' The words seemed to fall out of his mouth against his better judgement. I ignored him and turned away.

I stepped on to the green, towards the church garden. I looked ahead for the bright yellow coat but saw nothing.

I got as far as the gate to the garden of remembrance. And then I stopped. Standing on the cracked pavement, I made myself face it: she wasn't there. I'd imagined it.

At home, I went to retrieve the egg from the hedge. But when I got there, all I found were shells and the sticky remains of dried yolk. It had taken weeks to get the egg and, distracted by a boy, I'd fumbled it.

TWENTY-ONE
Keeper of the forest

As we prepare for Elizabeth's game in the woods, I find myself changed. My hair is lank and my eyes have taken on a glassy sheen. Sleep eludes me.

AdC

The next night was the party at Harkness House. Huge vases of white flowers – lilies, gladioli, lisianthus – were dramatically arranged. At the centre of the white room, on a pedestal, was her orchid.

It was so different to grove parties at Maeve's house, which usually ended up with music and dancing. I just didn't see this crowd breaking into a perfectly coordinated drunken set dance while Aisling cringed from the side.

I stayed at the edges of conversations, unable to find a way in. I held champagne that I didn't drink, the glass growing warm in my hand. Drifting through the crowd, I caught snippets from the guests, many of them girls my age: a new clothing range at Brown Thomas, a group of hot guys busking on Grafton Street. And punctuating their words was laughter as tinkly, as sharp as the chandeliers that hovered above.

Like the party at the Huntsman, I wasn't sure why Cassa wanted me there. I didn't fit in with the shiny judge girls, nor did I fit in with the crowd that arrived from the village. The Kilshamble girls grouped together, awkward, as if they feared that the heavy, beguiling scent of the flowers could lure them to poison, to madness.

As if it could make them sleep for a hundred years. Make them do things they both feared and longed for.

Aisling came in with a boy. I greeted her with a polite half-smile, like I wasn't her dark twin who'd slept beside her as a child. As if she were an ordinary village girl who meant nothing to me. I hated that we weren't talking, and that I didn't know who this boy was. His fingers trailed down the bare skin of her arm. Aisling was brittle and beautiful. I didn't linger.

The everyday chat in that bright room with its cloying scent was surreal. And at the centre of everything was Cassa. The circles of girls gravitated to her as though performing an obscure dance. They watched jealously to see who she spoke to next, her disinterested gaze sweeping over the girls and then releasing them.

And then she turned and saw me. Her eyes lit up and she

smiled from across the room. A warm, deep smile, her eyes holding mine, ignoring the swell of girls around her.

Hot and dizzy from the flowers, I made to leave the room. Just before I passed the double doors, I noticed something for the first time.

There was a pencil sketch on the wall. Arabella. I examined her delicate features, the haunted eyes and defiant chin. Her hair fell in waves, half up and half down, the intricate style come undone. Filigree hair combs ineffectively held her hair, and examining them, I saw that they were nearly identical to the lucky hairpins that Maeve had given to me. The picture was signed E. Gallagher.

Leaving the hall, I went outside to the iron table in the small courtyard. On a good day it was a suntrap and I often sat there, the honey cobblestone teasing my spinny eye. But it was different at night, and the dark, indeterminate shapes of the trees and bushes were almost sinister.

The bench was an invisible boundary. I'd never ventured beyond, never walked through Cassa's garden. Somewhere behind the trees was the cottage where Tarc lived. The garden was old and beautiful but it had always seemed forbidden. As if there were dangers within. As if two-headed snakes coiled around trees, waiting to tempt foolish girls.

But my longing must have told, because I heard Cassa say, 'Do you want to see my garden?'

'I've never explored that far.' I turned my head and saw her right behind me.

'It's so lovely at night,' she said.

She stepped back into the house and the garden lit up with hundreds of hidden lights.

'Come, I'll show you.'

'I'm cold,' I said, my feet rooting to the ground. I didn't want to go with her. I didn't know why I was suddenly afraid.

Almost motherly, Cassa draped her coat over me, her hands briefly squeezing my arms. She walked into the garden, looking over her shoulder.

'Come.'

I followed. With each step it felt like I was leaving the ordinary behind. With each step, I walked into something different. Something brushed with magic more intense than I'd ever known.

Slipping my hand into the coat pocket, my fingertips touched rough grit. I looked at it under the light. Soil.

Cassa was in front, the edge of her ivory dress trailing the ground. Ahead was a wall, hidden by the dark outline of trees, and she went towards it. Opening a door concealed by ivy, she revealed a small walled garden.

When I first felt the buzzing, I thought it was the hum

of the lights. It took a few seconds to realise it wasn't. That crackling feeling, like we were close to some resting power.

The garden was a nemeton.

A judge nemeton, and I'd been invited in.

I wandered between the flower beds. Though most were dormant, some plants were in bloom, despite the harsh winter.

There was something unnatural about the garden, magnificent as it was. It reminded me of the judges, of Harkness House, with its bold, aggressive beauty. But underneath was dirt. Underneath, slimy things writhed and wriggled. Things rotted. Creatures crawled and burrowed, feeding the beauty above.

At the heart of the garden, Cassa sat on a raised soil bed the size of a grave, her pale beaded dress on the mucky ground. She reminded me of my peony vision of her in the earth. It had scared me then, but now I couldn't imagine why. She looked serene and the flower bed with its turned earth seemed soft and luxurious.

'You don't like me,' she said.

'I don't think you care whether people like you or not.'

She smiled. It suddenly occurred to me, for whatever reason, that I pleased Cassa. And that made me both proud and repulsed.

'You asked me once before why Arabella went to live in the woods. I will tell you, if you're sure you want to know.'

Her words were a dare.

'What do you want from me in return?'

'Only that you listen. Really listen.'

'I want to know.' I felt a dizzying rush as I spoke. Like I'd climbed something high and stood at the edge. About to fall.

She moved on to her knees, then edged a little closer. The beads on her dress collected grains of soil. A coffee-coloured stain seeped up the hem. She touched her hand to my chest.

'Listen not with your head, but your heart.'

I thought I saw a streak of dirt on the side of her mouth, her lips stained with wine or earth. I couldn't be sure in the dim light.

'I'll try.'

'This will resist.' She touched my head. 'But the heart knows.'

Those endless seconds, Cassa's hand on my heart. It felt familiar, right. It felt like a mother's first touch.

'Arabella went to the woods because she became the Bláithín.' The little flower. 'She changed into the girl of leaf and petal.'

Using her finger, Cassa traced a pattern in the soil.

'Like the tuanacul?' I said, remembering that night when

Tarc's lips on my cheek seemed to summon the people of the woods.

'The Bláithín is something stronger, more powerful. It's not a fairy story.' She drew the five-looped knot I'd seen on the Ogham sheet. 'What Arabella experienced was the metamorphosis that happens under the wickerlight.'

'Wickerlight?'

'Threshold time, just as some places are threshold spaces. It's time when anything is possible. It can last minutes, hours, or even days.'

Wickerlight. Like wickering, the soft mesmerising draw made by familiar patterns. It made me think of the soft afternoon light that fell through the latticework shutters in the office. It felt like my time at Harkness House had been spent in wickerlight, an uncertain in-between time where anything could happen. Both terrifying and strangely gentle.

'The girl of leaf and petal doesn't have twig arms and bark skin,' Cassa continued. 'She is human, but inside, the power of the forest and fields runs through her veins. She is queen of the meadow, lady of the garden. She is keeper of the forest.'

I opened my mouth to speak, but she stopped me, touching her hand to my chest again. 'Listen from here, and you will know the truth of what I say.'

The gate to the garden opened, and we both turned. Tarc stood there, watching Cassa on her knees while I perched on the low flower bed. He paused only a second, but it was enough to know that he didn't like what he saw.

She beamed as he moved towards us.

'Cassa, could I have a word?' He glanced at me and waited.

Excusing herself, Cassa went to him. Angled away, Tarc's voice was low and I strained to hear. But my spy skills were improving, because I could make out: 'We need to discuss ... David's concerns ... a plan to steal nemeta ...'

'Not you too, Tarc,' Cassa said with fond exasperation. 'David's suspicions are unwarranted.'

'It won't hurt to investigate.' Tarc was firm.

'All right.' She held up her palms in mock surrender. 'It's a waste of time. But look into it.'

It struck me how unfair it was, when David had said the same thing she'd chewed him out. But not Tarc. Cassa was different with him. Away from the others, I glimpsed the woman who was also a mother. I'd heard Laney say that Tarc and Cassa's son were tight, that they'd grown up as close as brothers.

'You should go back in,' Tarc said to her, still not looking at me.

We still hadn't talked, not after the awkwardness in Kilshamble. After the kiss.

Momentary blip, I reminded myself.

I didn't know how long Cassa and I had been out there, away from the sparkling wine, the fairy lights and bright laughter of the guests. I'd lost all sense of time.

As we left the walled garden, I put my hand in Cassa's pocket again, feeling the gritty soil.

TWENTY-TWO
One of us

*After dark, when everyone is asleep, I slip outside to
Lady Catherine's garden. There my senses are
heightened and I feel an immeasurable peace.*

AdC

In her garden, Cassa's wool skirt was pushed up over her
knees. Her bare legs were covered in muck and her feet
buried in the earth. And she raised her face to me and I
saw that her mouth was stuffed with soil. She chewed and
swallowed. Her hand was already raised to her mouth and
she stuffed the next mouthful in, not taking her eyes off
mine. She swallowed again, then reached out a hand filled
with muck towards me.

'Want some?' she said and smiled. The horror of her dirt-
covered smile shot through my legs and curled my toes.

I woke up. A slight tingling in my mouth. The smell of
soil, rich and heady.

It was just after eleven. I was meant to attend my third

circle meeting in fifteen minutes. Grabbing my clothes, I was halfway in my jeans when I saw it. Or rather, didn't see it: the doll wasn't on the chair where I'd left it. Every day that small niggle – had it shifted a little to the side? But that morning, it wasn't on the chair, or the desk or the floor.

Maybe Sibéal had taken it. Maybe she wanted to make one like it.

Maeve was in her kitchen, preparing a tray of tea. It always kind of irked me that even though she was ard-draoi, she still got the tea.

At the table, Sibéal was taking photographs of her clay sculptures. Sadhbh, the girl who'd been turned into a deer. Fionnuala, daughter of Lir, with swan wings pushing out of her back after her stepmother had cursed her. All of Sibéal's sculptures were of girls coming undone.

'Wren,' she said. 'Give me a hand here when the meeting is finished.'

'Sure,' I said, relieved. Whatever she saw in the garden at Harkness House, she didn't hold it against me. Maybe it didn't look as bad as I thought. Just as well she didn't see what happened in the lane.

'Have you ever heard of dolls that are magic? Or cursed?' I said to Maeve as I grabbed an apple from the bowl and bit into it.

'Magic doll?' Maeve looked up.

'Magic doll?' Sibéal repeated. Then she smiled at me, serene.

And I felt a beat of fear. There was something wrong with her sugary smile. When Sibéal was cross or peeved, she'd stomp her feet and rage. Shout to the heavens for revenge. This sweetness was infinitely darker and more frightening.

'How is it magic?' Maeve said.

'I don't know. I think it moves. Not a lot, just small shifting around. Like it's trying, but struggles.' The words spilled out. 'She invades my dreams with her rustling and the scratching of her leaves.'

'Leaves?'

'Not doll, a brídeog. She came on Brigid's Day.' I realised it sounded like the doll decided to pay me a little visit. That she'd parcelled herself up and couriered herself to me. 'I'm being haunted by a doll of leaf and cloth.'

And as they were spoken, the words reminded me of something. I stood at the fridge, holding the milk in my hand, trying to remember why those words sounded familiar.

'A brídeog wouldn't do that. Brídeogs are good and protective. They bring the goddess into your home.' Maeve frowned. 'They're not about nightmares. And I've never heard of stories about them moving around. Whatever that is, it's not a brídeog.'

She paused. 'It could be … well, you are under some stress.'

'My mind playing tricks?' I swallowed the last of the apple. I'd looked it up and apparently the cores were good for you. Sort of. Apart from the cyanide in the pips.

Maeve gave a small smile as she lifted the tray. 'Bring the milk, will you, honey?'

In the good sitting room, the circle were waiting.

'Wren's time at Harkness House is drawing to a close,' Maeve began once we were all seated. I was on the same chair as last time, and felt like I was being interviewed.

'We should be able to form the Daragishka Knot very soon. Everything has gone remarkably well.'

Simon was looking at Maeve with something that resembled hostility. He was reading her, the way she sat there with her knees together, her hand flying up to tuck away an errant curl.

And I understood. Simon was ambitious. He wanted to take over as ard-draoi sooner rather than later, bringing in his *innovative* ways. All the subterfuge with Aisling had been about undermining Maeve, whose old-style leadership he obviously didn't respect. No one would expect Simon to get the tea.

'Has it?' Simon spoke lazily from where he sat. 'What exactly have we achieved?'

'We'll soon tie the Knot.' Maeve's eyes were flinty.

'Really?' he said. 'Do we have the stones?'

'The first stone has been secured. We've narrowed in on the second, it's within reach. And the third, well, that only Wren can do.'

'And after?' he continued in that same deceptively lazy drawl. 'What happens once the Knot is tied?'

'We'll be in a better position with our nemeta, Simon,' she said. 'We'll be stronger.'

'And Wren?' he didn't look at me.

'Wren will be fine.'

She turned from Simon to me. 'What's happening with the divining hen?'

'I don't have an egg.' I sounded meek.

'None at all?' Maeve's irritation was rising. 'I must get on to them about that hen. We should have had something by now.'

'It broke.' I'd been so careless, only thinking about getting into the car with Tarc. I should have taken the egg inside when I'd found it.

'Broke?' Maeve said. 'You let it break?'

'We need to ensure that we're able to protect ourselves in the aftermath,' Simon interrupted, steering Maeve's ire to himself. 'There will be some very angry judges when they realise what we've done.'

'We'll soon have the Knot, Simon,' Maeve repeated, as if

the words alone could ward off dangers. Again, I looked between them at the now obvious tension.

'And that's not going to be enough, Maeve,' he said, mimicking her exasperated tone.

'Well, Simon does raise an important issue,' Cormac O'Reilly intervened, trying to negotiate away from whatever was brewing between Maeve and Simon. 'We do need to think more about what happens after. What can you tell us about the judges, Wren? Have you learned anything more about Birchwood? Do you know why they're coming over here? And when?'

'Only what I told you the last time.'

'Anything more about their magic?' The question was shot from another corner of the room. Colm Wood.

'Nothing new.' I shifted slightly and looked up to see Simon watching. He knew I was lying.

'Heard anything about the Raker?' Cormac spoke again. 'A competition?'

'No. What's that?'

'What about the gardeners?' Smith said, sipping his tea.

'The gardeners?' I was confused. 'The chatty guy who does the flower beds at Harkness House?'

'You need to give us more, Wren,' Fidelma Walsh, swinging a crossed leg, smiled at me, but it didn't take the sting from the words.

'Are you sure you're telling us everything?' Cormac said, tapping his pen against the arm of his chair.

'I –' I began but couldn't answer. I wasn't telling them everything. But the questions were coming thick and fast, and it was hard to sift through what was irrelevant and what promises I needed to break. Fidelma's red kitten-heeled shoe swung back and forth.

'Cassa say anything about a third ré órga?' Dermot Walsh took off his glasses. He breathed on the lenses, then wiped them with a small cloth.

'There's a third one?' I'd only heard about the two golden ages. The tapping pen was louder, more regular.

'You're missing things, aren't you?' Maeve slapped her hands on her legs.

'Perhaps we need to jog your memory?' Colm paced from the fireplace to the table.

I glanced at Dermot: breathing and wiping.

The barrage of questions kept coming, relentless and with the aim of wearing me down. Their movements were irregular and discordant but with an underlying rhythm. This was one of the more aggressive forms of wickering. Instead of soothing or seducing, this pattern of words and actions served to unravel, and it was much harder to resist.

'You're holding back. Why would you hold things back?'

Cormac said. Table back to fireplace. Red heels. Hands. Sip of tea.

I felt pummelled by the questions, by the dissonant pattern they were setting with their words and movements. With each question, I came a little undone. My head was bursting, a deep sorrow moving to the surface. But I knew they were doing it to unsettle me, to jog my unconscious. It wasn't meant to be as hostile as it felt. They were doing it to help me remember.

'Have you seen this?' Colm Wood dropped a sketch on my lap before resuming his pacing.

'It's the symbol for the Bláithín.'

I thought of Cassa tracing the loops in the soil. I should tell them about the walled garden. But before I could, I was swept into the next question.

'Where have you seen it?' Maeve said as Colm reached the fireplace.

'Cassa drew it for me.'

'Why?' Red swinging shoe. Hands. Tea.

'Because … because I think she wants something from me.'

The steady beat of Cormac's pen against wood.

'What does she want from you?' Colm was back at the table.

'I'm not sure.' I couldn't put it into words. Too difficult, it drained me to even try to explain her predatory stare. That tapping was driving me demented. I wanted to throw Dermot's glasses across the room. To grab Colm and make him stop pacing. Fidelma's swinging leg, Maeve's jagged movements, even Smith's regular sips. All of it was too much.

'What are Cassa's weaknesses?' Maeve stood up. I was hanging on by a thread.

'Tarc.' The word was ragged. 'Cassa has a weakness for Tarc.'

And it stopped. I was limp when Maeve pulled me into her arms, smoothing my hair.

'I'm so proud of you,' she murmured.

They gathered round me. Fidelma drew me to her soft chest and told me how strong I was. Colm said I was a credit to the grove. Cormac was sure I would go down in augur history.

And my mind was reeling with untethered thoughts that I couldn't work through: gardeners, the symbol, my betrayal of Tarc, the Raker.

From across the room, still slouched in his chair, Simon watched.

'Smith.' It was late afternoon and we were alone in the cottage. 'What did you mean earlier when you asked about the gardeners?'

He looked up from his book, his bible: *The Art of War.*

'The gardeners?' His voice was weak and he looked so old, and I felt a sudden jolt of fear. I remembered how Aisling had run her eyes over him, as if there had been something that jarred.

'You're all right, aren't you, Smith? I mean, you'd tell me if there was anything wrong?' I scrutinised him. What I saw was the same as always: the intelligent blue eyes, the smattering of hair on his chin that was less than a beard and more than stubble, the long elegant frame folded up in the armchair.

'Just a little creaky,' he said, clearing his throat.

'You said something about gardeners?'

'You remember, we spoke about them at your first circle meeting. Long ago, the gardeners were the warrior unit of the brithemain, the forefathers of the judges. The law needed muscle to implement its rules.' From his chair, he reached out to touch the tips of my hair. 'Colm Wood told you how they would single out their victims with the kill mark.'

'Did we have a warrior unit in the old days?'

'Of course. But the gardeners were in a different league after the first ré órga, when they developed a brutal system of hard warrior training. Only the strongest, most ruthless men were able to complete it. Sons would follow in their fathers' footsteps, and having generations of gardeners in a family would earn them a place in the judges' elite. But when the judges were nearly wiped out in the eighteen hundreds, the gardeners became defunct. Just as well, modern society wouldn't approve of their methods.'

'And they never regrouped? The warrior units?'

Smith rapped his book. All through my childhood, he had quoted the Chinese general Sun Tzu at me. 'Remember, war becomes art when you master the ability to conquer your enemies without fighting.' He tapped his head, 'Strategy, now there's where true skill lies. Not in brute strength.'

'Why were they called gardeners?'

'Not because they lovingly tended shrubs and planted little bulbs. On initiation, these men would receive a set of pruning tools. Implements for torture and murder. They were called gardeners because they would cut down, cull and eliminate anything that threatened their territory. They would fight each other to become the Raker, the most heartless warrior of them all.'

'Why didn't you tell me about the gardeners before?' I said, moving across the worn rug, fighting the rising dread.

'I didn't think you'd be interested.' Smith's voice was mild, aimed to temper my increasing agitation. 'It's nothing to do with us.'

I looked at the war table in front of me. One army surrounding a village. A farmhouse completely unaware of the soldiers lurking in the trees.

'Ah, Wren.' His voice was gentle. 'I would have told you if you were even vaguely curious about the history of the judges.' He looked over to where I stood at the war table. 'It's not an apostrophe.'

I couldn't muster a smile. Whenever something bothered me, Smith would listen, then say 'It's not an apostrophe', which was apparently how the five-year-old Wren had tried to say 'catastrophe'. It did make me wonder why I was talking about catastrophes at five.

But Smith was wrong. Right about the history of the judges being of little interest to an augur child. But wrong that it was of no relevance to me.

'My father —' I struggled with the words. 'Was he one of them? How is that even possible?'

'You think your father was a gardener?' Smith said. 'What gave you that idea?'

'I just know,' I said. 'Always have. I thought that was his job. A travelling gardener.'

The hushed whispers before the grown-ups realised I was there: brown as a bear, sell condoms to a nun. Cheat. Gardener.

'I don't know much about your father.' Smith shut

his book and put it on the armrest. He watched me carefully.

'But you know more than you've told me.'

'They came from abroad. India, I think.' Smith was reluctant. He stood up, moving towards me. 'He was adopted into a powerful judge family as a young child when his mother married one of them. A family who'd earned a place in the elite with their history as gardeners.'

'I'm from a family of killers?' I was too loud. 'Did my father –'

'Don't you worry about the gardeners, Wren. That's all ancient history,' he interrupted, then put his hands on my shoulders as if to steady me. 'Your father wasn't a killer. He was a rich, entitled boy who took what he wanted without any thought or sense.'

'But he was a judge.' Stepping out of his grasp, I saw the farmhouse, the tank trained on it.

'Yes,' Smith breathed the word in. 'He should have known to keep away from an augur girl.'

'I'm half judge.' Terrible words to utter.

All my life I'd heard how awful they were. Bloodthirsty, unscrupulous, with a burning lust for power. Greedy and hostile towards us. And now I found that which I'd been raised to revile was part of the pattern that formed me.

'You should have told me.'

Smith flinched at my tone. We never raised our voices. Maybe my judge self was unleashing. Maybe it had been hiding inside, selfish and ugly, waiting for permission to come out.

'You are an augur from the line of Mug Ruith,' Smith spoke sternly, his words snapping me out of my wallow. 'You're one of us. You have an augur talent. You are not a judge. You're nothing like them.'

Had I not enjoyed Cassa's casual cruelty towards David? Did I not, if only for a moment, think he deserved to be punished?

'Your father doesn't matter.' Smith spoke gently, as if trying to call me back.

'If he doesn't matter, then why didn't you just tell me? Why keep it a dirty little secret?'

He reached out to me but I held up a hand.

'I'm going for a run.'

I set off to the woods, channelling my anger into pounding the ground beneath me. I didn't want to be this strange in-between thing that didn't fit. I didn't want to be like Arabella, who'd ended up alone in the woods.

But there I was, alone in the woods.

TWENTY-THREE
Looking for a girl

I am vexed by that doll.
AdC

I eyed the black hen with trepidation.

Smith wanted her gone. The front drive was regularly spattered with chicken shit, almost as if she did it to deliberately provoke him. He'd been muttering about Southern fried, and from the dark look on his face, his patience had run out.

'I think you're just misunderstood,' I said to the hen. 'Smith giving you a hard time?

She fixed me with her beady black eye. Her feathers were black with an iridescent sheen. Across the grass, a solitary magpie hopped down from the roof of the shed to the ground.

'Now,' I said to the hen, 'I'm asking nicely. Will you please lay a damn egg and not eat it? Seriously. That's just manky.'

She took a few cautious steps.

'I get it. You want some privacy.'

I swept a generous hand. 'Go on. I won't look.'

Unbelievably, the hen walked past the direction of my hand. Unnerved, I called her back, 'Here, Henny.' She stopped and turned to fix that evil eye at me.

'Go on.'

And then she disappeared down the side of the house. I leaned against the wall, thinking about the children of Lir. Swans were more elegant. There was something plain demonic about certain hens.

After a little while I went in search of her. Reaching the front drive, I could hear her screeching from across the road. A minute later, she put a dainty foot out on the potholed tarmac. I checked the hedge where she'd been and, bending down, I retrieved the egg.

The plant doll waited on the couch, watching for me to come home. She rested on a cushion, the smidge that might be a mouth having darkened into something more. Something hungrier. I had to swallow down a lump. I'd thrown her in the wastepaper basket.

'Wren.'

Aisling startled me. We'd been avoiding each other so carefully.

'What are you doing?' She frowned at me standing there in the middle of the room.

I'd been watching the not-brídeog. It had to be Sibéal playing tricks. When I'd asked if she'd moved the doll, Sibéal had denied it. But of course she would, the game wouldn't work if she confessed.

'Can we talk?' Aisling said.

'Sure.' I forced a smile. 'Can we get out of here?'

We walked towards the village. Never had we gone this long without speaking.

'How's it been? Harkness House?' Aisling broke the silence.

I shrugged.

'I miss you so much.' She threw her arms around me, her body wracking with sobs. 'I wish we'd never started any of this. I wish we could go back to that morning before the Ask.'

She looked at me with watery eyes. Puppy eyes. The eyes of a loyal friend.

'What is it, Ash?'

But she shook her head and smiled through her tears, 'Let's get something to eat.'

We went to the Gargoyle, and I was glad to erase the memory of that awful fight. At our usual table, beneath the ugly gargoyle faces, I gave an exaggerated bow in greeting.

'Has anything happened?' she said tentatively as I sat down. 'It looks … intense.' She circled a finger in the direction of my head.

Was I a little more unhinged? Probably. I'd found out I was half judge, I was either haunted by a doll or forgetting things. And I'd kissed Tarc. I must have been sending out all kinds of odd vibes.

'Smith is concerned,' she said. 'It's not good for him, all this worry.'

'What exactly is the matter with Smith, and when were you planning to tell me?'

'What do you mean?' Aisling was suddenly unable to meet my eye.

'Ash?' I was no stranger to fear, not after years of David's game. But this kind of fear was different. It felt like my blood had frozen. Like everything around me had stilled while I waited for her to reply.

'It's his blood pressure,' she relented.

'Did something happen?'

'Back in January it went scary high. If I hadn't been there, he would have had a stroke. I took him to the hospital. And as long as he stays on meds, doesn't overexert himself or get too stressed, he'll be OK.'

'Why would he hide that from me?' I said, trying to control the rising panic. Smith couldn't die. I couldn't lose him.

'You've a lot going on. He didn't want you to have something else to worry about. Smith promised he'd tell you when this is finished. High blood pressure is common. I'm watching it. He'll be fine.'

'What can I get you girls?' The waitress appeared at our table, her upbeat tone jarring.

'You should have told me,' I said when the waitress left.

'I wanted to.' She fiddled with her hair. 'But I worried it would guilt you into soldiering on. That if you knew Smith was sick, you'd keep going until you were completely lost.'

But it was Aisling who sounded lost.

'Have you seen this?' From my pocket, I pulled out the sketch of the Bláithín symbol Colm Wood had dropped on my lap.

She wavered, and I thought she would say no. But she was feeling it too, that gap growing between us. A gap that started with a white tulle dress and a folded square of paper taken from a box. A small perforation slowly tearing bigger and bigger.

'There's an old story,' Aisling said, staring at the symbol. 'Centuries ago, in the days of open warfare, an augur girl stumbled upon a judge settlement. From behind the trees, she saw a beautiful boy. Hidden, she would watch him every day. She loved seeing him cut wood, fetch water from the river. But unknown to her, other judge boys noticed her returning day after day and they thought she was spying on them.'

The gargoyles seemed to lean in closer. Aisling had always said they loved a good secret.

'Eventually the beautiful boy caught her,' she continued. 'He knew she was an augur but they fell in love, meeting in the hollow of an oak. But one day, as she was leaving, the other judge boys followed. Certain she was a spy, they chased her through the forest, into a field and through a meadow. Desperate, she begged a circle of oaks to shelter her. They took mercy and disguised her as a meadowsweet plant.

'Months later, after a brutal battle between judges and augurs, her judge boy was horribly injured. The girl found him among the dying on the battleground and dragged him to the oaks. She begged them to heal him. This time there was a price: she was to become one of them as they'd grown very attached to her. So she became meadowsweet for three years. He was healed, and when she was girl again, she joined his gairdín.'

'She abandoned us?' I was appalled. What could make an augur turn away and embrace her enemy?

'But she was never the same. Even though she looked the same, sounded the same, she'd lost part of herself when she became meadowsweet. She had metamorphosed into someone who was part plant, part woman. The Bláithín.'

Aisling looked at me intently, like she was telling me

something beneath her words. Above her, an open-mouthed gargoyle looked like it was bursting with glee.

'You know their golden ages? How the first ré órga brought a military revolution and the second brought ridiculous wealth? Some judges believe that each ré órga is linked to a Bláithín. The first one revolutionised their military. Arabella de Courcy brought back their prosperity. Now there's talk of a third.'

And I finally understood what I'd known for some time.

'Cassa's looking for a girl.' But those words were inadequate to convey what she was really after.

'Cassa believes that when the third girl turns,' Aisling said, 'she will bring a reawakening of strong, pure magic. The third ré órga.'

'How do you know all this?' I said. Judge lore was hard to access. I'd spent months at Harkness House and only managed snippets.

'Simon.'

Light flutter of her hand to her neck. She was uncomfortable. But if something was happening between them I'd be delighted.

'All judges anticipate the third ré órga,' she continued. 'But most don't connect it to the myth of the Bláithín. Rather, they link it to the decline of augurs. Some of them are keen for a bloodbath because they believe our ruin will bring on their golden age. Word is, they're getting impatient.'

The waitress appeared with our pizza and Aisling fell silent. When she left, Aisling was so intent on her plate it looked like she was counting the pepperoni.

'There's something else. Mam said it would distract you. Confuse you. It's about the doll.'

'The not-brídeog?'

Aisling flushed red. 'There's a judge tradition where girls are given tree and flower dolls by older women in their family. It's a keepsake, and the dolls are often handed down through generations. The story goes that if the doll comes to life, then the girl has been chosen. By the original Bláithín.'

'That's supposed to be a quaint family tradition?' I felt sheer terror. 'Sounds like a fucking nightmare.'

'It's just a story. Like Santa. The doll never comes to life.' She looked distressed.

'I heard a few girls in the village received dolls just like yours.' The way she looked just then, her bright, open face, I was reminded of what Laney had said. A daisy. Aisling was a daisy. Her fresh, easy beauty.

'Cassa sent the dolls. She thinks it could be you.'

⟞ TWENTY-FOUR ⟝
Won't even see it coming

*It feels as though all the bones in my legs and
arms have broken and are trying to re-form
into something else.*
AdC

The day of the fire, Cassa was hosting an Arabella de Courcy
coffee morning at the historical institute. Most of the team
were with her. In the office, Laney was on the phone,
ruining someone's day after finding mistakes in the glossy
Arabella brochure. Ledger Man was fixing the Foundation's
crashed website. I'd used Cassa's absence to snoop downstairs for the stone but found nothing.

Now, at my desk, I searched recent news. I'd found
damaged standing stones and a ring of burial stones
defaced with paint. I guessed that the orchard at Newton
Grange, the fire that had distressed Tarc so much, was a
nemeton bonded to the judges. The axed beech tree in
Wicklow appeared to be ours. There was no question that

someone was vandalising nemeta. But I couldn't see why, if both judge and augur nemeta were targeted.

Trying to make sense of it, I gazed out of the tall window. Desecrating a nemeton, any nemeton, was the most sacrilegious thing draoithe could do. And we certainly wouldn't damage our own, so who was doing it? Who would know where to find them? The only thing that made sense was if there were still bards around. But that was impossible.

Consumed by thoughts of zombie bards hell-bent on revenge, I didn't register the smoke at the edge of the window. Rushing over, I saw hungry orange flames rising from the heart of the garden. From Cassa's walled garden.

Calling for help, I ran out of the office, through the hall and out of the garden door. I heard Laney shouting behind me. The smell of smoke and fire was thick in the air.

The fire was contained within the walled garden. I'd seen pop-up sprinkler heads inside it, so I knew there was an irrigation system but I had no idea where the valve was. I couldn't see any pipes outside the garden. It had to be inside. Taking off my cardigan, I held it over my mouth and nose and opened the door.

I hadn't gone far when heat and smoke began to overwhelm me. Eyes burning, I followed one of the pipes, edging further into the walled garden. And then I couldn't. Fighting for air, I had to get out.

I collided with Tarc. His hoodie was tied around his face and he ran on, heading for the wall.

I was wheezing towards the door when the sprinklers piped through the garden came on at full blast.

Tarc ran down the path, pulling me with him. Outside the walled garden, away from the smoke, we took deep breaths through sore, swollen airways. I bent over, resting my hands on my knees.

In the distance, the sound of approaching sirens.

Tarc had pulled off his now sodden T-shirt. I couldn't help casting a glance at the ink peeking out of the low-slung waistband of his jeans. I could only see part of it, but I recognised the bare outline of the symbol for the Bláithín. His hidden tattoo.

Tarc caught me staring at his ink and my cheeks burned. He turned away from me, taking a dry hoodie that Laney held out to him. He seemed almost embarrassed, like he didn't want me to see it.

'This will break Cassa's heart,' Laney said. There were tears in her eyes as she watched the last flames burn. The garden was a mess. Her beautiful flowers, the carefully tended plants were replaced by an ugly cropped black. 'It's taken her years to grow it.'

In silence, we watched water vanquish flame. My clothes were drenched and clung to my skin. And, as the last of the fire went out, I realised the buzzing I'd felt so strongly the night of Cassa's party, the buzzing of a powerful nemeton, had been entirely quenched too.

In the afternoon, after the medical that Cassa insisted I take, I found her standing over the charred remains of her garden. There was nothing that told; her face was without expression and her body appeared relaxed. But she was devastated. It was precisely because she cared so much that she wouldn't let it show. I knew that beneath her controlled surface, something was simmering. I could almost feel it, the strength of her emotion.

'I'm sorry about your garden, Cassa. I know it was special to you.'

She nodded. 'It was. But I will grow it again. Better than it was before.'

'It will take time.'

'Most things that matter do,' she said, and her voice was suddenly fierce. 'I can choose to be the kind of person who just burns and that's the end.' I had a horrible image of a wicker man. 'Or I can choose to rise from the ashes.'

'I suppose.' I wasn't convinced it was that simple. Sometimes you just burned whether you liked it or not.

'I want to make you an offer,' Cassa said, looking at the flower bed where we'd spoken on the night of her party, the smell of fire and wet, burned plants still pungent. 'I want you to stay on here at Harkness House. You can work part-time at first, while you study, if that's what you want.' And again, her easy words belied that passion I'd sensed before. 'You'll get a good salary, paid tuition.'

'What would I have to do?'

'Learn about Arabella,' she said. Then she looked at me, with the burned garden behind her, a hint of fire in her eyes.

She was offering more than just a job.

'More than you dreamed possible.' She left it there, the words heavy with meaning.

Before I could respond, she held up a hand. 'Don't answer just yet. Think about it.'

Then she turned, leaving me alone in the burned garden.

I left Harkness House early, wearing clothes borrowed from Cassa's wardrobe; I smelled of smoke and her perfume. I moved from bus, to road, to Luas tram as if in a dream.

I was at the Luas stop when I saw her, my ghostly Sorcha, her yellow oilskin ill-suited to the sunny afternoon. There was something almost inevitable about it, like she was waiting for me. The flow of people closed around her and then opened again. And still she was there, wearing her blue flower dress and yellow raincoat. Ladybird earrings in her ears. She looked across at me, a horrible little smile on her pale face. She raised a hand.

Making my way towards her, I kept my eye on her as best I could. But I knew that by the time I got there she would be gone.

There was no sign of the bright raincoat. I didn't bother looking. There wasn't any point. The realisation had been a slow dawning: the figure from my milk dragon vision had stepped into the world. The Sorcha with the dead eyes and wan skin wasn't the real, breathing, living Sorcha. It was my worst manifestation of my mother, brought into being by overusing my talent. Made stronger, more fleshed out every time I lost myself in a picture, until I could no longer tell what was real. Where waking life was invaded with dream creatures.

This was how it would drive you mad.

At home, I entered the cottage in the middle of an argument. Sibéal was furious and, hands on hips, she was staring down Maeve. The smell of honey-baked ham filled the kitchen, its sweetness at odds with the mood.

'What's going on?' I murmured to Smith, who was busying himself in the kitchen. I'd never see him peel carrots with such fierce determination before.

'Domestic turmoil.' He held up his hands. 'I don't get in the middle of two strong-willed women.'

'You're such a hypocrite,' Sibéal was saying. 'I don't see why I shouldn't tell it like it is.'

'It must be kept a secret.' Maeve's face was flushed and pinched. 'You can't just go announcing yourself as an augur in Kilshamble, even if the judge kids at school piss you off. I've explained this many times before.'

'All these secrets,' Sibéal spoke with distaste. 'I don't understand why you need to have all these secrets. It's like you're ashamed of who we are. Of what we'd do to protect ourselves.'

'I know that the secretive nature of this grove frustrates you,' Maeve said, her voice low and calm. 'But with it we have stealth on our side. You should know that by now. When we act, they won't even see it coming.'

I watched Maeve and Sibéal facing each other as they argued. For all that they looked different they were so alike. Suddenly, for the first time in ages, I felt a kind of peace. There was something comforting and familiar about Maeve and Sibéal's argument. I'd seen versions of it more times than I could remember. Watching them squabble put me back in my place in the world. The smell of the ham crisping in the oven. Smith butchering carrots with a blunt knife. This was where I belonged. I could almost forget about Cassa and her obsession, the fire that had burned down the walled garden. I could almost forget about the doll that moved around the cottage. About Tarc, my mother. My father, from his proud line of killers.

Almost.

'I think Cassa wants me to metamorphose into a flower,' I blurted. 'And there was a fire in her walled garden today.'

Sibéal and Maeve abandoned their argument mid-sentence. Smith looked up, knife in hand. Sibéal narrowed her eyes, 'Whose clothes are you wearing?'

'Here, pass that cloth,' I said to Smith, ignoring Sibéal's question.

'Wren,' Maeve said. 'That's big news.'

'Doesn't matter, does it?' I said, lifting a hot heavy pot that smelled of boiled pig, trying not to gag. 'That metamorphosis is never going to happen. We're nearly done. Soon our nemeta will be regenerated and we'll be able to do all the rituals we need.' I emptied the hot water from the pot, steam filling the air. 'Besides, it isn't real. A girl can't turn into a flower. Can she?'

'There is no proof of it ever having happened,' Smith said.

'Magic is about design. It's a spider spinning her web,' Maeve said. 'Even for judges it's a slow, deliberate orchestration. It's not clicking your fingers and suddenly there are dragons and flower girls.'

Putting down the pot, I went towards the passage.

'Dinner soon,' Smith called.

'Not hungry, thanks.'

'Wren, you have to eat,' Maeve said.

'Later, OK?'

'Wren,' Sibéal said.

'What?'

'I think you should do it, the metamorphosis. You'd be crazy not to.'

I shouldn't have been surprised. Ordinary was Sibéal's most damning insult. But it was the detached way she spoke to me that bothered me. The coldness that had touched our friendship ever since I started at Harkness House.

'That's not the plan,' I said, looking at Maeve and Smith, who were pretending to be absorbed in taking out plates and pouring water into glasses. 'Is it?'

'No, honey,' Maeve said and glanced up. 'That's not the plan.'

I turned to go, but her voice stopped me.

'Only, don't refuse just yet. It might work in our favour to keep her wanting something from you.'

'Any idea where that stone is, Maeve?' I said, not turning to look at her.

'I'm doing my best, honey. It's been harder than I thought.'

'Maybe I should do it?' I said, thinking of Sorcha in her yellow raincoat.

'I'm better at this kind of reading. And I'm getting close.'

I went upstairs to my room. Cassa's clothes had suddenly become uncomfortable. Wrong-fitting. I had to get them off. Scrabbling at the buttons, I stopped in my doorway. The plant doll was lying on my bed, as if she'd done the rounds. This bed is just right.

Wakens the doll.

I was skeeved out. Light-headed, sick, I went through all the traits I ticked: almost an orphan, Kilshamble grown, from the line of judges. And now the doll.

It's impossible, I told myself. Magic doesn't work like that. The moving doll is a game. Sibéal is trying to wreck my head.

On the bed, that blank face looked at everything and nothing. Red floral skirt stretched out neatly. As I stepped closer, my eyes were drawn to the face with a macabre fascination. Was that the faintest impression of a smile? I picked up the doll and threw it in the wastepaper basket. It must have been a smidgen of dirt.

TWENTY-FIVE
So close to the finish

Wickerlight draws close. We are going to the woods tonight.
AdC

I felt the weight on my bed before I woke up. A light touch passing over my arm. I opened my eyes, panic shooting through me.

But it was only Maeve, sitting on my bed. The early morning light streamed in through the window, catching her wayward curls.

I sat up. 'You gave me an awful fright.'

She held up her hands. 'Just me.'

Drawing the covers up over my bare arms, I said, 'What is it, Maeve?' She looked troubled. She reached to my bedside table and picked something up.

'I wanted to talk to you. Alone.' Her voice was low, just above a whisper.

'What is it?' I said. 'Is Smith OK?'

'He's fine.'

I leaned back on the headboard. My eye caught the not-brídeog on the desk. She was sitting exactly where I'd left her. On her best behaviour. As if she hadn't been rasping a little song in my ear all night long:

Beneath the great oak my love does lie
A sword through his heart and arrow in his eye
Blood in his mouth, blood on my hands
I tie the great knot
He will not die. He will not die.

'Wren?' Maeve frowned, then turned to look at the not-brídeog. I could still hear the echoes of the song that had repeated through my dreams.

'What?' I said.

'Did you find out if Sibéal will get a talent?'

'No.' I shut my eyes. 'I forgot.'

'You forgot?' She sounded so disappointed. 'It's her birthday in two weeks.'

'Well, we'll just have to find out then.' I sounded snappier than I meant. Maeve looked like I'd kicked her kitten.

'Sorry.' I sank down to the pillows, feeling guilty. Sibéal and her birthday had completely slipped my mind. What kind of a friend forgot that?

'I can't get a reading on the last stone,' Maeve said. 'Cassa's blocked it somehow. Like they do with the nemeta so we can't scry for them. I've tried, and some of the others in the grove have tried. It's impossible.'

I pushed back the covers and got out of bed. At my wardrobe, I stared blindly at the clothes and said, 'So, what now?'

Maeve looked down at something in her hand. I pulled out a skirt, black tights.

'I saw something else. Yesterday, while watching the clouds and asking for the stone, I had a clear image.'

Seeing an image in the clouds, rather than reading through light, formation and position, was Maeve's talent at its strongest. But only if the image was distinct and without ambiguity.

'I saw the symbol for the Bláithín.' The word sounded strange coming from her lips. Wrong. 'Large and clear. And as I watched, it shifted into the Daragishka Knot.'

'What do you think it means?' I said, queasy. I knew what she was going to say. The guilt I felt about Sibéal twisted into something that made me want to shout, 'All right, all right! I'll do it.' Just so I could stop feeling like this.

But I didn't want to do it.

'It's obvious,' she said. 'We'll find the last stone if you do what Cassa wants.' Maeve was looking around my room: the pile of clothes on the armchair, the books on the desk, the things I'd collected from outside on my bedside table.

'The clouds don't tell you the future, Maeve.' But her roaming eye was making me uncomfortable.

It felt like she was sniffing for patterns in my room. Trying to sense what was anomalous. I was being paranoid. While there were exceptionally gifted augurs who could intuit the patterns that made a person, Maeve wasn't one of them.

'You're right,' she said, standing up and reaching a finger to the not-brídeog. 'But this isn't the future. It's very much the present. It's telling us we already have the answer. Cassa's offer.'

Her hand halted, like she was reluctant to actually touch the doll.

'Absolutely not,' I said.

I went into the bathroom, glad to get away from her.

'Think about it,' her voice called after me. 'If you do this, Cassa will give you anything. You'll get the stone no problem.'

Downstairs, Smith stood in the square arch between the kitchen and the living room.

'Wren,' he said as I passed him. 'We're so close to the finish line.'

I ignored him as I filled the kettle, took out a cup. I stood there, arms folded while I waited for it to boil.

'I can't do it,' I said.

'The Bláithín isn't real. Cassa is obsessed with an illusion,' Smith said. 'Going through with it won't change you, if that's your concern.'

'But what if you're wrong?'

And there it was, the thing that hurt so. That Smith would put me at risk of some unknown magic. Sure, he didn't believe. But what if there was the smallest chance that Cassa was right?

He shook his head. 'There is no danger. I promise.'

'The Bláithín is meant to bring on the third ré órga,' I said.

'And do you think we'd be keen to hurry that on? The golden age of judge magic?' Slight smile as he put his hands on my arms. 'I've studied the myth. Cassa's wrong. The third ré órga happens at the decline of the augurs. They eat our magic and it makes them stronger. And that's what we're trying to prevent.'

'How do you know this?'

'I once knew someone, long ago, who had access to judge papers.'

'The circle always knows more than you might think.' Maeve's words sounded like a warning.

I turned. 'There has to be another way. I can't be there with them. I hate lying. I just want to be home again.' I fixed on the thick dust layering the skirting, unable to look at them.

'I can't understand why you'd just give up when it's nearly over. Unless,' Maeve said, 'you're feeling a little confused about him? That Gallagher boy?'

My head snapped up. 'What do you mean?'

'Seems like you're getting on well with him.'

'I'm supposed to get on with them. That's the plan.'

I turned to Smith, feeling Maeve's gaze on me. But he looked away.

'You're spending an awful lot of time with him.' Maeve held out her hand. On her open palm was Tarc's lucky acorn. She'd taken it from my bedside table. 'It can get confusing. Is there something you need to tell us, Wren?'

'I'm not confused.' I wanted my lucky acorn back.

'Sibéal says he's smitten,' Maeve said, slipping it into her pocket.

I remembered Aisling saying how she loved that word. Smite. I very much doubted that I'd smote Tarc.

'Did you send Sibéal to spy on me?' I felt heat rush to my face. And something clicked.

'Wren,' Smith said. 'We're worried about you.'

'You mean you're worried that I'm not doing exactly as you say.'

'Do you feel anything for him?' Maeve was beside me, taking up the boiled kettle.

An impotent anger coursed through me. It was none of her business how I felt about Tarc. And yet, it was. If my feelings interfered with the plan, I should tell her.

'You don't have to worry about Tarc.'

'I think I do,' Maeve said, her voice rising. 'Look how you've just forgotten about Sibéal, about her birthday. I asked one thing from you, Wren, one thing. And you couldn't do it.'

'One thing?' I exploded. 'What do you mean one thing? You and Smith, you've asked everything of me.'

All the pent-up anxiety and agitation that had been swelling inside me over the last months wanted out. Hurt, because she didn't seem to see how it was costing me. How it felt like I was coming undone.

'All of us do what we have to for the grove,' Maeve shouted back at me.

'I've been there with them nearly every day. Worried, afraid. Lying. While you get to go on as normal. So yes, sorry if I've been preoccupied.'

I pushed away from the counter, my hand catching a cup. Falling. Broken shards on the floor.

'Don't push me, Maeve.' I headed for the arch.

'And you stay away from that boy,' she shouted as I walked away.

⤙ TWENTY-SIX ⤚
I like peanut butter

Something terrible has happened.
AdC

The white peonies on my desk were furled shut. They'd begun to rot on the inside, a slow brown seeping from the core.

Laney and Ledger Man were talking in hushed voices. I couldn't hear much, but Laney said something about irreparable damage. Hacked with an axe. Another day, I might have inched closer, but that morning I couldn't make myself care. Not after the argument with Maeve.

The security boys came into the office, hair damp and smelling like soap. They grabbed drinks, as they always did after their training session, except it was after lunch, not ten in the morning. Looking up, I saw the scowls. Ryan bumped against David while he downed a shake.

'Watch it,' David said, menace clear in his voice.

Cillian murmured something, and then David had a fist to his face. Dissention in the ranks.

Taking a sip of his drink, Tarc called his boys to heel. David released Cillian, well exceeding Smith's bad language quota. When Cillian stepped back, I saw that David had been in a scrap, his face roughed up.

The boys had polluted the room with their dark mood. Grabbing my coat, I went out for fresh air.

I was near the end of the hallway when David caught up with me. He stood closer than was comfortable. I could read the accusation in his face, like whatever had been hacked with an axe was all my fault. He loomed over me, bruised and angry. Reminding me of the promise he'd made when he took my hair.

Tarc appeared down the other side of the long hall.

'David.'

'Gallagher.' David turned to him. Tarc didn't say anything, just walked closer. David stayed where he was, watching Tarc advance. It was the first time I'd ever sensed defiance from him towards Tarc.

'Go.' Tarc glowered.

David scowled at him, then scarpered off.

'Something get in the water today?' I said. Whatever had come over the security boys that morning still held Tarc in its grip.

'Things are a little tense.' He was restless, like he couldn't be sure if he wanted to stay or go.

'You're fobbing me off with "a little tense"? I'll take nothing less than tempestuous, thanks.'

Tarc hesitated. Then: 'It's not your concern, Wren.'

I gave him the dagger eyes and walked away. Five steps, then he caught up with me.

'Sorry,' he said.

And, looking at him, I could see the anger, the sadness. But more than that, I sensed he was afraid.

'I don't know what's going on,' I said, 'but if people are getting hurt, maybe you should report it to the guards. You're awful young to carry such a weight.'

I walked down the hallway to the garden door. Out to the courtyard, beyond the bench and into the garden. I passed Cassa's blackened sanctuary to a cement bench adorned with stone roses.

I stayed out in the weak sunlight, watching the dark clouds moving in.

And without warning, he was right behind me. He took my wrist, pulling me to my feet. Wordlessly, half yanking, half pleading, Tarc led me into the cluster of wet trees.

Hidden by the trees, I couldn't see the house. Still, Tarc spoke in a low voice as if we might be heard.

'Please don't do what Cassa asked. Please don't go along with it.' He held on to my wrist.

'Why shouldn't I?'

'Because doing the ritual changes things.'

'You don't really believe that I would transform into the girl of leaf and petal, do you?' I said, pulling away.

Tarc took a deep breath. 'No. I don't know. I don't know what I think. Cassa's obsessed over this for years. None of us really believe. But I don't want you to take the risk.'

'I haven't decided.' Meaning, I was doing my best to resist being pressured into doing it.

'It doesn't matter whether it was real or not,' he said. 'It damaged Arabella. I don't want it to damage you.'

'Maybe she was drawn to the ritual because she was already damaged.'

'I want to help you understand. What do you need to know?' Tarc said. 'About Cassa, me. Any of this,' he spoke quietly and urgently, 'I will tell you anything you want to know.'

'You don't trust me.' I nearly added: you shouldn't.

He frowned at me like I was a riddle carved in stone. I tried to think of all the things that had vexed me these last months. My mind had been brimming with questions, but they all fell away. There were things I needed to know.

Things I had to do. But that was the beauty of this: he wasn't another of the things I had to do.

This was the wrong time, wrong place, and it gave me a thrill.

'Beneath the trees, remember?' He gestured to the canopy above and smiled. 'Go on, ask me something.'

So many questions but, foolish girl that I was, I could think of none of them. Instead, deliciously irresponsible, I wanted to know about him: what did he like to do? Did he sit on a comfortable chair in the sun, reading a book? Did he lose himself while jogging in a green wood?

I pushed those thoughts away, trying to remember what I should ask. The things that didn't add up. What was he doing at night when he did Cassa's security work? Why had he been so angry with Moleskin? Who had beaten up David? What was happening with the nemeta? The words were on the tip of my tongue. Then he stepped forward, closing off the space between us. I stepped back, and again, until I felt a tree against my back. My questions dissolved.

'Ash tree, good choice.' He smiled, and seemed so light and carefree. He pressed his legs against mine, his chest brushing mine. 'I'm waiting.'

So was I. Would he get on with it already? But I was enjoying the anticipation. The uncertain certainty of what would happen next.

'For what?' I leaned into the ivy that draped itself around the split trunk. I felt embraced by the tangly branches of the just budding tree. A heavy cloud moved over us.

'Your question.'

'I'm thinking,' I said.

And I was thinking that this was the wrong story. I was thinking that this was not meant to happen. Everything in me was braced to step away. To move one inch closer was a betrayal of Smith, Aisling and all the others I loved. To confirm the accusations that Maeve had thrown at me just that morning.

But then his hands were in my hair and his lips were fierce against mine. All those things we hadn't said to each other suddenly didn't matter. He was telling me so much more, with his hands, his legs, his lips. The way his body curved over mine. And in those minutes, for the first time in months, I felt right.

This was the promise that I'd seen in my topaz vision down in the quarry: Tarc and me, beneath the trees. That feeling of right. I hadn't dared hope that it was anything but skewed. Then, before I was ready, he pulled away.

'You're vibrating,' he said. And I realised it was my phone. Smith. No way could I speak to my grandfather just then.

'I should get back.' But as I turned to go Tarc held my

arm, his fingers closing over the puckered skin beneath my cardigan.

'Skive off with me,' he said. 'I'll show you my woolly hat collection. We can compare letter openers. Play Monopoly.' He glanced at the dark cloud above us. It would break any second.

'You really know how to sweet-talk a girl.'

'You know you like it.' He tugged gently.

And he was right. I did. I was never going to be wooed with love songs and roses. Not chocolates, nor cards with red hearts and sugary verse.

I followed him through the trees until we reached his cottage.

'Do you want to come in?'

My phone started again. Maeve. It was like they somehow knew to keep interrupting. I hesitated; if I answered there was no way I'd go inside. This exquisite madness would draw to a close. *Stay away from that boy*, Maeve had said.

But I was done doing what they told me.

'Yes.'

Lacing his fingers between mine, he led me inside. I stalled at the entrance, trailing my other hand over the threshold. Hiding the draoi blessing in a casual gesture before pulling the door shut behind me.

'These used to be the old stables,' Tarc said. 'Now it's the security quarters. There's room for the others, for when they need to stay over, but I'm the only one who's here all the time.'

I peered down the hall, half expecting to see David.

'They're not here now.' He moved towards me, tentative. Suddenly, uncharacteristically shy. 'I can make you tea?'

'No tea.'

Outside, the rain. It streamed against the large windows, the wet trees beyond. Just the sound of rain against glass, and Tarc.

'How is it that I have only known you two months?' he said, almost in wonder.

'You don't really know me that well.' I dropped my face, letting my hair fall to hide my shame as he took my coat.

'I want to know you.' And the look on his face, the longing there. It startled me, the ferocity of his desire to know me.

My mother left when I was a baby. The words were at the tip of my tongue, fighting to be let out. *I was named Wren for the druid bird. My first memory is of trees. I am an augur with a spinny eye, which is a curse, not a blessing. I am here to steal from you. I love peanut butter and running in the woods, but never with the boys behind me.*

I'd never wanted to tell anyone the story of me as much as I did just then. I wanted to offer that to him. To stop the traitorous words, I kissed him, pushing him down on the couch. I sat, one leg either side of him.

'I like peanut butter.' Inadequate, but it was all I could give.

'Peanut butter,' he said, touching my face as if I'd told him my deepest secret.

I kissed him again, my hands exploring his hard arms, running up to his shoulders, then inching between the couch and his back.

'Bleak, abandoned industrial areas,' he offered in return. 'Broken windows in forgotten factories.'

His hands were warm through my thin cardigan, my black tights.

'Really loud songs with swear words in them,' I said, feeling his laughter in his shoulders, on my mouth.

'Grey hair. Lined skin.'

'The swirling colours in marbles.'

'Purple skies. October.'

He flipped us around, so I was lying down with him on top.

'The snitch of Velcro pulling.' The tips of his fingers at the hem of my tank.

We kissed, exchanging details about ourselves. We matched each thing discovered with a new touch, growing closer. Until, 'My mother left when I was a baby.'

My words were a whisper, my hands on his skin. I wasn't sure he heard them.

But suddenly his attention was taken by something beyond me. He moved away, saying, 'David.'

I sat up, looking through the window, and there he was, coming down the path towards the cottage. I was grabbing my cardigan when Tarc spoke, 'Where did you get that?'

He stared at my arm, at the puckered skin from my stone snakebite.

'Accident. Got careless while poisoning weeds a couple of years ago.'

'An accident in a garden?'

'Sort of.'

Marked by the garden. I knew that's what he was thinking.

'You don't believe it, do you?' I said.

'No.' But there was a shadow in his eyes.

David turned the door handle. The latch was on.

'Gallagher,' he pounded on the door. I heard the clink of keys.

'I don't want to see him.' I didn't want him to see me. He'd take one look and know we hadn't been playing Monopoly.

'This way.' Tarc pulled me down the passage and into his room. 'I'll drive you home when he leaves.'

'Gallagher,' I heard David calling from the living room. Leaving me inside, he shut the door.

In his room I could smell that indefinable scent of Tarc. There were books on the desk. Photographs beside the bed.

The stone. It was possible that Tarc, as Cassa's security, kept the stone in his room. I examined the desk, the table beside the bed. I ran my eye over his bookshelf, knowing it was a shitty thing to do after what we'd shared.

The door opened slightly, the draught running through the house probably did it. I went to shut it.

'The old power station?' Tarc was saying.

'It's supposed to be a surprise.' David's laugh sounded hollow.

Quietly closing the door, I went back to the bookshelf. Something there had caught my eye. It was on the bottom shelf, under a pile of books. The symbol for the Bláithín was small and clear. Pulling it out, I saw a case made of brown leather. I paused, reluctant. But Maeve had seen the symbol in the clouds; what if the stone was in here?

Snapping the latches on either side of the case, it opened. Laid in cream silk was a set of sharp utensils. They looked old-fashioned: there was a double-bladed instrument, a sickle, a wooden handle with a sharp brass tip, a small saw, a strange object with a large flat half-moon blade. A hand spade, which I picked up, feeling the hard steel. I recognised the forerunner to garden shears with its sharp pointed edges. And three knives with carvings on the handles. There were indents beside the knives, suggesting two had been removed.

Smith had told me about pruning tools, how they were used for murder and torture. And if there were pruning tools in his bedroom, that meant Tarc was from a family of gardeners.

I picked up the small card slipped into the side. 'For Tarc, on passing your exams. These were your father's and now they are yours, that you may follow his path as Raker. With love, Cassa.'

Not just from a family with a history of gardeners, Tarc was a gardener. A brutal killer from the warrior elite.

Worse, he was meant to be the Raker.

Smith was wrong, the gardeners hadn't disbanded. They were very much around. And, very likely, I was alone in a house with two of them.

'What are you doing, Wren?' Tarc's voice was tight as he stood in the doorway.

I turned to face him, the spade still in my hand.

He stepped closer, as if he was the one holding the sharp instrument. His face was impassive, but taking everything in. He was seconds away from figuring it out. That I was his enemy. That I had lied to him all this time.

'Stay back.' I waved the spade at him. 'Why do you have these?' I wanted him to tell me that Cassa had insisted. That he'd hidden them on the bottom shelf because he couldn't bear the sight of them.

'They belonged to my father. And to his father before him. And his before him. Now they're mine.'

Any hope I'd had dissolved with those words.

'You hurt people?'

'I protect.' The look on his face suggested that sometimes they were the same thing. Tarc stepped towards me. 'You were looking through my things. Why?'

My hand clenched around the spade.

'Put it down, Wren. You don't understand what those are.'

'I know. I know you trained as a killer. That you mean to be Raker. And I know who you'll end up hurting.' I couldn't hide the tremor in my voice. 'Here's your chance. You have the enemy in your bedroom. Do your worst.'

And he finally understood.

He looked utterly, utterly crushed.

I saw disgust flit over his features when he realised what I was. How I had lied. Just for a few seconds, he let me see how he really felt. The disappointment, the sadness. The longing for what might have been otherwise. Then it seemed like he packed his emotions away.

'You're one of them.' He shook his head with a bitter

laugh. 'David warned me that something wasn't right. I refused to see it.'

Another step closer.

'Was this,' he gestured disdainfully between me and him, 'part of whatever it is you're doing here?'

And closer.

'I told you to stop.' I held the spade in front of me. My hands on the hilt were shaking.

'Was it you who leaked the locations of our nemeta?' He prowled towards me. 'Are you the reason they've been damaged?'

'I would never allow damage to a nemeton,' I gasped, sounding ridiculously uptight. I raised the spade a little higher. 'I don't even know where your nemeta are.'

'Put it down, Wren.'

'Stay back,' I said again. But he came closer.

I tried to find the Tarc I'd come to know over the last two months, the Tarc with whom I'd laughed and talked and kissed. I could still feel the ghost pricks of stubble against my chin.

But in his place was this hard, cold person who would one day be Raker. He reached for me and I felt like that girl. The one who stumbled through the forest with boys at her back. The victim.

So I lashed out, meaning to warn him off. But, despite

everything, he must have trusted me, because he stepped forward instead of away, and the sharp edge of the spade hit him on the temple. Blood trickled down his face. He touched it in disbelief. I could barely believe it myself.

'I told you to stay back,' I lowered my trembling hand. Then made myself hold it up again, poised to strike.

But before I could move he tackled me, taking me down to the ground. He grabbed at the spade, and I pushed out from under him, rolling on top. He flipped me over, pinning my legs with his.

'I don't want to hurt you,' he said. Holding my wrists with one hand, he tried to prise the spade out of my hand with the other. As his fingers unpeeled mine from the spade I tightened my grip. I wrenched my arm away and whacked him again. It was a weak strike, but it allowed me to push him off. I got up and ran for the door. I made two steps before he pounced at me from an awkward angle, hanging on to me around my waist while I strained towards the door.

'Let me go,' I shouted.

I felt him freeze, then his arms released their hold. As he let go, I felt myself lifted out of his grip and swung across the room. The spade clanked to the ground. I saw David's face before I hit the wall, my jaw catching the edge of a shelf. His boots pounded the floor towards me.

'David, no,' I heard Tarc say.

As he approached his face was a mask of calm anger, and yet I sensed that David himself was missing. It was as if something else had overtaken him.

He raised a fist. But before he could strike Tarc shoved him away, pinning him face down on the ground.

'David.' His voice was hoarse. 'Come back.'

My head fell against the wall, aghast at what I had done. Blood streamed from Tarc's temple where I'd hit him. From down the passage came the sound of footsteps.

Ryan appeared and surveyed the scene in Tarc's bedroom. 'Canty called. They're moving tonight.'

Taking advantage of their distraction, I got up and ran. I wrenched open the lane gate and sprinted down the road, trembling as I pulled my phone from my pocket. My bag was inside the office, which would be locked and alarmed by now. I pulled out the emergency tenner Maeve insisted I keep in my phone case and began to make my way home. It was wet outside, with heavy rain that reminded me of my first days at Harkness House.

At the cottage, Maeve and Smith were waiting, anxious.

'What happened?' Maeve cried when she saw the bruise on my face. 'And don't tell me it was dreams.' Her voice was fierce.

'They know I'm an augur. I've fucked it up, Smith.' I let out a ragged breath. 'I'm sorry.'

Smith pulled me, sodden clothes and all, into his arms. For the first time in ages, I felt tears start. But it wasn't because of the plan or the months of deception. I wanted to cry because of the way Tarc had looked at me when he realised what I was. But I couldn't cry for that. Not when he was a gardener. Swallowing hard, I wiped the tears away.

'I found Tarc's pruning tools.'

I sat on a stool beside the fire, feeling the heat warm my face.

Looking into the flames, I told them that Birchwood had to be the gardener training school. That far from defunct, the gardeners were very much around. If the rumour of judges from Birchwood coming to Dublin was true, a bunch of gardeners were on their way over. And that likely meant trouble.

Smith touched my arm. From the resigned look on his face, I guessed this wasn't exactly news.

'Why didn't you tell me?' I said. 'That they were still around?'

'Because you were so upset about your father,' he said. 'And because I didn't want you worrying about soldiers who posed zero threat to you, when the real danger was always Cassa.'

'How did it happen?' Maeve crouched beside me. 'Where did you find his tools?'

My shame was as intense as the fire at the side of my face.

'They were in his house.' I stood, my wet clothes hardening uncomfortably. 'Can we talk tomorrow?'

'His house?' Maeve said.

'Another time.' Smith was firm. 'Wren's had an awful shock. I'll put on the heat upstairs and you get dry. This can wait.'

I stayed in my room, where I could hear their agitated murmuring. I heard cars arriving, doors closing as people came and went late into the night. In the dark, I lay in my bed, shivering. Nothing could warm me up.

I ignored the soft knocks at my door as Aisling tried to lure me out with promises of hot tea, rich gravy and sweet cakes. Simon whispered at the door, his voice both comforting and safe. But it wasn't him I wanted.

I pulled the covers over my head, burrowing into the darkness.

I'd let everyone down. All their intricate plans. Two months at Harkness House and for nothing. Eventually, I fell into broken sleep, weighed down by the shame of my weakness. By the burden of my failure.

TWENTY-SEVEN
Pinned to that tree

Since the game, my body knits itself into something
different. I am changed. My skin glows and my
eyes shine. Something like power surges
through my veins.
AdC

The next three days were awful. I resisted the urge to hide in my room, away from Sibéal and Maeve's grim disappointment. Instead, I made myself work. I cleaned the cottage, scrubbing tiles and toilets and floors like it would atone for my lapse in judgement.

I would not think about Tarc. I wouldn't think about how he'd kissed me, or the feel of his skin and muscles beneath my searching hands. Not the shape of him above me, his face as he looked at me on his grey couch. I would not think about how the boy I liked too much was going to become the Raker, in charge of soldiers tasked with killing augurs at the slightest provocation. I didn't dare linger on how he, more than my family, had cautioned me about Cassa's ritual. Had worried about the risk to me.

He and Aisling.

'I think I can see my reflection.' Aisling stood over me as I washed the dust-covered skirting in the living room.

I kept on scrubbing and didn't realise I was crying until I tasted the tears.

'Don't cry, Wren.' She slunk down beside me, not minding the water I'd sloshed. She pulled me into her arms.

'I'm so glad you found a way out,' she whispered in my ear. 'I'm glad it turned out this way.'

'I let everyone down,' I said.

'It should never have been all on your shoulders.'

'But now we won't get the third stone, and our nemeta will go to shite and we'll end up like the bards.'

'We'll find another way,' she said. 'Don't tell Mam, but Simon and I have an idea.'

I sat up straight. 'Your last idea was a disaster.'

'Shhh, there's nothing to worry about. We haven't decided anything.'

A short, sharp knock sounded at the door. I was due to report back to the circle that morning. Whatever happened, I wouldn't lie. Maeve knew I'd been in Tarc's house. I wasn't looking forward to clarifying that really I meant his bedroom.

Or why I was in his house at all. My gut twisted as I thought about admitting this to the circle. To Smith.

'Fix your face,' Aisling said. 'Don't let them see you cry.'

But it wasn't my summons to the circle meeting. I opened the door to find Tarc standing there. He was wearing black cargos and what looked like a fitted waxed jacket with an insignia on the sleeve. The symbol for the Bláithín.

I guessed there was nothing to hide any more.

He didn't come in, it would mean too much. His eye flicked over the small spider on the upper inside door frame. The hard line of his jaw as he looked back to me tore something inside.

'Cassa wants to see you.' He was civil, the anger from a few days ago had dissipated. 'She's here in Kilshamble.'

Aisling hovered behind me.

'I don't like this, Wren. You don't have to go.'

Tarc cast a disdainful look at her. 'You don't think much of us, do you?'

'Won't bother to answer that one.' She gave him her sweetest smile.

'Ash,' I said. 'I'm not going to skulk away and hide.' I moved to get my coat. 'This shouldn't take long.'

'I don't trust them.'

Tarc shrugged. 'I won't hurt her.' He sounded almost bored.

Aisling stared at him. 'Yeah, *that* I might believe.'

My coat and boots on, I gave her a quick hug.

'If I don't hear from you in an hour,' she said, 'I'm sending in the troops.'

'Yeah, good luck with that.' Tarc murmured, barely audible. But, along with his uniform, it reminded me what he was. And how much stronger they were.

It was quiet as we marched along the path.

'Cassa's at Arabella's cottage,' he spoke over his shoulder.

We walked in silence through the woods. He said nothing, seemingly more interested in the line of trees and listening to the birdcalls.

Beneath the trees, he'd once said. But whatever trust we'd shared was shattered.

How afraid I'd been of the judges and their punishments. How troubled I'd been about David's blood fine. And now I knew that for me there could be no punishment worse than this. More brutal than his blazing anger was Tarc's indifference. As if denying anything had grown between us over the last months. He looked at me like I was nothing to him.

I squared my shoulders and hardened my heart.

'They're here.' I heard Laney's words travel down the slope as we approached the ruined cottage.

Inside the broken walls I saw Cassa. Outside the ruin, Laney and David stood a short distance away. I'd expected him to show some kind of triumph. Smug that he'd been right to question me. But David seemed lost inside himself, barely looking up.

'Cassa,' I said, and stepped into the ruin. There were fresh flowers in the corner. Peonies.

'Wren,' she said. 'You came.'

'I'm sorry.' I took a few steps towards her. 'I should have told you who I was.'

Tarc moved to the wall, standing upright. A soldier on guard.

'You did tell me,' Cassa said. 'Not with words, but I've known you were an augur for a while now.'

If Tarc was surprised, he didn't show it.

'You knew?' I said. 'How?'

And why didn't she call me on it?

'Augurs look at things differently. They're always dissecting and designing their surroundings, searching for visual patterns. Augurs are all about art, and that's impossible to hide.'

'I'm not like that.' But I wasn't going to explain my wonky to Cassa.

'You underestimate yourself.' She remained still, barely moving at all. Behind her, the trees stood tall and silent and it felt like I was on trial. But I wasn't sure what my crime was, nor what was at stake.

How I might be punished.

'I want to know why you came to Harkness House.' Cassa's words rang through the forest. A crow flew from a tree, squawking loudly.

I paused, trying to organise my thoughts. I couldn't tell her the truth. I dithered, suddenly unsure whether the story I'd prepared would be enough.

But then the words popped into my head, almost as if they were whispered to me.

'I wanted to know about Arabella.'

'Why?' Cassa demanded.

Again the words were clear in my head. I could almost imagine a girl with white petticoats standing beside me, leaning in and saying the words close to my ear.

'Because we are alike.'

'And how are you alike?' Cassa's eyes gleamed. She stared hungrily at me.

You know.

'You know.' Loud and bold.

You tell me.

'You tell me.'

'Because you are also a judge,' Cassa said.

From the corner of my eye, I saw Laney and David turning to the ruin, Laney letting out a small squeak of surprise.

'How did you know?' I sounded so weak. I felt weak, beneath the gaze that missed nothing.

'I knew your father.' Cassa spoke to the flowers. 'A long time ago. Before he … went away. You have his eyes.'

'You knew my father?'

Suddenly I was too aware of the others. I could sense them all watching the unfolding drama, silent witnesses to a different kind of metamorphosis. Girl turned augur turned judge.

'Many years ago.'

So many questions, I didn't know where to start.

'My grandfather said he was a cheat.'

'I barely knew him at all.'

From the wall, Tarc watched. There was something like shock on his face. I guess he hadn't been expecting this.

'Leave us.' Cassa held out a hand towards the other three. Tarc nodded to David but didn't move from the wall. Laney stayed close beside David as they walked down the slope together.

'You too, Tarc.'

'Cassa, I can't do that,' he said.

'Don't challenge me, Tarc.' But it was a question, not an order. 'Five minutes.'

'I'll be over there.' He pointed just beyond a tree. 'No further.'

Cassa nodded. Tarc came to me, running his hands down my arms and body. Then down my legs in brisk, efficient sweeps. He pulled out a long sharp pin and my hair fell down my back. His touch was all business, and it hurt.

'Now, I don't think you have ill intent,' Cassa said once he'd left, 'but it won't do any harm to inform you that Tarc has excellent aim with his throwing knife. He would have you pinned to that tree before you could draw some cleverly hidden weapon. But we're not here for that, are we?'

'No.' I swallowed.

'How are we going to fix this, Wren?'

'I'll collect my things. You won't hear from me again.'

'When the judges learn that augurs infiltrated Harkness House at the same time that many of our nemeta have been damaged, they'll be pushing for action. I'm not sure I can hold them off.'

'I've nothing to do with that,' I said.

Cassa studied me. 'I believe you. You don't have it in you to damage nemeta. But that doesn't solve the problem. The judges, and they will find out, will want blood.'

I hesitated.

'These are your choices. You could leave now and I will do my best to contain the inevitable hostility, but I can't guarantee there won't be retaliation.'

'And the alternative?'

'You show your commitment to the judges by becoming the Bláithín. Become one of us, the girl of leaf and petal who brings the third golden time, and you will change your story. You'll no longer be the girl who deceived us when our nemeta burned. You will stop retaliation from the gairdíní. You will prevent a war.'

I thought about everyone I loved. I looked at Tarc and David, alert and ready. I thought about the warriors from Birchwood making their way here. About boys like Simon, who would stand up and fight. Who would be outnumbered and outclassed.

'And you will achieve what you set out to do. You will learn about Arabella. And more about who you are, about the judge in you.' She moved closer to me. 'I think you don't realise how strong that desire is. How much you need to complete the pattern, to connect to your other side.'

Her voice was soft and lulling. 'It's augur nature to find the balance in a design.'

'When did you realise what I was?'

'From the start, there was something that niggled. Your eyes were so familiar, and there was that day you stared through the peonies.'

And I knew what she was thinking: *she sees what isn't.*

'But it was impossible to be certain. So, not until that night in my garden.'

I leaned against the broken wall, feeling cool moss through my dress and on my thighs. 'And what about my family? If I do it, I'll want to see them.'

'Your loyalty will be to the Rose Gairdín.' But she nodded her agreement.

I could stay with Cassa for a few weeks. Long enough for her to see that her metamorphosis didn't work and for the dust to settle. The gairdíní would soon lose interest in me.

And in the meantime, the groves would be getting stronger with the Daragishka Knot formed, and soon enough I'd be back home where I belonged.

I leaned against the wall for a long time. I felt the cold of the ruin seep through my dress into my skin. I thought I heard something whisper: *do it do it do it.*

There wasn't really a choice. It was my fault, my lapse in judgement that had caused the plan to unravel.

'Yes,' I said.

I expected the earth to tremor and the walls of the cottage to shiver, so charged was the air around me.

Cassa smiled. She drew nearer.

'You chose the right thing.'

I bloody hoped so.

'Wickerlight is drawing close,' she said as she took my hands in hers. 'The equinox is approaching. Last night there was torrential rain.'

I remembered walking from the bus stop in the dark, wretched and wet, numb. In bits.

'A thunderstorm last week.' Cassa continued to list weather conditions, visible constellations, and she may have mentioned a bunny-shaped cloud, but I couldn't be sure.

'What happens afterwards?' I said. 'To me?

'You'll still be you,' Cassa said. 'But more so. The girl of leaf and petal has the power of nature humming through her veins.'

Upgrade to Wren 2.01 and eliminate the wonky. Except I knew now that I quite liked my wonky. That I preferred to keep it, thank you very much.

But it didn't matter. I didn't believe it. Magic was subtle, quiet. It worked through patterns. It wasn't this rush of power that Cassa was describing.

'You would have it all,' she said, picking up soil from the ground. She rubbed it against my palms, soothing the ache there. Last, she raised her hand to my mouth, the smell of it rich and earthy. She put a small bite of soil inside my lips. It felt cool. Fresh.

I don't believe you, I wanted to say. I didn't think anyone did. Not Laney, who so meticulously organised the information that Cassa had collected. Not Tarc, whose gentleness towards Cassa made me quite certain that he felt sorry for her. That's what her money could buy: her own private fairytale, acted out for her with full cast and costume.

And afterwards we would say, *Oh the wind blew wrong*. Or *Mercury was in retrograde* or *The cloud was a koala, not a bunny*. Sorry. But we'd all know that it hadn't worked because it couldn't.

My mouth full of dirt, I said nothing.

'You probably know that there are material benefits to this,' Cassa was saying. 'I would treat the Bláithín as my own. And I am very generous.'

'I don't want any of that. I don't want your money or things.' I spoke with a gritty mouth.

'Do you have any idea what you're refusing?' She examined me curiously. 'Are you not even a little tempted?'

'No.' Then I paused. 'There's a problem. With the list I gave you.'

'The definitive traits,' she said. 'Almost an orphan. Grows where the last Bláithín trod. Steals the love of one from the garden. Marked by the garden. Wakens the doll. Sees what isn't there. From the line of the judges. Brings the golden time.'

'They don't all apply to me,' I said. Tarc hated me and I hadn't a clue how to bring about a golden era. 'So it probably won't work.'

'I think you'll find that they do.' Cassa spoke quietly, and then she walked out of the ruin.

Tarc started after her, then paused. He looked at me, and there was such sorrow on his face. Our eyes locked. Then Cassa called and he turned away.

At home, Aisling was waiting. I must have had muck on my cheek because she touched a hand to it saying, 'Wren, what have you done?'

~ TWENTY-EIGHT ~
There's a good girl

Since agreeing to Elizabeth's game, I feel oddly detached.
AdC

Since agreeing to Cassa's metamorphosis it felt like I was moving underwater. The normal chat of everyone at home was strangely muted. I couldn't hear them, I couldn't reach them. Perhaps it was an underlying shock. It didn't matter that nothing would happen when I did the ritual. Because something already had. In having that conversation with Cassa beneath the trees, I'd chosen to be a judge. Which meant that I'd chosen to not be an augur. And it didn't matter if it was all a trick and a lie, the trees had heard me.

I moved between Carraig Cottage and Cairn House, trying to absorb the familiar comforts. Cassa had invited me back to complete the internship. Smith and I agreed that I would continue at Harkness House for few weeks after I'd done the ritual, so I could find the last stone. This way, I could make a discreet exit that didn't cause the judges to bay for blood. Cassa was right, by doing the ritual, the judges wouldn't know about my deception. Instead, I would be seen as Cassa's failed experiment with the halfling.

But I couldn't shake this fear that I would never find my way back. That if I moved to Harkness House, our cottage would never be my home again.

'Wren honey, you're here.' Maeve came in while I was standing in her kitchen, staring at the empty table. Her eyes looked worried, as they had been since I'd started listlessly ghosting through the two houses. I wouldn't go to the woods, I had this weird idea that the trees would whisper along messages to Tarc. At the Foundation, I avoided him. And he avoided me. Each of us barely able to look the other in the eye.

'You're not going to the party?' Maeve said, carrying bags of groceries.

'What party?'

'Ash and Simon went with a bunch of others from the grove. You should go. You can still catch up with them.'

'Nah. I'll stay home. Watch TV.'

'But you love the old power station parties,' Maeve said.

'There's a power station party?'

The old power station had been abandoned for decades. It was boarded up, with no one permitted inside because the building was in a bad state. The parties happened maybe three times a year and weren't authorised. Maeve must be really concerned if she was trying to send me to one.

'That's right. Simon and some of the other boys are going. I figured they'd watch over you and Ash.'

I was so listless I didn't even attempt to reprimand Maeve: if the building fell down, it wasn't like Simon could hold it up with his boy muscles.

'Didn't they tell you?' But Maeve was now putting the shopping in the fridge, the ice cream in the freezer, and wasn't paying me much attention.

Something niggled. Something about a power station party.

Then I remembered. David had been talking about a surprise at the power station. Maybe it was perfectly harmless. But I didn't like the thought of them all at the same venue together. Especially since it was odd that Aisling hadn't dragged me with her; we'd always gone together.

'Maeve, I think I will go. Would you mind dropping me there? I'll catch a ride back with Ash and Simon.'

'There's my Wren.' Maeve was delighted. 'Of course I'll drive you. Now go and put on something pretty. There's a good girl.'

At home, in the middle of my bedroom floor, was the not-brídeog. I almost didn't notice her any more.

Instead, my attention was taken by a short note in Aisling's handwriting on the bedside table.

After I'd changed, I went downstairs, clutching the doll. Outside, I handed it to Maeve. 'Please, get rid of this for me.'

In my other hand I held the crumpled-up note from Aisling: *Wren, I'm sorry.*

The abandoned power station was a solitary building out on the marsh, two villages over. A long time since it had been in use, the building was near derelict.

Inside, a crush of bodies danced in the blue light. It was packed, much more than the last time I'd been here, which was a shame. The desolate half-empty space mixed with wild music had been part of the appeal.

I searched through the crowd downstairs. The blue light changed faces, made them almost grotesque. I pushed through people dancing, people at the bar, but I couldn't see anyone I recognised.

Near the stairwell was a chill room with a mandala light show playing on a large screen. The mandalas formed slowly with a jagged line of light, then disintegrated until a single strand remained and then re-formed into a new shape. At the best of times mandalas were irresistible: they invited meditation and were a tool for inducing trances. At an impromptu club where the lights made me feel a little trippy, it was impossible not to be drawn in. I went to the doorway and stared, feeling a prick of excitement. That hunger.

Around me, people danced in the light: blue, red, then blue again. I focused on the image so intently that I became lost in the creases and folds of the lines that moved from squares to triangles to rectangles. That pricking in my palms and heart. The tingling started, and it felt so good.

But I saw nothing. Instead, I suddenly felt a pain so intense that I doubled over. My bones breaking, then melting into a hot liquid as they re-formed. My skin tightened, hardened. I felt light-headed, like I might escape from the top of my head and wisp away in the lights and smoke and music.

'You all right there?' said a voice beside me. A boy stood there, frowning with concern.

'I'm OK.'

As I straightened, I saw Laney a few feet away. Her white-purple hair took on the colour of the lights. She was walking towards the other end of the large room. I followed her through the crowd. She went down the length of the room and then slipped through a partition. Waiting a moment, I did too.

There, staying within the darkened recess, I saw David and Tarc facing each other. They were both bare to the waist, caught in a strobe of blue light. Covered in sweat, they were breathing heavily and giving each other the stink eye. They'd been fighting. Cillian stood between Tarc and David. Around them was a circle of boys, maybe a dozen, all stripped to the waist. Watching them, I felt that taste of soil in my mouth, that cool, earthy tang.

'Round two?'

They both nodded. David spat on the floor. And then they were at each other, fists pounding, the sound of hands smacking against skin. The music from the other side of the partition was loud, the beats punctuating their blows.

Laney walked around the circle of boys, heading for Cillian.

David cracked his fist against Tarc's jaw, and from the way he twisted it obviously hurt. Tarc launched at David, bringing him down. As he fell I saw that David had the lines of the Bláithín symbol tattooed near his hipbone. Just like Tarc.

Agitated, Laney was talking to Cillian. He held out his hands, turning away from her. But Laney grabbed his whistle and blew it hard. The boys broke apart.

'Stop,' Laney called. 'We can't do this tonight. They're here.'

'We'll sort them out afterwards,' said David, getting to his feet.

'There's a crowd of them. More than we thought,' she said. 'You can't fight them with cracked ribs. And you can't pull your punches when competing for Raker.'

'Don't worry, Davey,' Tarc said, reaching for his shirt. 'I'll beat you up another time.' He turned to Laney. 'Where are they?'

'Upstairs, behind the bar.'

'What are we waiting for?' one of the gardeners called. The others started shouting.

Tarc let out a single piercing whistle and they shut up, gathering around him. I retreated through the partition, shaking. It was worse than I thought.

This *was* an apostrophe, a big fucking apostrophe.

TWENTY-NINE
Girl of leaf and petal

*I have not seen Elizabeth since wickerlight. I think that
she is jealous that I was chosen.*

AdC

Pushing through the crowd, I went to the stairwell, past a
couple kissing on the stairs. Through the dance floor to the
upstairs bar, and there they were. Simon and Aisling. A
bunch of guys with them. I felt a pull, telling me I was near
strong augurs.

'Wren.' Aisling was wide-eyed when she saw me. 'What
are you doing here?'

'What's going on, Ash?' I looked at the augurs behind
her. They were restless, waiting to move. Whiskey in hand,
but poised. Alert.

'I know you care for him,' she said as she looked at me
sadly. 'I'm sorry you've been put in this position.'

'You have to get out of here, Ash.'

'We're doing this for you, Wren,' Simon said. He

seemed older, like he'd been carrying a heavy load this last while.

'Doing what? What's going on?'

'It was foolish, attempting to kidnap Cassa,' Aisling said. 'Much better to get her where it really hurts.'

Tarc. I'd told them Tarc was Cassa's weakness.

'She'll do anything to protect him,' Aisling went on. Give up nemeta, tell Simon where the stones were. 'Pay anything in ransom.'

It was a more decisive plan than Smith and Maeve's. It was also far more wrong.

'They know you're here,' I said. 'They've known all along.'

'So, they're expecting us.' She shrugged but her mouth was a tight line. 'We're not afraid of a fight.'

'It's not just Cassa's boys.' My voice was low with urgency. 'The crowd from Birchwood are here. You can't take on all of them. Not here. Not without hurting innocent people.'

'That's not what Canty said,' Simon interrupted. 'It was supposed to be Tarc and David.'

I looked at the four guys who'd come from Abbyvale. And about three from our own grove. There were way more gardeners downstairs. Trained fighters who delighted in their history of brutality.

'It will be a bloodbath, Ash. You can't do this.'

I looked at the boys behind her. They were ready, adrenalin pumping, excited to release years of pent-up frustration by getting into a fight with Cassa's boys. It had been coming to this all along. I didn't know why Smith was so adamant we could avoid violence. It seemed inevitable to me. But not tonight, if I could help it.

Aisling looked away.

'Get them out of here, Ash,' I said. 'Before it's too late.'

If it wasn't too late already.

Aisling hesitated. Then relented.

'Come on,' she called to the boys. 'We're leaving.' And then to me, 'You with us, Wren?'

'I'll find my own way back.' I had to talk to Tarc.

Aisling fixed her eyes on mine, a slight raise to her eyebrows.

'Who are you trying to save tonight? Us? Or him?' And then she walked away, the augur boys following behind.

'We're going to do this, Wren,' Simon said as he passed me. 'Not tonight, but soon. This is going to happen.'

I closed my eyes for a moment as they left. Then I followed a little way, watching them walk towards the wide staircase where a line of boys were coming up. Gardeners. And they were looking for trouble.

For a minute, I thought my attempts to avert the fighting had been in vain. Augurs walked down while gardeners stood like sentries every second step, watching them go. The hatred was palpable. I stepped back, keeping out of sight. I could see the physical restraint it took for them not to tear into each other. I could only guess they'd been told not to act until Tarc gave the command.

During that long minute the tension was unbearable. Then the augurs were gone. Two gardeners followed to make sure they were leaving. The rest talked among themselves, then started downstairs, either to drink or fight.

'Tarc,' I said, stepping forward. He'd been lagging behind, checking upstairs for stray augurs. And there I was.

'What are you doing here?' He came towards me, pulling me out of the line of vision of the remaining gardeners. 'Were you with them?'

'I came to stop them,' I said. 'I don't want anyone hurt.'

There was a long silence.

'Yeah? Too late for that.' He turned to go and I lunged at his shirt.

'Wait.'

He was too close.

'Why are you here?'

'I'm working, Wren.' He sounded tired. Fed up. I was too.

'Working or fighting?'

'You saw?'

'A little. Why would you want that, Tarc? Why would

you want to be the Raker, the most ruthless and brutal killer? Isn't being a gardener enough? Must you be the biggest badass too?'

'All for you.' He gave a mock bow.

'This has nothing to do with me.'

'I have no desire to be the biggest badass, as you so eloquently put it. Becoming Raker is my worst nightmare. After my dad … I wasn't going to compete.'

'So that's why you were beating the crap out of David downstairs.' I folded my arms.

'That fighting you saw? We're battling it out for the girl of leaf and petal. Because that's what the Raker does. He's protector of the Bláithín.'

'The Bláithín has a special protector?' Cassa hadn't told me this.

'Do you know that David ranks second in our class?' he said. 'Do you know what happens if he wins? The connection between the Bláithín and her protector is for life.'

'You shouldn't.' I realised what Tarc was doing. For me. 'Not if you dread it so much.'

He lifted his shirt and pushed down his waistband, showing me the five-looped tattoo. 'This is only the outline. It means I'm a contender, because of my family. It's not complete. It will only be filled in if I win the title. All my life, this is what has been expected of me. My parents, Cassa. This is all they wanted from me.'

I touched my finger to the tattoo, tracing the top loop.

'I'd hate it if it's David.' Even though I was planning to leave at the first chance I got, that bond would chafe.

'I know,' he said. 'So would I.'

'Do what you must. But don't do it for me.'

I didn't want Tarc to become something that might destroy him. Not when he called it his worst nightmare. Not for me, anyway.

There was no quiet around us that night, not with music pumping through the speakers, drunk kids shrieking and laughing. Someone lurched beside me, spilling her drink with a loud 'Whoaaa'. But I didn't know what to say, and my silence was laboured.

'I'm sorry,' I said eventually. 'For not being honest with you. And because you now have a bunch of augurs out to get you.'

'That was always going to happen.' He made me hear it. That he was my enemy. That there would always be hostility between us. He stepped back. 'They're waiting for me.'

'What happened between me and you wasn't a lie.' The words spilled out too quickly before he turned away. 'I wasn't using you like that.'

He stood there, like there were all these things he wanted to tell me but couldn't get them out.

A loud, particularly sweary song began. He couldn't seem to help the smile that now shaped his lips. The lights flashed to red, and for a short while, I wanted to pretend.

'Come on,' I reached out to him. 'Dance with me. We can go back to being all awkward with each other on Monday.'

'I should go.'

But before he could leave, I grabbed his hand. I held it firmly in mine, feeling the callouses, the hard, long fingers.

I drew him to the edge of the dance floor. A light drizzle of glitter rained from the centre of the ceiling.

And I danced in the falling glitter. Drawn by my movements, Tarc danced with me. As we moved together, his hand hit my hip. The first time it was probably an accident. Then it landed there and he pulled me closer. He dipped his mouth to my ear.

'I should go,' he said again, hardly audible through the music. But he didn't.

Something had changed in the room. There was a feeling of a shared frenzy as the throng jumped up and down. Only we were slow and sure in a crowd gone wild. The lights changed to a steady ice blue. The glitter fell faster and harder. People turned gold and silver.

'I should go,' he said for a third time. And still he didn't move. Grudgingly, he took his hand from my hip and closed it over my fingers. Two steps forward. I dug my heels in. I didn't want this to end.

'I don't like the mood here.' His mouth at my ear. We went another two steps.

The crowd had surged towards us. They jumped up and down in a steady rhythm, as if beating the floor with their feet. The very foundations seemed to shake with the fury and passion that swelled. Then, right before my eyes, the ground opened. The floor gave way, taking with it a large crowd of dancers in a cloud of dust. One minute they were dancing, jumping and shaking. And the next, they were just gone. Nothing but the rising dust swallowing the swirling glitter, and the sound of screams below and around me. The fall shook me, and it took a moment to find my balance.

For a second I wasn't sure if I'd imagined it. But the screams went on, the furious push of the crowd away from the huge crater. The boy from earlier in the evening, the boy who'd asked if I was OK, dangled from the edge and then fell the long drop to the floor below. The ice-blue light flickered: now you see it, now you don't.

'Tarc!' I shouted, but my cry was swallowed by the noise.

Through the dust, people ran screaming towards the stairs. A gaping hole yawned where the dance floor had been just seconds ago. Where the throng of dancers had plunged twenty feet. A few people were clinging on, their hands clutching the broken edge. Tarc was trying to help someone up. I moved towards the girl closest to me as she tried to heave herself over.

People surged forward and pushed into me. I felt a sharp jab against my back. Trying to stay on my feet, I was carried along in the tide moving to the exit. I turned round, pushing against the swell of people. But it was useless; another shove and I went down, falling between the running legs and feet.

I broke my fall with my hands and tried to get up. But the crowd kept coming in a relentless wave. Someone stamped on my hand causing me to cry out. A heavy foot on my thigh.

A hand grabbed on to the back of my dress and yanked me to my feet. I tried to see who helped me but I couldn't. I surged forward with the crowd, and in the next lull I moved to the side. I surged forward again, and then to the side.

Now at the edge of the crowd, I couldn't see Tarc anywhere.

I'd been to the old power station a few times, and as luck would have it, I'd kissed a nice boy in the fire escape on the other side. There was an emergency exit and a narrow flight of stairs on the opposite side of the chasm. I could cross at the bar area, but everyone was pushing towards the main exit. I'd be going against the tide and I'd get nowhere. Or I could cross an extremely narrow, insecure strip of floor along the opposite wall.

The crowd still pushed and pressed towards the stairs. It didn't seem that they were moving at all. From below, I smelled smoke.

I moved towards the narrow strip and began crossing, shuffling one careful foot and then the other. I pressed my back against the wall, trying not to look down. As I crossed, I could feel the pulsing light on my face and hear the sounds of screaming and the stink of burning.

There weren't many people on the far side. The few that remained stared down into the void, transfixed. One sat down, sobbing. Another ran around aimlessly, shouting incoherent words.

I took a last look around the room. I had to believe that Tarc would find his way out. I swept my eye over the crater and saw a figure hanging on to the edge with both hands. He was trying to climb up, but it was hard with the floor so unstable. I took a step towards him, uncertain. If the floor gave, we would both go tumbling down.

And then I saw it was David.

I hesitated. It would be easy to let him fall. He'd never bother me again. I watched him hanging over the smoke-filled pit. I could see the jagged edges of snapped metal rods. I could hear people screaming with pain.

David's fingers slipped.

I lay down flat, reaching out both hands. The floor

beneath my arms strained as he pulled. It felt like he was dragging me in. But just as he gained purchase, part of the floor fell away and I screamed. David was let loose, dangling worse than before.

Then I felt the hands on my hips as someone pulled me back. And as I retreated, David pushed with his forearms while gripping my hands tightly. My hips were weighted down by someone holding on to them from behind. I couldn't turn to look, but I knew who it was. He held me strong and secure. David's head emerged above the floor. I sat up to help him as he crawled to safety, then he fell down on his back. I scrabbled away from the edge like a crab. David lay still, his chest rising and falling.

'We have to get out of here,' I said, getting to my feet. My lungs were tight. Tarc's hand clamped down on my wrist and he pulled me up.

'Let's go.'

'This way,' I said, pointing to the corner of the room.

'The stairs are over there.' He pointed to the opposite end of the room, across the yawning gulf, where bodies still pressed too close.

'Emergency exit,' I said, and the two boys followed me.

Tarc looked sceptically at the door like I was about to drag him to a storeroom. Grabbing a chair, I propped it open and pulled him through. On the other side was a narrow stairwell. We ran down to a door with a crash bar. I pushed against it but nothing happened. David and Tarc both worked at it but there was no give.

'It's jammed,' David said, pointing to a mangled Allen key that had been inserted in the bar, presumably to lock it at some point. The building was abandoned, whoever supervised it was probably more concerned about keeping people out than the proper procedure for emergency exits. The two boys heaved and pushed against the door until it broke. We fell into the cold marsh outside and away from the smoke and dust. I took in big gulps of the clean air.

It was raining, large, almost painful drops. At the front of the building the emergency services were arriving. Cold, ragged partygoers watched in shock. I didn't want to think about the people inside.

'I need to get away from here,' I said. I felt panicked by my need to escape.

'Me too,' Tarc said. He looked pale, unsettled. David was on his phone, and from what I could hear, Laney and the other gardeners were on the far side of the building.

I texted Aisling, relieved when her message pinged to my phone, saying they were at the Lacey farm.

Before he set off to find Laney, David shuffled uncomfortably.

'Thanks.'

Across the marsh were ambulances, guards and a multitude of vehicles whose flashing lights signalled the horror of what had happened.

A helicopter circled and we ran off into the wet night, losing ourselves in the marsh. We made it to the road when the rain stopped.

'Where's your car?' I said, shivering.

'I came with David,' Tarc said. 'I'll get you a taxi.'

'I want to walk.'

'It's too far.'

'Just for a while.'

We trudged through quiet roads, passing a petrol station, a row of shops where blank-faced mannequins stared out of the windows. We'd been walking for about twenty minutes when I stopped suddenly. I bent over with the weight of it: that awful lead in my gut. I closed my eyes, hearing the screams of the people who had fallen.

'You're soaked. I'm calling a taxi,' Tarc said, taking out his phone.

We'd stopped in a small tunnel beneath a bridge. From the motorway above, I could hear the muffled sound of zooming cars. The tyres crossed the expansion joints, and from the tunnel it sounded like a heartbeat.

But I didn't want to go home just yet. I didn't know how I could sleep without seeing all those people who'd been dancing in glitter and fog, not realising what would happen in the next minute.

Another car drove above us, and the heartbeat thumped again.

'Do you think they're OK?' I said. 'All those people who fell?'

'Some of them will be.' Which meant that some of them wouldn't. Thump, thump from the cars above us.

'There's something you should have,' Tarc said. He pulled a small book from his jacket pocket and handed it to me. 'Arabella's journal. Read it before you do the ritual.'

I took it from him. The rain had washed away the dust, but silver and gold glitter still clung to his face.

'Don't tell Cassa I gave it to you,' he said.

'Tarc,' I began. There was so much to say, but still I couldn't. I stared down at the book, wishing I could explain.

'Yes?' But his voice was cold and whatever truce we'd called had come to an end.

'Thank you.'

My taxi turned the corner. As I walked from under the bridge, I heard the last heartbeat as a car on the bridge crossed the expansion joints.

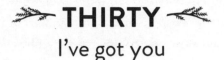

THIRTY
I've got you

*They come to me all the time now. They are drawn
like moths to a flame.*
AdC

The next day was the equinox, and I had to read the egg
from the divining hen.

On the fridge, held by a small magnetic photograph of
Smith and me, I found Maeve's instructions, which included
fasting, incense and dancing in the forest. She'd also left her
flowery bag with a hip flask of sherry and a vial of something that smelled disgusting.

I was glad Smith was out. I didn't need an audience for
any part of this. Looking through kitchen drawer, I found
the cones of incense and frankincense tears. Maeve's instructions, bafflingly, called for a pure stone. There were some
stones I'd brought home long ago from a beach at Spiddal,
and I went to look for them in the shed.

Smith must have cleared it out. The floor was pristine,

no bird shit anywhere. But there were new tools, tins of paint in the corner. Stone in hand, I shut the shed door. Somewhere inside the cottage my phone rang, but I ignored it.

In the bathroom, I burned frankincense on the flat stone and stepped into the hot water. Easing down, I immersed myself in the heat. I opened Arabella's journal, breaking several of Laney's rules for handling old books.

It was a slim book, written in a neat, old-fashioned hand. The diary entries were erratic and not chronological. It seemed that Arabella eschewed the left to right page order and chose to write entries in the middle of the book, at the back or three months earlier. It didn't help that not all the entries were dated. The effect was a jumbled mess. But there was one thing that Arabella was adamant about: *I am not mad. I am in full possession of my faculties. I choose an alternative way to frame my experiences of this world. I am not mad.*

The journal half read, I put it down and got out of the bath. The game in the woods. That's what she called it. I dried myself, still mulling it over, trying to make sense of the non-chronological order. I was more than a little unnerved by Arabella's strange cravings.

Wrapped in a towel, I went to my bedroom to find a white dress. There was only the old one that had once belonged to Sorcha.

Maeve had said to keep my mind focused. There was one purpose to this reading: I was looking for faster ways to forge binds to the nemeta. Maeve had warned me that if there were too many questions crowding my mind, the egg reading would be confused. I had to stay clear. Push away unnecessary thoughts. I had to focus on finding a faster way to bind to the nemeta, that was all.

Purified and dressed in white, I headed out into the twilight to read the egg.

In the trees behind the cottage, I placed the bowl with the egg on a stump and burned the incense. Waving my arms, I walked three times anticlockwise, as demanded by the instructions. Feeling the cold wind through the dress, I took a deep glug of sherry.

Three times clockwise, my arms swaying exuberantly. A jaunty shake in my step. I might as well enjoy it.

Opening the vial that Maeve had prepared, I drank it down. It tasted as bad as it smelled. The next step was 'letting go', so I twirled and danced between the trees. Raising my arms high, I began the invocation of the ancestors that Maeve had written out for me.

I drew the knife along my palm then opened my hand over the bowl. Blood dripped into it. Mumbling the rest of the words, I picked up the egg and cracked it. I didn't understand the Old Irish but Maeve had assured me it was a call to my ancestors to guide me. I hoped that I hadn't accidently called a plague upon myself by mispronouncing one of the unfamiliar words.

The yolk spread and mixed with my blood. Maeve had warned not to go all spinny eye on the egg, but to read the position of the yolk and blood in relation to the bowl, the direction it faced, how it ran or glooped, much as the ancient augurs had read the flight patterns of birds.

Staring down into the bowl, I began to feel light-headed. My hand was still bleeding. Egg white, yolk and blood swirled at the bottom. I tried to read the slobbery muck, but it was just an egg mixed with blood.

It was nearly dark and I was getting nothing. I should probably have had a practice round with a normal egg. I reached in the flowery bag for my Lego Wonder Woman key ring that shone light from her feet. Maeve had said five minutes to get a reading. Otherwise it was a dud. I pointed Wonder Woman into the bowl and stared harder.

'Is there a faster way to bind to nemeta?' I whispered the question again and again.

And felt myself slipping. I tried to stop it but hunger, the stink of incense and the loss of blood meant I had little resistance. The strange drink combined with the sherry had made my head foggy. I tried to examine them separately: the egg yolk, the stringy goo of the chalaza. The blood trailing through the yolk. But as I clung on, I could feel my grasp slipping further. There was a small shard of shell in the bowl, stabbing the centre of the yolk.

When it hit, it was harder than any other I'd experienced. Bliss and despair rolled through me in an awful mix.

The trees around me receded and I could see a lamp, the lines of an armchair behind it. I was screaming, my voice hoarse. A tangle of dread was fixed in my chest. I saw Tarc with a gun. The trees and the ghost living room blended together, the room with its furniture now superimposed on the woods. There was a look of determination on his face. It was Tarc, and I barely recognised him. Cold and unyielding, he looked straight ahead, ignoring my screams. The gun in his hand was pointed at Smith.

And then it all turned to black.

Crumbled on the forest floor, the living room had receded. But I could still see Tarc in front of me, as if he'd been snatched out of the vision and brought into the woods.

'I've got you,' Tarc said, helping me up.

I wanted to say something, but my teeth were chattering. Instead, I looked away. All around was the evidence of what I had been doing. The bowl with blood and yolk. My cut hand hastily bound with a piece torn from his shirt. I reached for the bowl, the knife and the incense. I couldn't pick them up because I was shaking too much. I hadn't felt cold during the ritual but it hit me now with fierce, juddering shivers. A vicious pain sliced through my head and it took everything not to sink to the forest floor and hold on to it. Tarc took off his hoodie and draped it around me. In silence, he picked up the things I'd left on the ground. Drawing me to his side, we walked towards the cottage.

I'd failed Maeve. I didn't get the answer she needed.

At the edge of the woods, at the small path that led behind Maeve's garden to Smith's, we heard a voice in the near darkness.

'That's far enough. I'll take it from here.'

Maeve stood there, short and dumpy, yet strangely magnificent. She wore her puffy winter coat with its line of fake fur that hid her curls and her face was blotted out by the light from the cottage behind her.

'She shouldn't have been alone,' Tarc said.

'She's not alone.'

'I'm fine,' I said to him. I still didn't understand why he was there or how he'd found me. 'It's better if you go.'

He looked at me like he was fighting back words.

Then he said, 'Cassa sent for you. It's time. Wickerlight will happen tonight.'

THIRTY-ONE
The end of the world

Elizabeth, I am sorry. I wish you could hear me now.
AdC

I was aware of Tarc's gaze on me every now and then as
we drove out of the quiet road and away from Carraig
Cottage.

I leaned against the headrest, my eyes shut, hoping it
would ease my raging head. But when I closed my eyes, all
I could see was Tarc aiming a gun at Smith.

'Are we going back to the city?' I said.

'The ritual will take place here in Kilshamble.'

It made sense that it would happen in the ruined cottage.
I didn't mind that so much. I liked the cottage, I felt at
peace there. I closed my eyes again.

After a minute, Tarc spoke. 'What did you see back there
in the woods?'

'The end of the world.' I kept my eyes shut.

I could sense that he wanted to ask more questions. I

could feel his curiosity about what I'd been doing, about augur ways.

The car stopped, and when I opened my eyes I saw we were parked on Kilshamble's main street, near the church. As I climbed out of the car and looked across the road, I saw Cassa and Laney ahead.

'No,' I said, staring at the village green. The old shambles. 'Not there.'

Tarc looked at me. 'The old slaughter grounds are exceptionally fertile.' His voice sounded dull and suddenly, even though he was right there with me, I really missed him.

He went to the boot and swung a large duffel bag over his shoulder. Down the road, another car approached.

Cassa was standing on the green, her face turned up to the full moon. I couldn't see the colour of the grass, but I didn't need to. I remembered its vividness. The faint metallic smell.

'Let's go,' Tarc said.

I hesitated. I didn't want to end up in a cottage in the woods. I didn't want to end up haunting gardens at midnight and trailing my coat through the muck.

The approaching car stopped on the main street.

'Who else is coming?' I said. I'd thought it would be just Cassa, Laney and Tarc.

'David,' Tarc said. 'Cillian. Brian and Ryan.' He shifted. 'All the newest gardeners.'

I looked down at Sorcha's white dress beneath Tarc's hoodie. Virgin sacrifice duty. I looked at Cassa on the green, the boys tumbling out of the car. Their laughter boomed across the green. I remembered the feel of crumbs of soil in Cassa's pocket.

'I can't do this.'

David and Cillian stood beside their car, David looking in our direction. He stood there, legs apart and folded his arms across his thick torso.

'Tarc,' I said, keeping my eye on the boys. 'Your snake tattoo. Why two heads?' The words tumbled out in a hushed urgency.

'The mark of the gardener warns there is always danger in the garden. The forked head suggests things might not be as they seem.'

'All the gardeners defend the Bláithín, but the Raker is her special guard. So you, or David, or maybe one of the others, would be the protector? And I would be the fragile flower?'

'Some might see it that way.'

'Sod that,' I said, and he almost laughed.

'I told you it would change things.'

'I can't do this,' I said again. Across the way, Cassa and

Laney were conferring, her fair head leaning towards Laney's white-purple. They were deep in discussion. The boys were on the green, moving towards us. Towards me. David kept his eyes on me as he advanced. Cillian at his heels.

And I knew what Cassa's ritual would be like. We'd been there before: in the ghost housing estate the moment before they caught me. Trapped in the forest.

Doing this ritual, I would be passive and stuck. The boys would leer, and afterwards they would grab a beer and the last, unfinished wren hunt would finally be complete. David would fulfil the promise he made when he took my hair: I would be defeated. I would submit.

'You should run,' Tarc said suddenly. And I knew that he saw it too. 'Get out of here. Before they get you.'

I looked up at him. There was something gentle and beautiful about the way his eyes fell upon me, searching my face.

'Run. Go to the cottage.'

I didn't need to be told a third time.

Shrugging out of his hoodie, I set off through the main street. An exhilarating freedom worked its way through my veins as my Converse pounded the asphalt.

'Stop her,' I heard Cassa shout.

And then I heard them behind me. First, the running feet

in the distance. Then the whistling call. David and the boys were on the hunt.

I left the road and went into the woods and in between the trees. If I stayed off the path; they would have a harder time finding me.

I pushed on, going faster. I felt a stitch tear through my side but I couldn't stop. I would get home first. I would outrun them.

As I ran, I reached that point of near bliss, where my body no longer felt anything. Not the piercing pain in my head, not my burning lungs.

And I knew this pattern, one that went beyond the meanness of boys or hostility towards augurs. The chase had always been part of something bigger. Like a spider spinning her web and knowing intuitively how to make that perfect shape.

In all those years of running, I'd read the future through a pattern. When it repeats, it gains significance. All the other hunts had been rehearsals. They had happened only in anticipation of – in preparation for – this chase.

The boys didn't matter. They never had. It was my run towards freedom, my acting to ensure my safety that mattered now. Tarc had been wrong: it was not doing the ritual but refusing to do it that changed things. I'd been persuaded to do so much that I didn't want to, and they all added up: stealing information, breaking into the archive, telling a hundred little white lies. But like a slow water leak, every small drip led to irrevocable damage.

Caught up in my thoughts, I didn't see the boulder until it was too late. I was running at full speed when I tripped and went sprawling to the ground, smacking my ribs against a large rock. Tumbling down the slope, I rolled over stones and sticks. The sharp edge of a twig pierced my calf. My face and arms were scraped by the floor of the forest, almost as if it were offended by my refusal. I felt Sorcha's dress ripping before I came to a stop. I sat up, stunned.

Slowly, I picked myself up. It took almost a minute before the dizziness subsided. I started jogging slowly, feebly. My ribs were aching something fierce. I'd come back to my body with a bang. And it hurt like never before. I paused, feeling the air claw into my lungs. My legs shook, refusing to take my weight. I clung on to a tree.

When they caught me it was almost a relief. I couldn't run any more. I'd pushed my body as far as I could. But during the chase, I'd found the clarity I needed to say no to Cassa, to Smith, to Maeve. I'd found the strength to stop running. I knew how to stop being hunted.

'All right,' I panted. 'I'll come back. I'll talk to Cassa.'

But David launched himself at me, tackling me to the

ground. He knocked the air out of me, his weight on my aching ribs.

'Get off,' I said, my hand, still wrapped in Tarc's torn shirt, loosely grabbing on to a stone.

But David didn't seem to hear me. He didn't move and I lay trapped beneath him.

'Get off,' I yelled again, smashing the rock – it was bigger than I thought – hard against his face.

He fell over, grunting and swearing. I stood up slowly, still holding the rock in my hand, and shouted at the others.

'I told you so many times. Just leave me alone.' My voice echoed clear through the woods. The boys watched as I walked away.

Dropping the bloodied rock, I limped through the woods.

No one was home. The lights were on and I let myself in through the back, calling for Smith.

In the kitchen, I stood at the sink and chugged down two glasses of water before hearing the front door open. A cardigan hung on the back of a chair and I pulled it over the torn dress.

'I'm in here,' I called, smoothing my hair and wiping at the dress with a tea towel.

Still dabbing at it, I went into the living room. But it was

Tarc, not Smith, who'd come in. He waited there, the shape and size of him incongruous with the room. I was used to seeing him in the wide, bright halls of Harkness House. Tarc seemed wrong in this room, with its faded wallpaper and cluttered bookshelves. From her spot on the wall, Sorcha smiled at him.

'I meant the ruined cottage,' he said, breathless, as if he'd run all the way. 'I looked for you at Arabella's cottage.'

'Was Cassa very upset?'

He came towards me, examining Sorcha's torn dress. The graze on my face. My mussed-up hair.

'What happened?'

'I fell.' I turned away.

He moved closer, until he was in my line of vision. Forcing me to look at him.

'You can't be here,' I said, feeling that rise of panic even though we were alone. 'My grandfather.'

But Tarc's attention had shifted. He was looking past me, at Smith's war table.

'Wren, what is this?' His voice was steady and yet I heard the alarm there.

'That's just my grandfather's hobby. He's not really planning a big war.'

'Hobby?'

'The war table. It's just a game.'

Hands on my shoulders, he turned me round to face the war table. The rivers, hills, woods and farms were gone. No soldiers, no tanks. In their place was a long, thick rope looped into the Daragishka Knot. At the centre of the first loop was a smooth, oval river stone. In the second, a rough mountain rock. The third was empty. Another smooth stone right beside it.

He turned to me and there was such gentleness in his eyes. 'You don't know, do you?'

'I've never seen this before.' I said, moving towards the table. 'Why would they put it out here?' On the top side of the knot was a sprig of dried meadowsweet, on the left a sprig of whitethorn, and opposite, the new bud of an alder tree. At the core, the lucky acorn that Tarc had given to me.

'They're forming the Daragishka Knot.'

'But we don't have the stones.'

Tarc brushed the hair from my face. 'To make the Daragishka Knot you need a stone from a river, one from a mountain and one from the sea.'

'No, that's not how it works,' I said patiently. Couldn't blame judges for not knowing augur traditions.

But Tarc was touching the first stone. 'The only thing that matters in forming the Daragishka Knot is naming the stones. The first is Betrayal.'

And I saw that the stone had been marked in Ogham.

Even my rudimentary grasp of the alphabet could make out that 'Betrayal' was a very possible translation.

'Then Sacrifice.' He traced the lines on the second stone. 'S, A, C ...'

'No. You've got it all wrong.'

'Naming the stones can only happen through action,' he continued. 'They have to be big gestures. Betrayal, sacrifice, surrender on an epic scale. The betrayal has to cut deep. The sacrifice has to hurt. The surrender has to be a leap into the unknown. Otherwise it won't work. And the bigger the gesture, the more power it has.'

'Maybe that's how it is for the judges, but it's different for us. The Daragishka stones are named for the Crimson River that flows red on Hy-Breasil. Ruairí Ó Cróinín found them.'

'No,' Tarc said. 'The Daragishka Knot is named for the river that flowed red with blood, where the Bláithín found her beloved dying after a battle. The Knot was formed when the Bláithín begged the forest for her lover's life. In return, she had to sacrifice an augur soldier who was injured on the battlefield. She turned her back on her people and surrendered herself to the forest, where she lived as meadowsweet for three years.'

'You're confusing your myths with ours.'

I looked back at the knot on the war table, trying to

think how to begin explaining this to Tarc. I reached out a finger to the rope, then picked up the beach stone.

'Wren, we should leave.' Tarc was right behind me.

'Leave? This is my home.'

The front door pushed open and we both turned, startled.

'What's going on, Wren?' I heard Maeve say. She came into the living room and hung her coat on the row of hooks. She stopped to take off her boots. But her movements were stiff and wooden. My eye fell on the acorn.

'Why's he here?' She placed her boots on the shelf. I slipped the lucky acorn into the slim pocket of my cardigan.

'Tarc was just leaving.' I tried to steer him away but he wouldn't budge.

'What's the sacrifice, Maeve?' Tarc said. 'Who did you betray?'

Her eyes were cold little pebbles. 'Get out.'

'What did you ask for in return? What could be that important?'

'Leave,' Maeve roared. 'Now.'

Tarc made to move, but stopped.

'Come with me, Wren,' he said. 'Please.'

'Go on,' I urged him. He had to get out of there. 'We'll talk tomorrow.'

'They've been lying to you.'

'Out,' Maeve spat.

'Explain to Wren how you tied the Knot. How you named the stones.' Tarc stood his ground.

'Maeve?' I said. 'Tell him he's got it wrong.'

Tilting her head, she turned towards me. I waited for the comforting words, the reassurances. For that way Maeve alone could calm me.

'Have you ever listened, really listened, to Smith talk about his hobby?' Maeve fixed her eyes on mine as she gestured to the table. 'Have you heard him say that warfare is built upon deception? That to truly strike at your enemy you have to make her believe that she has nothing to fear from you?'

'I don't understand.' But a slow terror had started from my gut and was spreading through my body.

'Wren.'

I turned round when I heard Smith call my name and was confronted with a sight so utterly bizarre that I was sure I was in the middle of another vision. Like I'd been staring too long at Maeve's dress, with its wild white daisies.

'Move away from my granddaughter.' Smith spoke from the other side of us. He stood in the wide arch to the kitchen. With a gun.

He aimed the gun at Tarc. 'Move. Now.'

Tarc stepped away from me, towards Smith and the gun. 'Stop,' Smith commanded.

'What are you doing, Smith?' I said. 'Put that down.' His blood pressure must be rising. I didn't want Tarc shot, and I didn't want Smith to have a heart attack.

'Smith?' Tarc said. 'This is your grandfather?'

I looked at him, confused. 'Yes.'

'Oh, Wren,' Tarc said.

And with those two words, something inside me broke.

When I was little, Smith and I had watched a solar eclipse together. We'd sat on the foothills near Kilshamble village and watched as the sun was slowly swallowed by the moon. The day leached of light and I began to feel afraid. It was as though all the light in the world had been drained through a small dark hole. It was different to the usual cloud cover where sunlight was still there but hidden. I was sure that it would never be bright again. And it terrified me.

That was how it felt watching Smith point a gun at Tarc.

'Up against the wall,' Smith said. The way he spoke, the ease with which he held the gun, I could tell that he'd handled one before. In a few easy steps, he was beside Tarc.

Gun to his head, Smith searched him, extracting two knives and another sharp instrument. Then, still training the gun on Tarc, he backed away.

'Put it down, Smith,' I said. 'Please.'

'Go upstairs, Wren. You don't understand what this is about.'

The recognition came quickly: the standing lamp beside Smith and the armchair. I should have known. I should have realised that it was Carraig Cottage in my egg vision. But I'd got it wrong again. It wasn't Tarc who aimed a gun at Smith. It was my grandfather threatening to shoot the boy I'd come to care for more than I should.

I stepped into his line of fire.

'Out of the way,' he said.

My feet were planted to the floor. I understood what he said, but I couldn't do it.

'Move, Wren.'

'No.'

I stood firm, watching as my grandfather held a gun aimed in my direction. With exasperation, he said, 'You're more like your mother than I thought.'

'What do you mean?'

Smith examined me carefully. And when he spoke his words were calculated and precise: 'What do you think I mean?' Each word aimed to hurt. 'I took you from her because I thought I could save you. So you wouldn't turn out like her.' To impose maximum damage. 'But it looks like I was wrong.'

All through this conversation it had felt like last night at the old power station. The ground uncertain beneath me.

'You stole me?'

And this was the moment where the floor gave out. The pain was physical. I wanted to curl up and wrap my arms around myself, because it felt like I was unravelling.

'Sorcha had cut ties with the grove. You were an augur child, I couldn't have you growing up ignorant of who you were. That's why we came to Kilshamble. It was the best place to hide.'

'You took me from my mother?'

'I did it because I love you, Wren.' His voice softened. 'She wasn't suited to motherhood. I wanted the best for you.'

He stood tall, those familiar blue eyes fixed on me. His lean, wiry body had always been a source of warmth and comfort.

'And now, please go upstairs while I sort out this mess.'

He was watching and I realised what he wanted: me paralysed with pain, and out of the way so he could reach his real target.

'No.'

Inexplicably, or perhaps it was a long time coming, I found myself standing between Smith and Tarc. Between augur and judge. In the line of fire.

As he trained the gun on Tarc behind me, I searched Smith's hands for the smallest tremor, his face for cracks in the hardness that encased him. What had Maeve said to Sibéal? *When we act, they won't see it coming.* She was right. Not even I'd seen this coming.

I heard Tarc step to the side, away from the shield of my body. I moved with him, keeping between him and Smith's gun. I could sense Maeve moving too, but I couldn't take my eyes off Smith. I could see him calculating the possible speed and distance. How to shoot Tarc without hurting me.

A car pulled up outside. I heard the doors slam, Aisling laughing.

'Please, Smith,' I said, glancing to the door. 'Put the gun down.'

Footsteps sounded outside the front door, and the girls continued their animated conversation.

And he did. Just before they opened the door, Smith put the gun in his back pocket.

I was shaking when Aisling and Sibéal came in, carrying shopping bags and a huge tinfoil balloon with 'Smokin' Sixteen' on it. It was Sibéal's birthday tomorrow. Their silence was abrupt, almost comic as Sibéal cut off mid-sentence.

Maeve rushed towards Tarc, aiming the cast-iron kettle at

his head. He whirled round catching her hands, obviously reluctant to hurt a lady in a floral dress and stockinged feet. She sank her teeth into his wrist. While he tried to extract himself without hurting her, Smith raised a hurley stick.

'Tarc,' I warned him.

The hurley came down hard against his head. He turned to hold off Smith, but I shouted, 'Don't hurt him.'

I'd seen him fight. I knew the damage he could do.

Tarc held out his hands, palms forward.

'He's sick.' It was little more than a whimper. 'Please.'

'I'm leaving,' Tarc said, hands still out in surrender.

'I'm afraid I have a problem with that,' Smith said. 'I can't have you telling Cassa about any of this just yet.'

'He won't say anything,' I said. 'Just let him go.'

'Wren,' Tarc said, turning slightly towards me.

'You have to go. Please.'

'Come with me.'

I hesitated. 'I can't.'

But he shouldn't have let me distract him. Smith was fast with the hurley, smashing it against Tarc's head. He raised it again, but Tarc caught it, holding the stick until Smith was forced to release it.

'Go!' I screamed. 'Get out of here. I'll find you.' I hoped he understood that I'd meet him at the ruined cottage.

Dropping the hurley, Tarc charged for the door.

Smith pulled the gun from his back pocket and fired. Three shots. Tarc was out of the door and gone. Aisling flattened herself against the wall. Sibéal watched, the balloon bobbing in her hand.

I turned from the door frame with its bullet wounds to Smith. He braced himself against a chair, catching his breath. I didn't recognise the man I saw there. A man who would shoot someone from behind.

Aisling leaned against the wall, pale. Her eyes caught mine, wide and afraid.

'Is Cassa's ritual finished?' Sibéal said.

They all turned to me, realising I was meant to be at the old slaughter grounds.

'I didn't do it,' I said, glad for the rebellion.

'What do you mean you didn't do it?' Smith said.

'I couldn't go through with it.'

Maeve spoke gently. Her special voice that always talked me down. I could almost recognise her. She said, 'Wren, honey, you need to go back there and do the ritual.'

And then it was clear.

'This was always about me becoming the Bláithín,' I said.

I'd never been looking for stones. The plan hadn't changed; this was the destination Smith had mapped out months ago.

'It was last May when I saw the Bláithín symbol in the

clouds,' Maeve said. 'And watched it shift into the Daragishka Knot. I haven't been able to read anything since.'

She came closer, careful, like I was a skittish animal that could bite.

'It was a strong vision. Of the future. A deviation from my usual pattern. I couldn't ignore it.'

She reached a hand towards me, lightly touching my arm.

'That was when I realised what we needed to do.'

Maeve's eyes were beseeching. She wanted me to understand.

And I did understand.

Tarc was right. My family had used me to name Betrayal by lying to me and turning me over to the enemy. Then they named Sacrifice by giving me up to the plan, knowing my augur self would unravel as I moved from Harkness House to Carraig Cottage. But only I could name Surrender. And I wasn't going to do it.

'It should have been me.' Aisling spoke through her tears.

'Did you know, Ash?' I was terrified of what she'd say.

'No,' she cried. 'Simon and I could tell something was off. That they were hiding things. But we didn't know it was this.'

I began to understand how Simon and Aisling had tried

to help. Through their crude attempt to kidnap Cassa and then Tarc, they'd been trying to come up with a counterplan.

'The circle agreed it would be best to keep this from Simon, given your special friendship,' Maeve said, sounding utterly reasonable.

'Why, Maeve?' I said. 'What did you get in return for me?'

'If you had any real sense of pattern, you'd feel it,' Maeve said. 'When the judges are strong, we weaken. When we are at our best, they diminish. This is what we asked from the Knot. This is how we become powerful.'

I looked at Smith. 'How could you agree to this?' He just shook his head, shoulders slumped.

'It's not too late, Wren.' Sibéal came up to me. 'Go back. Do the ritual. This is our big chance.'

'But at what cost?'

She shifted, impatient, and said, 'You can't blame us for acting to save ourselves.'

'Was it you, Shibs? Did you set the fire in Cassa's walled garden?' I said, suddenly bone tired.

She held her chin square and nodded.

I looked around the room at the people I loved: Smith who'd stolen me as a baby for some kind of twisted salvation; Maeve who'd betrayed me; Aisling, who'd tried to kidnap Cassa. Even me, who'd hit Tarc when he trusted me. Who are we? I thought to myself. How did we become this?

'And you think you're innocent?' Maeve spoke out. 'You lied to Cassa. You lied to Tarc. You spied on Harkness House. You used your position to leak information. You told us that Birchwood was the gardeners' training academy. You broke into the archive. You stole the master list of the judges' nemeta. You leaked it to the people who destroyed these sites and you think your hands are clean?'

She came a little closer. 'What do you think Tarc will say about that?'

'I didn't know,' I said, my voice weak as I realised that the map I'd stolen revealed the nemeta locations. Nemeta that were now destroyed.

'That's no excuse.' Maeve's words were hard. 'You chose to lie. You chose to steal. You are every bit as involved.'

She was right, I had made those choices. I might not have understood the scale of what was happening, but I was guilty as charged.

'We've come this far, Wren. There's no point in stopping now,' she said. 'Just take that final step, and then it's done. Everything will be different if you do that ritual.'

'How is it that we're worse than them?' I said.

With the list of nemeta, augurs could weaken judges through continued attacks. I guessed that augurs were stealthily re-forming binds under the cover of darkness. The judges had stopped the Abbyvale three, but it would be a lot harder to contain if all the undamaged nemeta were targeted for rebinding. Especially if Maeve had found out how to forge binds faster, as she'd asked from the egg divination. And if I did the ritual, they would have an augur installed in Harkness House. I would be heir to half of Cassa's empire. And we would have formed the Daragishka Knot.

Maeve's eyes were shining as she moved closer to me. 'If Cassa's right about the ritual bringing on a magical revolution, then think what we could become. Both the Knot and the Bláithín would be ours. For the first time, we would be stronger than them.'

She stood before me and I looked past her, staring at the open door where Tarc had run out.

'We can use the very weapon she constructed to bring Cassa down.'

Not a girl who was like her very own daughter, but a weapon.

'You believe.' My eye on the bullet holes. 'You believe in Cassa's ritual.'

'Not at all,' Smith said. 'That's not the plan.'

'I think it is, for Maeve.' Two holes split the wood on the white frame.

Her chin proud, she acquiesced.

'I would have done anything for the grove.' I stepped away from them. 'Had you been honest, maybe even the ritual. But you lied. You gambled on my loyalty.'

They may as well have stuffed me in a wicker man and set it alight.

'And now you've lost.' I had nothing more to say to them.

I turned out of the house, gripped by a rising terror, and ran.

'Wren,' Smith called after me, but I didn't stop. I had to get to the ruined cottage. I had to find Tarc.

Two holes, but there'd been three shots fired.

And again that night, I found myself running through the forest. As I ran, I was lost in a loop of images that played through my mind. Pyjama bottoms with grey hearts. Greeting the gargoyles. Shouting for echoes in the quarry. Scrabble tiles forming impossible words. My hand entwined in Aisling's as we sat on my bed. Sibéal and Smith bent over the war table. Sugar buns and snapdragon dresses.

I was near Arabella's cottage when I heard the slight rustle. And in my head, that song.

Beneath the oak my love does lie.
A sword through his heart, an arrow in his eye.
Blood in his mouth, blood on my hands.

'Shut up!' I hissed.

And there at the foot of a tree was the bright-red floral cloth. In the moonlight, I thought I could make out the blank face, the plant legs and arms. The not-brídeog. Something twisted inside me. Going towards the doll, I picked it up and stared, before hearing the soft grunt. I turned to the cottage, wary. Cautiously, I went inside. And found Tarc.

His face was slick with sweat, his hair matted. He was lying there, unmoving, his breathing shallow. A pool of blood beneath his leg.

'Tarc,' I said as I bent over him, dropping the doll.

His eyes were open but unfocused. The way he'd run out of Carraig Cottage, I was so sure he was OK. That Smith had missed. But I was wrong.

'I'm here.'

I pushed a fallen branch under his leg to raise it. Using my dress, I pressed the heel of my hand to his leg. My other hand, sticky with blood, reached into his pocket and pulled out his phone. But before I called Laney, I paused, looking into the dark woods.

'I surrender.'

I spoke out loud, not knowing if it would work. I hadn't started the Knot. I didn't have a sea stone to mark in Ogham and place inside the loop. I didn't know if my request would be heard above Maeve's. All I had was the forest, the trees. The strength of my feeling. The idea that they'd looked on this boy with some favour at least once before.

I took the acorn from my pocket, warming it with my fingers. 'I surrender to the ritual. I will be the Bláithín, if you just save him.'

I pulled him closer. He felt so cold, Tarc whose skin was always so warm. Wrapping my arms around him, I called Laney and told her where to find us.

'My mother left when I was a baby,' I told him. 'I was named for the wren, the druid bird. I am an augur with a spinny eye. It's a curse not a blessing. My first memory is of trees. I first saw your eyes, your tattoo, the day I turned sixteen.' He lay there half on my lap, drifting in and out of consciousness, and I told him who I was.

'Wren,' Tarc spoke.

He was still weak, but his eyes were focused now.

'Easy there,' I said, touching my hand to his bloodied face. 'Looks like Smith's bullet got you.'

'What have you done, Wren?' Tarc said, his grey eyes more liquid than ever.

'Only what I had to.'

He looked like he wanted to say more.

'Shhh,' I told him, drawing him closer to me. 'Everything will be OK.'

I remembered Cassa's words in the scorched walled garden. You can choose to be the kind of person who burns, or one who rises from the ashes. I hadn't believed, I still wasn't sure I did. But that's what I was going to do. As long as I could keep moving, I would rise. I would soar.

That's how they found us, my body bent over Tarc like a question mark. In Arabella's cottage.

I couldn't believe how the village didn't see it. The circle of boys wearing only black jeans, their bodies marked with dark swirling lines. The fire that burned at the heart of the shambles. I couldn't understand how they didn't hear the low drumbeats, the chanting from the old slaughter grounds.

I was seated in the sea of unnatural green. Green as my eyes, green as my father's fingers. The cloying scent of perfume. The kiss of a thousand flowers. Beneath me, a bed of white peonies. My bones turned to liquid as the peonies seemed to twine around me. Their stems curling around my ankles, creeping up my leg.

Cassa's voice sounded all the while. She spoke in Old Irish, sometimes laying her hands on me, sometimes reaching out and pulling from the sky, the trees, the wind.

One by one, the gardeners came before me. As they kneeled, each of them whispered something I couldn't understand. A promise, a blessing. They touched my forehead with blood and dirt. Then my chest, my hands. They raised a crystal cup to my lips, one small sip.

When it was David's turn, he put his hands to my face, my chest. He cut his hand, dotted my forehead with his blood. As he raised the cup to my mouth I thought I saw something mocking in his eyes, a big final 'Gotcha.' But it was hard to be sure with his eye slightly swollen, the gash on the side of his face. Then, with the briefest touch to the ends of my hair, he was gone, replaced by the next gardener. And then the next. Until I was faced with Tarc.

Kneeling before me, he touched his blood to my forehead. Like my dress wasn't already soaked with it. Like it wasn't already on my skin. Under my skin. He moved deliberately, touching a hand to my chest, then held his hand to mine. Palm against palm. Caked blood on his face, his clothes soaked through. He whispered his promise to me, longer than the others, his eyes steady on mine. The drumbeats grew faster, louder. Around us, the gardeners started moving, half dancing, half fighting; fluid, graceful kicks and turns, squats and leaps. Fierce and exuberant. A celebration. I was filled with the vigour of boys.

Cassa handed me what was left in the crystal cup and I lifted it to my mouth, drinking deeply. A dark infusion of herbs, the taste of something rich and sweet.

I watched the gardeners move with the shadows of the flames, until the peonies drew me down entirely. Until the darkness claimed me completely.

THIRTY-TWO
You're awake

Since taking on the lily, I have never felt more in command of my own path. Where I will wander, I am certain I will decide.

AdC

The first thing that registered was the pain. It felt as though every bone in my body had been broken. Everything hurt as I tried to sit up in the bed.

I was in a room in Cassa's apartment. She was in the armchair beside me, her eyes shut. I shifted a little higher and grimaced. I remembered a boulder smacking my ribs. I remembered running through the forest. Cassa's eyes snapped open.

'You're awake,' she said.

Anxiety squatted in my throat and held me from speaking. Something was wrong. I had to call home. Smith would be worried. And Aisling could tell me if I'd hurt anything seriously and ... Then I remembered. The Knot laid out on the war table. Smith with a gun. Tarc pale and cold on stones and twigs and dirt in Arabella's cottage.

Everything had been a lie. Smith had shot Tarc. I gripped the sheets, feeling the blood draining from my face.

'Everything was just perfect.' Cassa's voice was low, soothing.

'Tarc.'

'He's fine. Anxious to see you.' She smiled at me, then reached out to smooth her hand down my hair.

And as she spoke, the door opened and Tarc came in. Seeing I was awake, he froze, his hand on the doorknob. His face had taken a beating, there were red and purple bruises on his temple, down his jaw.

'I'll leave you.' Cassa smiled and walked to the door, where she touched a hand on Tarc's arm.

'Nearly forgot.' She gestured to a potted blood-red peony. 'That's yours.'

And then she left.

'You're OK?' I searched Tarc's face for remnants of what had happened to him.

'I am.' He took my hand. 'I know what you did in Arabella's cottage.'

It seemed so distant, that night in the cottage. His body cold in my arms, his unfocused eyes.

He sat at the edge of the bed and opened his palm. 'This is yours.' The lucky acorn.

I took it from him and drew my knees up in the bed, wrapping my arms around them.

'I owe you my life,' he said.

'The trees saved you.' I had to believe that. I couldn't think of the alternative. 'They've helped you before.'

'Maybe.' He nodded, relieved to have an explanation.

It was my fault he'd been shot. Unable to look at him, my eye fell on the bedcovers, the small embroidered birds escaping their cage. For a long time, we sat in silence while I examined the blue and silver embroidery. The long sash windows. I thought perhaps I should cry, but there was nothing, except exhaustion and a numb anger.

'They betrayed you, Wren.' I felt his voice against my hair and the weight of him as he sat on the bed beside me. He pulled me into his arms. The smell of him filled my nose.

'And I betrayed you,' I spoke into his chest.

Later that week, I went down to the library. It was quiet, early evening light pouring in through high horizontal windows. Fresh poppies standing watch.

I drifted to the wide archive door, which was slightly ajar, and went inside.

Laney had finished unpacking all the boxes and sorting through the chaos. All the shelves had been neatly stacked and small laminated labels marked the cabinets. Soil and rock specimens had been arranged on a display table.

Tarc was there. He stood at the reading desk, looking down at a book. I remembered another time we'd been in the archive together: the day I'd stolen the map. Not the map of the Daragishka stones, but Basil Lucas's map of all the nemeta owned by the judges. And I'd handed it to the augurs.

'It was my fault.' I explained to Tarc how I'd inadvertently handed over the locations of the nemeta.

'We weren't aware that Lucas had compiled the map. There was meant to be only one master list, which Cassa keeps in her safe. He was sometimes a bit rogue.'

'If you didn't order the damage of the augur nemeta, then who did? And how did they know where to look?'

'We didn't,' Tarc said. 'Only our nemeta were damaged.'

'The spray paint on the Lacey stone? The beech tree in Wicklow?'

'That beech was one of ours,' Tarc said. 'Cassa planned to retaliate. She sent Brian out to track down augur nemeta.'

And I tried to remember that night, how Maeve had let me assume that it was an augur tree without saying it outright.

'All those nemeta damaged,' I said. 'Because of what I did.'

Looking over his shoulder, I saw that he was reading a leather-bound copy of Arabella's journal.

'You didn't start a fire, or raise an axe or throw a can of paint,' Tarc said as he shut the book. Before it closed, my eye fell on a line: *Where I will wander, I am certain I will decide.*

'Let's get out of here,' he said.

I was glad to leave. The room was too bright and stylish. Really, I needed a dungeon, some place suitable for misery.

As we walked, Tarc explained. 'We tried to prevent the damage. But our informant wasn't reliable. Some nights we were in the wrong location or got there at the wrong time.'

'Moleskin.' I remembered Tarc holding him up against the wall. 'That was your informant.'

'Yeah, Canty. He played us. Sometimes he'd be spot on, and other times it felt we were on a wild goose chase.'

'He was meeting with augurs too.' I remembered Simon talking about him at the power station.

'The night they damaged the dolmen, we got there as they were leaving. Got into a fight.'

I remembered the morning after, when David had clearly been beaten up.

'As we fought, one man was standing to the side. Just watching. The others listened when he called them off. I heard one of them saying his name. Smith. When I heard you call your grandfather, that's when I knew for sure that the damaged nemeta were linked to what was happening with the Knot.'

Dizzy, I leaned against the wall, feeling it hard and straight on my back. We stood in Cassa's passage, the light streaming in from the tall windows.

'Do you hate me for it?' I asked.

'You didn't know.'

'I lied. I stole.'

'And you've paid a heavy price.' He didn't look at me as he spoke.

'But is it enough?'

We stood there, the weight of the last months between us. Both of us hurt, and the bruises and brokenness on the outside only the barest indication of the damage beneath.

Down the passage, David came in through the garden door. He paused when he saw us, then gave a brief nod. He was uncomfortable.

'Who's going to be Raker?' I asked Tarc.

'Cassa wants me to wait until I'm properly healed before we compete.' From the look on his face, I could see it was a source of tension.

'Hey, David,' I called down the hall. The pink tone in his skin seemed more pronounced than before. 'How many judges does it take to change a light bulb?'

He glanced at me, uneasy. A slight shrug. Then eyes back to the floor. I realised that I unsettled him. That since the ritual, he saw me differently and that perhaps he wouldn't want to be Raker any more. It was almost a reversal of the wren hunt. Since that night when he kneeled before me, it was David who seemed caught.

'Just one.' I smiled. 'To hold the light bulb in place while the world revolves around him.'

David immobile at the garden door, uncertain. Trapped. I stood my ground, staring him down until he was forced to look up. Wresting his eye, I saw something that I'd never seen there before: panic.

'Let's go.' Tarc took my hand. Over my shoulder, I saw David looking furtively in my direction.

As the days stretched out at Cassa's house my body healed. I no longer felt anxious to leave. In those first days, I'd been certain that I needed to find my own place. Maybe leave the city. Find my mother. Cassa might be able to connect me with my father, but I wasn't ready to ask about that yet.

'Stay here, for as long as you need,' Cassa said. 'You'll always have a home with me.'

And I stayed because it was easier. My life felt blank, everything was new and undecided. There was comfort in being with familiar people.

We said nothing about Carraig Cottage. Once, when sitting outside, I reached out my hand to Tarc and said, 'Please don't do anything to them. Please don't let them get hurt in any way.'

He didn't say anything.

'Promise me you'll avoid it as best you can.'

He examined me, my bony grip on his shoulder, and gave a nod so short I almost didn't see it. Maybe I didn't.

I spent much of those weeks outside in Cassa's garden. Little by little, I felt put together again. Less woolly-headed. My sense of taste had been restored and I no longer had an appetite for banana peels and apple cores. I didn't see that much of David and his boys. He was still wary and kept a distance. The others followed his lead.

Of Cassa's ritual in the old shambles there was little evidence. Every morning I would wake, testing myself to see what remained the same. But it was hard to tell because everything had changed. At night, I would scream through tortured dreams of being snared by the forest. I had nightmares of people stepping out of trees and welcoming me into their fold. In my dreams, they fed me soil and rubbed bark on my bare skin. Smeared petals into my hair.

But I did not feel invincible. I did not have it all.

'See that flower,' Cassa had whispered over my shoulder, after placing her orchid beside my new potted peony. 'Cast all your weakness on to it. That flower is still and pretty. You are so much more.'

I stared at the peony. One closed bud. I felt it, the pull of the peony, as a judge might to her totem. But nothing more.

I was in my room brushing my hair at the mirror, my peony on the dressing table. My skin was clear and my eyes bright after months of looking dull. The stress of the deception must have taken a physical toll and I was glad to be free of it. My hair fell in rich waves over my shoulders. I was glowing.

Tarc came into my bedroom. He slipped his arms around my waist, those golden forearms with their fine muscles, and pulled me against his chest. I touched my fingers to his skin, and in the mirror I saw him dip his lips to my neck.

'You ready?' He stepped away, holding my eye in the mirror.

'Yes.' I was meeting the Rose Gairdín for the first time. Because of my father, Cassa had assured me there was no question that I belonged. 'How could they not love you?' she'd said.

One of us.

I pulled up a strand of hair and pinned it with Maeve's lucky combs. I hadn't been able to throw them away.

'Remember I told you there'd been a break-in here before the security update?' Tarc said, watching me in the mirror.

I nodded, thinking of that long-ago conversation on the road to Kilshamble.

'Cassa lost a similar pair,' he pointed to the combs. 'Hers were a little different, a faded gold. They'd belonged to Arabella.'

I took a small pair of scissors from the dresser and scratched away at the surface, then I saw the dull gold emerge.

'They're hers.' I began taking the other one from my hair but Tarc stopped me.

'They're yours now.' And he seemed sad. I leaned towards him, my mouth right at his ear.

'I am exactly the same,' I whispered.

He smiled at me so brightly, as if he'd been waiting to hear those words. Then he kissed me long and hard.

Pressing his hand to my hip, we went down the stairs together. As we descended, he told me about the families

I would meet that evening. He seemed concerned, and it reminded me of that day when I'd held the pen so tightly in my anxiety. But that was long ago and he needn't have worried. I had never felt more in command of my own path. Where I wandered, I was certain that I would decide.

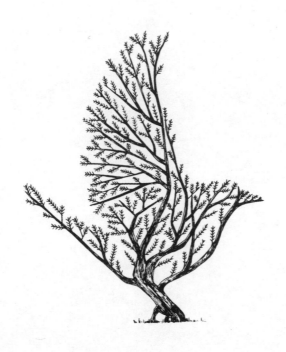

✿ ACKNOWLEDGEMENTS ✿

I am so grateful to Claire Wilson, who long ago sensed the story beneath with her spinny eye (magic eye), even when I couldn't. Who, with Ellen Holgate and her uncanny ability for discerning how to fix things, helped me get it right. You've both done so much: thank you for taking that leap of faith that meant everything. Thank you to all the wonderful people involved, both at RCW, especially Rosie Price, and at Bloomsbury: Lizz Skelly, Vicky Leech, Bronwyn O'Reilly, Hali Baumstein, Sarah Shumway, Grace Whooley and the rest of the team who do such amazing work. Thank you also to Anna Swan, Katie Everson and Tilda Johnson.

As always, there're a load of people that I question, prod and annoy while piecing together the background of a book: thank you. You can unblock me now. Go raibh maith agaibh Muireann Ní Chuív and Pilib Ó Broin for careful reading and especially for helping with the Irish. Thank you Strangers on the Internet who read opening chapters when I was uncertain: David, Carissa, Anna, Cat. Thank you to the lovely writerly women I met along the way: Emma

Heath for Project 10/10, and Ash Cloke. Nicole Lesperance, thanks for being the first reader. There's a range of information about historical gardens, druids, brehon law, folklore, Hy-Breasil and more, available both in print and online – I'm grateful to those who curate this knowledge and make it available, especially the original manuscripts.

Thank you friends and family. From those who were marched through Victorian walled gardens, made to visit stones and dolmens when you thought you were on holiday, to those who feed me bubbles and take me to the movies. Thanks David for chatting gunshot wounds, I just love how enthusiastic my in-laws are about their work. And always, thank you my gorgeous sisters, all Tilly's girls really, for being as mad as a box of frogs. You keep me light. I'm grateful to my children for their bickering because it drives me to my study to write. Just kidding. Kind of.

And this is not just the boyfriend thank you: Cathal, thanks for many conversations, for reading so many times, for taking boys on adventures. For caring about the small details and investing so deeply that words like 'tuanacul' and 'Kilshamble' matter (the English/Irish word origin mash-up there is on me). Thanks for your oblique references, your fine, sharp, dark mind and manly forearms, and most of all, your ability to suggest that one thing I'd never think of, which then somehow hits the perfect note.

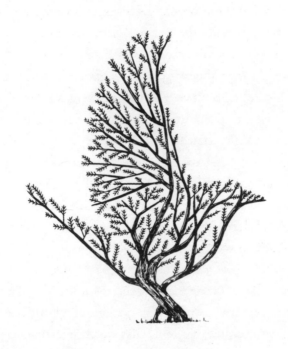

MARY WATSON is from Cape Town and now lives on the West Coast of Ireland with her husband and three young children. Highlights of her adult writing career include being awarded the Caine Prize for African Writing in Oxford in 2006, and being included on the Hay Festival's 2014 Africa39 list of influential writers from sub-Saharan Africa.

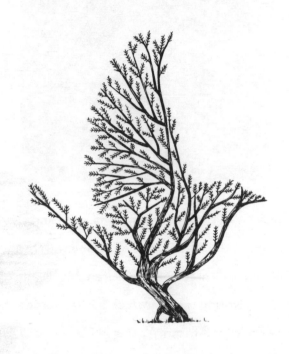